9-8-72

This Mysterious River

Books by Mel Ellis

THIS
MYSTERIOUS
RIVER
by Mel Ellis

HOLT, RINEHART AND WINSTON

New York   Chicago   San Francisco

Published simultaneously in Canada by Holt, Rinehart
and Winston of Canada, Limited.

ISBN: 0–03–091347–0
Library of Congress Catalog Card Number: 74–182753

First Edition

Designer: Bernard Klein

Printed in the United States of America

The Source

I HELD IT in the palm of a calloused hand, and my fingers, edged with ragging nails, trembled so the pearl quivered with light; and then and there any plans my mother had for making me into a concert violinist drained like rain off a hill to become one with my mysterious river.

Since that day I have always been planning to go back to see if the big, black clams still cluster where Wisconsin's Rock River sweeps the clay bottoms at the sharp bends, hoping to find one with a pearl luminous as the moon and worth maybe a thousand dollars.

But I never get there, and I do not even know if pollutants have killed off the clams and my dream is, after all, just that —a dream.

Once it wasn't. As a sunburnt crisp of a boy I opened and examined tons of clams to obtain a wine glass full of precious seedling pearls with which I was loath to part. There was no fascination comparable to spreading them on a card table, watching the light, like tunes of a song, play a hundred, a thousand variations on the same theme.

My precious pearls! What horizons they lighted! And then to lose them—all of them—down the huge, circular hot air register of my grandmother's furnace.

So I calculated the summer as a waste because I had not one seedling to show for the hundreds of hours I had spent pearling.

Only now, after so many years, I know all was not lost. Now I see the real value was not in the pearls but in the dream. I have never dreamed so grandly since, and in all the years between I have never been driven so ruthlessly toward an objective. Not once since have I been so completely immersed in any project. Nor have I come to any adventure with such a singleness of purpose.

My search for pearls, like the search for gold, consumed me, but in the driving fire of my desire I turned tough. And, in losing the pearls, I learned the hardest lesson—that all life is transient and only dreams can bridge the muddy rivers of despair.

M.E.

This Mysterious River

One

THE NEXT MORNING his buttocks still smarted. On the way home his father had turned into a cow lane, and cutting a hazel switch, whipped him. Later, when his mother had tried to comfort him, his father had brushed her aside and hurried him to bed. He had lain awake a long time, numb to everything except the sight of the switch sharp against the first softness in the evening sky, there in the lane, under the trees, close by the vines, with one retreating whippoorwill the only witness.

After awhile the numbness had given way to anger, and it had been a sharpness in his belly which finally came up his throat and was sour in his mouth. But the house had been quiet for a long while before she came and before he smelled the perfume of her soap. Then when she bent in the dark and kissed him softly, the anger dissolved in tears, and her warmth seeped down to still his churning stomach.

He heard her bare feet then, like whispers on the floor, as she went back to the bed she shared with his father. And he threw back the blanket because only a few days of spring had been sandwiched between winter and summer and already it was hot.

It was a heat that, given time, could of course, shrivel and kill, especially old men, but on this night it was being celebrated in every meadow and on every hill by every growing thing, and the frog chorus came to him on his cot on the screened porch like a heart beat—the pulse of a quickening world.

If it had been last night he still might have felt his own pulse quicken to the fertile rhythm because then he was so sure that his plan would work. Then, last night, he had been confident, even eager. So he had bolted his supper, pushed his plate away, and then asked: "May I please be excused?"

Mathew Drumm had looked up from his plate questioningly, but then he had said: "Go ahead."

The kerosene lantern he had carried to the marsh edge seemed to signal every mosquito squadron in the marsh. They came in clouds to singe their wings against the hot lantern chimney and to search out the boy's blood as he tore away with knife and pliers at the skins of the carp he had caught.

His face was soon smeared with his own and carp blood as he crushed mosquitos with the back of his bloody hands. They competed by the hundreds to get into his hair, nostrils, mouth. By the time the last carp was laid bare of its skin, and the big white bladders and intricate innards were on the ground, Ham was quivering with pain.

He quickly wrapped the reddish-white slabs of flesh in the brown paper he had brought and ran up the hill to a shack of cedar shakes. Inside, where it was dark, he dug blindly in the sawdust until his fingers felt the ice. Then he put the parcel of fish in it and covered the hole. Glad to come into the starlight again, he raced for the house. His mother met him at the door and handed him a towel.

"Down to the river," she said, and then repeated: "Down to the river."

He outran the mosquito horde waiting just outside the screen door, and on the gravel he kicked out of his overalls and jumped into the river. Still icy from spring freshets, and not yet accommodating itself to the warm air blanket above, the river tried for his breath and got it for a while, but then he got it back. He lathered once, rinsed, and then grabbing his overalls and the towel raced up the hill.

At the door he wrapped the towel around his loins and went

in. No one was in the kitchen so he darted out onto the long, screened-in porch where his cot stood.

Sleep was not long in coming. Once or twice he had the feeling that his mother was standing over him. Then the sun was over the valley hill, and he lay for delicious minutes immersed in the brief freshness night had wrought, and in the wonderment of being twelve years old.

But gradually, fact by fact, in successive slides of memory, he was dragged back down to earth. By the time he was headed for Greenville with the fish under his arm, it didn't make any difference anymore that the sun was shining and there were golden splashes of cowslips at the Creek Crossing.

In Greenville he went up the winding, dirty alley to the back door of Nero's restaurant.

"Fresh fish?" The dark-skinned Nero rested his palms on his protruding stomach. "Sure, I like fresh fish. How much?"

"Twenty cents a pound," Ham said.

"Let me see," Nero said, and Ham opened the package. "What kind are they?" Nero asked.

"Bass," Ham said, "black bass."

Nero's eyes lighted up. "Black bass! I give you twenty-five cents a pound," he said, patting the boy on the head. He hurried away to weigh the fish.

Ham wanted to leave while Nero was inside, to run away, but he pulled on his overalls until the suspenders were cutting into his shoulders as though that might keep him anchored to the spot.

Nero was back quickly. "Ten pounds," he said, handing the boy two one-dollar bills and a fifty cent piece.

"Thank you," Ham said, staring intently at his toes.

"Next week you bring more?"

"Sure." Ham nodded, backing away. "Next Friday."

He managed to walk until he was out of the alley. Then he ran.

After the two-mile hike home he took a long drink from the dipper and stared at the rust spot on the rim as though it had a special fascination for him. Well, he thought, it had worked. He had sold the fish. Perhaps he could sell more.

His mother was on the porch sewing. He could hear her humming softly. The baby was sleeping. He let the dipper slide back into the water pail, noted that the water level was low but decided against taking it out to the pump for refilling, and went out the door and walked down to the river.

Here where the banks sloped somewhat more precipitously to the water, the Big Pike River was a sleepy stream, hardly a hundred yards across. Mostly, in its travels it meandered among farm lands, pressed up against hardwood lots of much hickory and oak.

It was an unusually stable river, seldom rising too high nor yet again dropping too low during periods of drought. If sometimes its sand bars came naked to the sun, almost any rain of consequence helped cover them, or if a cloudburst gave it more depth and zest the new vigor was quickly dissipated.

All the way north, as far as Ham had ever rowed, it stayed securely between banks, but to the south it spread into a sizeable lake as the result of a dam at Huntingford.

From where Ham stood, the first widening of the river was visible. Big Pike Lake, named after the river which created it, was as treacherous as all large, shallow bodies of water, and strong winds were known to almost bare its bottoms and then send waves soaring across the tops of the smaller islands.

Ham knew the lake reasonably well, as well as any boy or man can know such a changeable place. He had landed on most of the forty or more islands, toured most of the big bays, pushed his boat into many of the shallow sloughs.

Both the river and the lake fascinated him. He learned their secrets like a dry slough sucks up water. But like the slough, it seemed he could never get enough. One wisp of wisdom only opened doors to wider horizons, and he discovered quickly that even old men never knew it all.

Squawk Island was in his line of vision, and there were the specks of many bird forms hovering above it, so he knew someone was down there disturbing the heron rookery. It was illegal to kill the blue herons, but some men did anyway.

They excused themselves by saying the big birds ate all the fish. Ham wondered who the fish belonged to in the first place.

His brother appeared, walking out from beneath the drooping branches of a weeping willow tree. Rock, their grizzled, gray dog of pony-like proportions, was with him.

Mort came over, nudged him hard with an elbow to remind him that, if not older, he was bigger. "Where you been?" he asked.

The dog dropped down with a grunt to the ground, stretched his legs, rolled his eyes and then closed them.

"In town," Ham said, feeling the sharp pain of his brother's elbow, but not putting his finger tips to the bruise. "Where you been?" Ham asked.

"At Rob's. He got to telling stories."

The Old Man had been a boy on the river banks long before there'd been much "except thousands of ducks, sloughs full of muskrats, and so many fish you could fill a boat as fast as you could pull them in."

"What'd ya do in town? Go up to the house?" Mort asked.

They had two houses—one in town, and the cottage on the river bank. Their father would have been glad to sell either or both, but times were such "you couldn't sell a potato to a starving Irishman because he'd not have the penny to pay for it."

"No, I just poked around," Ham answered Mort's query.

Ham wanted to drift away. He hoped Mort wouldn't follow. He had to be alone to think.

But Mort followed, and so they walked ankle-deep around the slough where fleets of slate colored mudhens with bobbing white beaks complained endlessly as they examined rafts of coontail and every floating bog for tendrils and water-living insects.

The dog went along, careening off to investigate every vagrant odor. Sometimes they could see over the tops of the cattail swords to where the carp swam, to where the muskrat feed beds were bright salad patches and where their last year's houses were rotting now in the summer sun like raisins wrinkling in the green frosting of a cake.

Already the slough was beginning to smell in the heat. Mort held his nostrils and made faces, but Ham relished the rich odor, especially the thin, sharp smell of reeds just lifting through winter's morass.

They went all the way around and came back—examining stones to see if perchance one might be an arrowhead, wading out to peer into a hanging blackbird's nest, whistling to make the gophers stand like sticks, and holding their hands like sunshades so they might see the hawk sailing, and skirting the fresh platters of cow dung, and treating their bare feet to water and dust, soft grass and cool mud . . .

And Ham forgot—almost—this that had been weighing on him, but it all came back again when they neared home and their mother called: "Mort? Ham?" Three times.

Then when they were near the door she said: "Your father is late, but he's always said we're not to wait." So they went in where the baby was propped in a high chair with a pillow, and Ham bent to feel her hands on his face before sitting down.

Mr. Drumm came in while they were eating. He didn't come to the table, but stood just inside the door.

"Hammond, come here!" the father ordered.

The boy's fork clattered to the floor.

"Hammond!"

"Yes sir," Ham jumped to his feet and started across the kitchen.

"What on earth is wrong?" Mrs. Drumm asked.

At the door the father took Ham by the arm and pulled him outside. He walked so fast Ham had to run to stay with him.

The engine of the Model T Ford was still running. Mr. Drumm pushed Ham into the front seat from the driver's side so he had to inch over under the steering wheel. Without a word Mr. Drumm got in and started the car toward town. The dust billowed up behind the car and then settled straight back down on the lifeless evening air.

Ham had to hang on at the curves. When the car crossed

the railroad tracks at the edge of town, Ham's head hit the roof fabric.

Right up Main Street the father drove, and at one crossing Old Oscar, weaving slightly, shook his fist at the passing car.

Across from Nero's restaurant Mr. Drumm stopped so abruptly he killed the motor. It was then Ham got his first inkling of the trouble which lay ahead. In Nero's store window was a huge white card, and in black lettering, the words: FRESH BLACK BASS TODAY!

Mr. Drumm took Ham's arm and catapulted him across the street. Through the front door glass Ham could see Gunnar Strong, the game warden. He was talking to Nicholas Nero. When they came through the door, Nero turned to them.

"What you do?" Nero asked Ham, spreading his hands in supplication. "Mr. Strong here say it is against the law to sell black bass."

Ham felt his insides shrivel. He felt the blood retreat from his face, his fingers. Hair on his neck stiffened.

"Well, what about it?" the warden asked. He looked straight at Ham, but his gray eyes were friendly.

Ham looked from the warden's eyes to the wildly flashing eyes of the frightened restaurant operator.

"You get me put in jail, boy," Nero said, waving his hands.

Mr. Drumm motioned for silence. "Did you sell him black bass?" the father asked the son.

Ham's tongue moved, but he made no sound.

"Answer me!" Mathew Drumm almost jerked the boy off the floor.

"Just a minute. Just a minute," the warden said, moving toward father and son. "I don't think they were black bass. I ate some of what was left. There were too many bones, and the flavor was different."

Mr. Drumm waited. When his son was silent, he said: "Well, Ham, what about it?"

The boy tried to work up some saliva. Finally he got enough to say: "They were carp."

The warden looked relieved. "I thought so," he said. "Well, there's no law against selling carp."

Ham felt momentarily relieved until his father's fingers tightened on his arm. "But there is a law," his father said, "about misrepresenting a product."

Warden Strong laughed. "Yeah, I suppose so. But that's not in my jurisdiction. The way I figure it, the whole thing is one big joke."

"Joke! You call it a joke!" Mathew Drumm shouted.

Nero had stopped shaking. He was smiling. He waved his hands expansively. "No, it's a joke. A big joke. A good joke. One on me. On my customers. They tell me law says no sell bass. But they always tease me. I think they tease today."

The warden started toward the door, but he stopped to watch when Mathew Drumm asked Ham: "Where's the money?"

The boy dug it from the watch pocket of his overalls. The bills were folded firmly around the piece of silver.

"Give it to Mr. Nero." the father said.

The restaurant operator protested: "No. I got my money. The customers pay me. They eat the fish."

Mr. Drumm pushed his son forward. "Give him the money!"

Nero stepped back. "No! I got my money."

Mr. Drumm said: "Put it on the counter." Ham stepped forward and put the wad of money on the counter. Then the smell of grease from the kitchen, or the fear of his father, or the amused look in the eyes of some customers who had gathered, got to him, and he felt faint.

But Mathew Drumm buoyed him up. "Come on," he said. "There's one little thing left," and with a jerk and a thrust he propelled him through the door.

As the car pulled away from the curb, Ham saw Nero taking the sign out of the window, and then they went jolting away to come careening to a halt in the cow lane where he saw the switch from a hazel bush raised high against the soft sky of a summer sunset.

Two

NEXT MORNING Ham waited until he heard the Model T clatter down the road before he got up. He drank a glass of milk, and then, knowing his brother could do the chores and before his mother could stop him, he ducked from the house.

As usual he was barefoot, and he walked along a dusty road. Ahead a green garter snake, still lethargic, crossed slowly. It disappeared in a tangle of roadside grass, reappeared briefly at the edge of a stone fence, and then where a wild plum was a white billow of blossoms, it went below—toward hell, the boy thought.

If the affair of the carp had been painful, it was nothing compared to the sin which had prompted the experiment. As if to erase away this sin, the boy smoothed the snake's trail in the dust with his bare feet. Then wearily, though the day had hardly begun, he trudged on down the road.

To be a thief was bad enough. But to have stolen from the church! His feelings of guilt were monumental, because he was twelve, and incapable of such mental subterfuge as might help him bury his sin in some rarely visited closet of his conscience.

And so his heart did not leap with the rabbit as it crossed the road. Nor did he see the bright oriole in an elm, and when a catbird called, he never looked for her nest in the prickly ash.

At Creek Crossing even the fresh smell of icy springs, melting through green cress like quick silver, went unnoticed. He saw only dust as it puffed at each step, merely marking that a barefoot boy had passed, a barefoot boy in faded blue overalls.

He had tried to get the money back after it had been spent. But Solomon, whom he had given it to, would sooner have sold his wife. In desperation he had even gone to his father.

"Ten dollars!" his father had roared. "Might as well ask for ten thousand!"

As usual his mother had separated them quickly by herding him out onto the porch. "These are hard times, Hammond," she had said. "Your father hasn't sold as much as a hay fork in weeks. We can't sell or even borrow on the house in town or on this river place. There is no money."

Ham had known it. His father went to the farm machinery equipment yard every day, but every night he came home with the same set face and the sometimes bewildered eyes.

It was 1932 and bacon had disappeared from the breakfast table. It was stew instead of steak on Sunday. His father smoked a corncob pipe instead of his usual fragrant cigars, and he grew more irritable each day, until it seemed to Ham his hair and mustache and even his mind bristled.

Mathew Drumm looked twice the height of his wife, Rose, and Ham sometimes thought their lives might be even farther apart than their ages. Mathew was fifty. Rose was thirty.

His mother was dark, red lipped. She had enormous black eyes in a tiny face. She wore her dresses just a little longer than was stylish, and still had black, luxuriant hair down to her waist because her husband wouldn't let her bob it.

His brother, Morton, with his brittle blue eyes, was the bristling image of his father, and though a year younger than Ham, he was at least an inch taller.

Mary, just beginning to crawl, looked like she might be another Rose. She was dark, shy, and lovely.

But if Ham inherited the dark sensitivity of his mother, he also came out of the womb with the obstinancy that had caused Greenville folks to call his father "a hard but an honest man."

The dust road ended. The gravel road began. The boy

walked past the sign which read: GREENVILLE POPULATION 1018.

When he came to the railroad tracks he turned north and tried to walk the rails, but settled for walking the ties. He went by the red depot, and when Chauncey Peters, the ticket agent, waved, he waved back. At the Greenville Lumber Company he turned to make his way back to the street.

As he was passing the square, box-like lumber company office, Mr. Van Stylehausen came out. Ham said hello. The man nodded, and then with sudden inspiration the boy asked: "You need a boy, Mr. Van Stylehausen? To stack lumber? Or sort nails?"

Ambrose Van Stylehausen, necked in an immaculate collar despite the heat, said: "Nobody wants lumber. Nobody wants nails." He was a gorilla of a man, and even though his suits were neatly tailored, the sleeves never seemed long enough.

"Just goes to show you," people had said, "how a woman can make a sap out of a man."

Van Stylehausen had found his wife while at a lumbermen's convention in Milwaukee. It was even rumored she was a divorcee. But if Ambrose Van Stylehausen had ever considered himself a sap, that time had long passed. He had come to accept the proud part his wife decreed he should play. So now even the heat couldn't wilt him.

"That's too bad," Ham said, referring to the lack of business.

Mr. Van Stylehausen rubbed his little eyes as though to see the boy more clearly. Perhaps he had detected real concern in the boy's voice, because he stopped to say: "It's worse than that. The lumber lays there and dries out. It has been there so long the sparrows have it so dirty I'm going to have to have every board scrubbed before I can sell it."

Encouraged, Ham offered: "Maybe you should cover it with canvas or something."

Mr. Van Stylehausen looked irritated. "You think I haven't! Every bum who rides the rails steals the coverings, and Lord knows, there's more people riding free today than pay for their passage."

[13]

The big man started away. Ham said: "I might be able to catch the sparrows for you."

Mr. Van Stylehausen stopped, started walking again, and then turned. "I sure wish someone would," he said.

The sparrows were everywhere. There were hundreds. They traded between the high, red grain elevator, the feed mill, and the siding where the boxcars always spilled grain—and, of course, the lumberyard where they roosted.

Even as the boy and the man stood in the glaring sun, the sparrows quarreled in the dust, perched in ragged brown rows along the hitching rail which still accommodated an occasional horse. They hopped among the cinders along the tracks, heads cocked for a missed morsel which their stomachs could magically turn to lime strong enough to eat the finish off an automobile.

"How much would you give me for killing the sparrows?" Ham asked.

Ambrose Van Stylehausen never hesitated. "Listen, boy," he said, with a thrust of a finger, "I'll give you ten cents for every one of those filthy birds you bring in. Only, bring them in dead!"

Ten cents! It was enormous payment. "I'll do it, Mr. Van Stylehausen," Ham said. "I'll do it!"

When the lumber dealer had walked as far as the next block, Ham sat in the dust and figured with a stick that twenty sparrows came to two dollars, fifty sparrows came to five, and one hundred sparrows represented the ten-dollar bill he needed so desperately. The ten-dollar bill which would free him— let him go singing back to the river.

The thought lifted him, carried him all the way up the street to where his father's equipment yard was shiny with tractors that no one wanted, mowers and hay rakes only waiting for some horse to pull, and even a threshing machine already three years old but shiny as the day it had arrived.

His father was nowhere in sight, so he crawled up on a Fordson tractor seat to wait. Old Oscar came over while he was waiting.

"Looking for your dad?" Old Oscar asked.

"Not exactly."

"Well, your dad said for me to keep an eye on the place. He said he had to get home in a hurry," Old Oscar said.

Ham wondered what had happened. Mr. Drumm never left the yard unless there was an emergency. He wondered if his mother might be going to have another baby. He didn't think she was. She didn't look like it.

Perhaps someone was hurt. Or sick. Or maybe his mother *was* going to have a baby.

He jumped from the tractor seat and started down the gravel road at a trot. Near the edge of town he saw the dust cloud and got off into the ditch. It was his father's car coming. He waved to intercept it.

The car stopped, and dust settled around it. His mother was in the front seat holding the baby. Mort was in the back seat. They had on their Sunday clothes.

"What's the matter?" Ham asked.

"Aunt Lucy had to go to the hospital," his mother said. "They think it might only be her appendix. But someone has to be there."

Lucy was his mother's sister. She lived in Milwaukee, the largest city in the state, more than fifty miles from Greenville.

"You go on home," his mother said. "I left a note for you on the kitchen table. There's plenty to eat in the icebox. Be careful when you light the lamp."

"Why can't I go along?"

"Just look at you, boy!" his father said. Ham did. He was barefoot, and his feet were dirty. His overalls, once blue, were bleached white. There was a tear in his shirt.

"We've got to go," Mr. Drumm said, putting in the clutch so the car edged slowly forward.

"You be a good boy," his mother called back as the car moved up the street.

He drifted to Greenville's park and looked for money beneath the bleachers. There was none. At noon he went back to the implement yard and Old Oscar gave him a piece of bologna and a piece of bread.

Then he drifted back to the lumberyard. The eaves fairly

bristled with sparrow nests, but he couldn't reach them. But below the two-by-fours that held the arching roof, there was ample evidence that scores of sparrows roosted. He could reach the two-by-fours from the piles of stacked lumber.

He went back uptown to where Old Oscar was on the bench in front of the Barber Shop.

"Got a flashlight I can borrow?" he asked.

Oscar shook his head. "But maybe I can get you one."

Oscar got up, and Ham followed him. They stopped in front of Jumpy Jones's place. Ham had never been inside. It wasn't allowed. There was a bar, and Jumpy made beer in the basement and whiskey in the attic.

Old Oscar went in. He was gone nearly half an hour, and Ham was about ready to give up when he came back out. His eyes were bright and brassy, but he had the flashlight. "I could use some paper sacks, too," Ham said.

Oscar went back in and came out shortly with two brown paper bags. Then he headed for the park, and Ham knew it was so he wouldn't fall asleep in the street and have to spend the night in jail.

Ham put the flashlight into one of the bags and walked to the north edge of town, to the old gravel pit shack where he had hidden the bicycle. When he opened the door he waited for his eyes to adjust to the gloom.

The bicycle was gone! The blue racer with the balloon tires and the silver trim and the rubber handle bar grips! It wasn't there.

He closed the door and started to walk away. Then he went back and opened the door, as if to see whether his eyes had been playing tricks on him. Only an old shovel with a broken handle leaned against the far wall, and while he watched, a mouse ran across the hard-packed earthen floor of the shack.

Then, after his first astonishment, he was surprised to discover that it didn't really matter. The bicycle had become too much a part of his sin. In a way he was almost relieved. The visible, tangible evidence of his transgression had disappeared.

He closed the door, turned away, and drifted back into town. He went down Oak Street to the park. Old Oscar was snoring gently beneath a giant, spreading oak. He drifted away, out of the park, to the far south side of town where Jim Backus had horses shipped in from the west for the fox farmers.

Silver foxes had been the rage. Before the crash two years ago, it seemed everyone was raising silver foxes, even in their back yards. Now (he'd heard his father say) they couldn't even feed the foxes, and "those without the guts to kill them are just turning them loose in any woods."

So nobody wanted horse meat for fox food, and Jim Backus had the horses and no money to buy *them* food. And they stood there, and he watched them, fifty or more, bony and tired of living, but not even worth killing now, and their heads hung in the heat.

He picked some dusty grass and held it out for a pinto near the fence. The horse looked at him balefully, but refused the grass. It was sad, he thought, and he walked far enough so that the horses were out of sight, before slumping to the ground to wait for night.

He thought he might have slept a little, because the sun seemed to come so quickly to the horizon. So he got up and went back to the lumberyard. Birds were flocking in from every direction. They were fighting for their favorite roosts —tumbling in combat, almost to the ground, before swooping off in separate directions.

Gradually they quieted. Shadows deepened under the V-shaped roofs to which no sides had been added. A rat ran across the tracks. Two cats came out of the dusty railside weeds and went between the stacks of lumber. It was almost dark, and he had been ready for a long time.

Three

USUALLY LUMBERYARDS smell sharply and pungently
of pine forests. But in this graveyard of trees there was the
smell of death—the overwhelming odor of old, old bodies
(birds and bats, mice and rats) down between the boards,
caught there to shrink and become as juiceless as the lumber
which had lain so long.

No wonder the men who rode the rails avoided it now,
and unless it was raining, slept in the open. There were hundreds in the course of one summer, and if they were rousted
from the park, they spread out across the fields and along the
condensery creek, preferring the sour odor of whey to the
musty smell of shrunken bodies and lifeless wood.

Ham climbed the first stack of boards at the south end of
the yard and then stood uncertainly. It was a place of mis-
shapen shadows. He flicked on the flashlight and ran it across
the boards. The grain of the wood had parted. It was wrinkled
and brown. Knots had popped from the lumber nobody could
afford, and when the eye of the flashlight crossed them they
looked like sockets in a skull.

He turned out the light and waited, as though to be chal-
lenged for this trespass by the ghost of Mrs. Cable, who
had been dragged here, raped, and murdered, or by the
specters of the tramps found stiff and cold and curled, still
clutching their bottles.

His body convulsed in one giant shiver of apprehension.
But it might be his only chance. He tried to steel himself, but

nothing would keep his upper lip from quivering. He bit down on it, digging his teeth in to stop it. The sharp pain helped chase away the ghosts.

In the dark he folded one bag and put it into his back pocket. He opened the other bag and held it with his right hand, the hand which also held the flashlight. He took a step. Even through the calluses he felt the grain, the roughness of the boards on his bare feet.

Then he turned on the light, lifted it, and a sparrow's eye sparkled. It was a male with a black bib. He could see every feather etched as if in wood. The bird was mesmerized by the light. He put out his left hand and the sparrow never moved. Then like a snake, he struck and had the bird. He had touched another bird and it went past his face and he could feel the feathers of its wing tips against his cheek.

He stood uncertainly, and then he tried to bring the flashlight down on the bird's head. It would never work. Not in the dark. Not standing there high on a pile of lumber.

Well, there was a sure way. He wedged the sparrow's head between two fingers wrapped around the flashlight. Then with a quick jerk he separated the bird—head from body.

He could feel the warm blood, sticky on his fingers. The wings shivered, convulsed. He could feel the tiny heart tick. Once again a shudder shook the length of him. Then he tossed the body to the ground, shoved the tiny head into the paper sack.

He couldn't stop now. If he stopped, he'd never be able to start again. He focused the light on another bird. He clutched it quickly. He separated the bird's life into two parts. Body to the ground. Head into the sack.

He took a step, heard a few sparrows flutter, thought he saw their passing shadows. But there must have been hundreds, lined almost solidly along the two-by-four. Almost all males because the females were probably on the nests.

The bright, white light hypnotized them. He caught another and killed it, then another. When he came to the end of the stacked boards he had ten.

He climbed down, drew himself up on the next stack, lifted

the light, got on with his grisly business. Systematically. From one pile of boards to the next. From one sparrow to another. Body to the ground. Head in the sack. Fingers slippery, sticky with blood.

Disembodied now. Fear, revulsion, pity—all pushed back. A harvester of heads. Calculating, cold executioner. Old. Old in minutes. Wings convulsing. Tiny heart ticking. Body to the ground. Head in the sack. Reach. Pull. Throw. Automatic. Keep it that way. Don't stop. Never stop. Sparkle of a sparrow's eye, frozen like glass by death.

When he came to the end of the last stack on the east side of the yard he let himself slump to the ground so he could breathe again. It seemed as if he had been holding his breath all the while, but, of course, that couldn't be true. Nobody could hold their breath that long.

He looked up and was amazed to see that the sky held stars. He looked around at the great shadows of freight cars on sidings, the bulge of box elder trees across the tracks, the signal light far down the tracks like a red eye.

He was about to get up from the ground when there was a frenzied scuttling among the piles of lumber in front of him. He had no room left for fear, so he turned on the light. Three cats came out from between the stacks in single file, each with the body of a bird between its jaws.

He turned out the light and got up. He went to the tracks. The cinders hurt even his leathery soles. So he walked the ties, toward the street where a single bulb was strung to cast pale light across an intersection.

Ham stopped at the edge of the circle of light. He sat again, breathing deeply, and marveling that the town hadn't changed and the hitching rail was still there and lights were coming from the houses on both sides of the streets.

He waited a few minutes, as though accommodating himself again to the world of the living. Then he opened the sack and rolled out the heads. One of the heads was still opening and closing its sharp, little beak. He arranged the heads in rows of five—all eyes open and staring at him—and there were ten rows and one head left over.

Fifty-one heads! A haul! Fifty-one. Ten cents apiece. Fifty-one. Five dollars and ten cents!

It was enough to shake him out of the tomb-like world where the dry boards hid the dead bodies.

He gathered the heads and put them back into the sack. His hands were black with clotted blood. He tried to wipe them on his overall bib. But the blood didn't all come off.

He got up and started up the street toward where the Van Stylehausen house was a stone fortress surrounded by several vacant lots. But now walking was too slow, so he broke into a dog trot. It took him the several blocks quickly, and he went up on the wide porch and rang the door bell.

The porch light came on and Mrs. Van Stylehausen opened the door. When Ham told her he wanted to see Mr. Van Stylehausen, she turned and called: "Ambrose, there's a little boy here to see you."

"Little boy?" Ham could hear the question in Mr. Van Stylehausen's voice. "What's he want?"

"Tell him it's about the sparrows," Ham said.

"He says it's about sparrows!"

There was silence. Then Mr. Van Stylehausen said: "Oh, sparrows. Yeah, all right. I'm coming."

When Mrs. Van Stylehausen left, Ham arranged the sparrow heads in rows of five so the lumber dealer could count them. When the man came to the door, he was in a purple velvet smoking jacket in spite of the heat. He looked at the boy first. Then when Ham pointed, he looked down at the sparrow heads.

"My gosh!"

"Fifty-one, and I'll get some more on another night," Ham said.

"Pretty good," the man hesitated, looked up, "but how do I know you didn't get them out of some farmer's barn?"

Ham's face fell. He bit down on his upper lip. Then he said: "But I didn't. I got them at your lumberyard."

"Okay. Okay." The man reached into his pocket and handed Ham fifty cents.

"But you said ten cents apiece," Ham blurted.

"Ten cents! Apiece! For each one! What do you think sparrow heads are made of? Gold?"

The boy started to speak again, but the man cut him off. "Look, Sonny, that's over five dollars. Now I know everybody thinks I'm the richest man in the county, but even if I had all the money in the world, I wouldn't go around paying ten cents apiece for sparrow heads . . ."

"But you said . . ."

Drawing back and away, the man shook his head. "I have to draw the line somewhere." He closed the door. Ham stood fingering the fifty cent piece and looking down at the sparrow heads. The porch light went out. Still he stood. Then he shined the flashlight on the sparrow heads. Some were streaked with blood. He shined the light on the fingers of his left hand. The blood was caked beneath his ragged nails. He examined the bib of his overalls. It was stained.

He kicked at the sparrow heads, scattering them across the porch. For a moment he wanted to cry, but then anger saved him. It started like a slow, burning fire in his neck, and he could feel his face get hot as the anger welled up. He jumped from the porch, thrust out his lower lip, and leaning far forward, trotted as though with a specific purpose straight back to the lumberyard.

There was no hesitation this time. He climbed to the first pile of lumber on the west side of the yard, and taking the extra bag from a back pocket, began scooping sparrows from their roost. But now he didn't separate their lives—head from body—but stuffed them alive into the sack.

In his swift anger he failed to notice that he had come to the end of a pile of lumber, and he stepped off into air. He turned an ankle and a wrist when he hit the ground, but his only thought was for the birds. He clutched the sack mouth so they couldn't escape.

Then he climbed the next pile of boards, and like a frog flicks insects out of the air, he flicked sparrows off their roosts. He stopped only once to pinch tiny air holes in the bag so his captives could breathe. Then he was off again collecting birds, and when the sack was nearly full he jumped off the

[22

lumber, hurried along the rails, and turned up the street toward the Van Stylehausen house.

In front of the house he stood on the sidewalk for a moment looking up and down the street. Then he crept onto the lawn, and hiding in a hedge, looked into the window. A sparrow in the bag fluttered. It started the others fluttering, but they soon quieted.

Mr. Van Stylehausen was half-asleep in a huge leather chair. A bottle of home brew stood on the end table beside him. Mrs. Van Stylehausen sat across the room, thumbing through a magazine. A child of about five was sprawled on steps which obviously led upstairs. She was sleeping. Their high school boy was at a small corner desk bent over a book.

Ham backed stealthily away from the window. He went around to the front of the house. Standing at the front door he tore a slit in the side of the bag. Then quietly, but quickly, he opened the screen door. He held the screen door with his hip. He put a hand to the door knob and tried it. It turned. Gently then he twisted the knob. Finally he braced himself and thrust the door open.

He got a glimpse of Mrs. Van Stylehausen's startled face, and then he hurled the bag of birds inside, slammed the door shut, and scrambled around to the side of the house where he could watch through the window.

By the time he was in position, sparrows were all over the room. They were clinging to the drapes, perched on the stair rail, sitting on a lamp, clinging to the moulding which circled the room. And they kept trading places—back and forth, around and around—one alighting on Mrs. Van Stylehausen's head and getting its spidery sparrow feet tangled in her hair.

The child who had been sleeping on the stairs awakened when Mrs. Van Stylehausen screamed. The schoolboy threw his book. It knocked over the floor lamp. Mr. Van Stylehausen made a grab at a bird hanging on the front window drapes. The drapes came down. A girl of about his own age appeared. She ran through the room, out onto the front porch, and then ducked back inside again.

Ham guessed there were between twenty and thirty sparrows loose in the house. They would be a while catching them all.

Mr. Van Stylehausen disappeared. He came back wielding a broom. He batted a sparrow down, scooped it up, and ran to the front door to thrust it outside. He came back and swung at one in flight. The broom whisked so close to Mrs. Van Stylehausen's head that she screamed again.

Ham could hear Ambrose Van Stylehausen shout: "Clara, you shut up!" Then he swung again. The broom hit the chandelier. The fixture fell. The room went dark, and there was only a little light from what must have been the kitchen. It was quiet. Abruptly quiet.

Ham hadn't laughed, but his anger had dissolved to fear. Instead of heading for the street, he ran through the back yard. A clothes line upended him. He gasped for breath, got it, and ran again, all the way to the end of the gravel road. Then when he felt the dust of the River Road between his toes, he walked, and a moon which had risen walked with him, right off his left shoulder, all the way past Creek Crossing, between the hills of hickory, dipping down to marsh bottoms, coming up the last slant—home.

The cottage was empty. They hadn't gotten back from Milwaukee. He tried to eat, but it made him sick. He drank some water. It was warm. He went to the porch and crawled onto his cot, turning just enough so he could see the moon, and before he slept a heron called down for landing instructions, and from a tree somewhere another heron answered.

Four

BUT THIS NIGHT no ghosts walked. Nothing could top the eerie lumberyard, so the branches scraping the side of the house were *not* claws, but only branches. The swish of wings was *not* the Holy Ghost, but a duck flock passing. The cruciform of light on the screen was *not* a sign from heaven, but only the angle of the moon. The sighing *did* come from the clump of spruce, and the groaning *was* only two basswoods scratching one another. The footsteps *were* only boats gently bumping as they swung at anchor in the current. And the buzz was *not* in his head, but only a mouse making a new door.

So he finally fell asleep and didn't awaken until the slant of the sun through the oaks, which stretched corrugated limbs around the screen porch, was dancing with dust diamonds.

He lay listening for clues, and he got them. His mother's voice: "Now, Mort, you leave that dog outside!" Then the screen door slamming. Finally the Model T being cranked and his father coughing from the exertion even above the roar of the engine.

Things couldn't be too serious for his aunt, he told himself, or his mother would have stayed in Milwaukee. It would be safe to get up now, and if Van Stlychausen planned any revenge for the rain of sparrows, that would come later. But it didn't frighten him. He didn't think Van Stylehausen would care to call attention to the fact that he had lowered his sparrow price from five dollars and ten cents to fifty cents. Above all else, Mrs. Van Stylehausen wouldn't want to be characterized as cheap—not by anybody, and especially not by a boy in overalls.

So he dressed and came out into the combination kitchen and dining room.

"Oh, look at you," his mother said.

"I'll change. How's Aunt Lucy?"

"Appendix. She'll be fine."

He changed overalls and ate a bowl of milk and oatmeal. When he got up Rock was waiting to wag him through the door. The dog followed him down the path to the outhouse and then picked a dust pocket in the path to lie in while the boy went inside.

Someone had left a seat cover off one of the holes. The squirrels had taken advantage of the invitation to gnaw for salt which perspiring bottoms had left in the soft pine.

He dropped his overalls, sat down, reached forward and pulled the door shut. A crescent of sun from the quarter-moon cut in the front door lighted up a corner web, lair of a fat spider.

Ham tried to spit as high as the web, but he missed. He tore off a corner of the Sears-Roebuck catalogue, wadded it into a ball, and tossed it into the center of the web. The paper stuck and the web reverberated until every strand was striking forth slivers of sun. Only when the trembling stopped did a spider, in a black and yellow suit, come hurrying like a clown on a tight rope. It stopped short of the speck of paper as though to test for temperature. Then it grasped the wad of paper with hairy front legs, felt it, and turning, hurried back to disappear in a crack between boards.

Ham looked into the tobacco box nailed to the side of the wall. There wasn't enough. He couldn't risk taking some. He didn't want to smoke anyway, not without someone to watch, because that was half the fun.

Plainly now it was Mr. Van Stylehausen's move. Perhaps he had already driven his Pierce-Arrow to the Drumm Equipment Company yard and told his father about the sparrow invasion. He supposed he'd know soon enough.

At least this time he'd be ready. It wouldn't be like it had been with the carp—a surprise lightning strike, a sharp switch cutting down out of an evening sky. He'd be braced, ready as he could be.

It occurred to him that he wasn't frightened. He wondered if this was because he still wasn't convinced that Mr. Van Stylehausen would show his hand, leaving himself open to ridicule from the community for being a cheap skate?

The spider was back, but Ham had lost his interest in the insect. He crumpled several sheets of the Sears catalogue, felt their rough edges, and then pulling up his overalls, stepped from the gloom of the two-holer out into the sun.

Mort had already finished the chores, so he headed for the fence corner where a stand of young cedars was being suffocated by nightshade, ivy, wild grape—all manner of creeping vines. There was an opening in the arbor, one he had made, so he crawled through it, and here where the sun could not shine and even on the hottest day the earth felt cool, he sat back and looked out.

Rock was trailing him down the slope. Ham whistled softly. Rock wagged his tail tentatively. Ham whistled again. The dog dropped to the ground and crawled through the opening, keeping his eyes on the boy.

"It's okay, Rock," the boy said, and the dog showed the tip of his pink tongue. "It's okay." The dog's tongue lolled and Rock showed his white teeth.

"Come on." Ham patted the ground. The dog crawled all the way then and stretched out on the ground. Although no grass grew there, it was none the less comfortable, with a shredding of dead cedar fronds.

But there was no peace in this quiet place, mostly because there was no peace anywhere—not with the thrust of his problem pricking his conscience like a thorn.

If he could only talk to someone about it. Lydia. If she had been here. But he didn't know. Maybe they wouldn't be back this year. Last summer the pearl harvest had been poor.

"It's the current," the girl had said. "Clams need current

to move enough to make the pearls round. The dam at the other end of the lake, it's stopped the current. The pearls aren't round anymore."

But Lydia wasn't here. So who was there? His father? His father would half-kill him. His mother? She'd be so sad she'd weep for a week.

He wondered about Miss Mallow—Myrtle Mallow, his teacher during last year's sixth grade. No. He didn't even want to think about her. But he thought about her anyway, and then a line of little sweat diamonds appeared just above his upper lip.

"You have lips just like a girl," Miss Mallow had said, applying lipstick so he could play the part of Charlie's Aunt in a school play.

Luckily no one had heard her, but after that he had taken a good look at his lips, and the upper lip did have a bow like a girl's. No amount of biting would straighten it.

"You've even got hair like a little girl," Miss Mallow had said, running her hands through his hair. And he did have. It was black, and not even a stocking cap would keep it from curling.

Luckily, he thought, his other features were boyish. His skin was dark like his mother's, his eyes were almost black, and he had high and almost severe cheekbones which he hoped made him look like an Indian.

Miss Mallow had run her fingers over his cheeks. "Your skin is so soft," she said, and then before he knew what she was about, she had bent and kissed him—not on the cheeks, but full and hard on the mouth!

It was enough to flunk him out of sixth grade, because he couldn't look at her, much less understand what she was trying to say. But she passed him, and twice she had embraced him when they were alone in the cloakroom, and once when he was walking past her apartment she had suddenly appeared out of the dusk and had his arm.

"Come on up, Ham," she had said. "We'll have chocolate cookies. Whatever you want."

She had propelled him halfway up the stairs, and then when

he held back, she had put her arms around him. When she kissed him he felt her tongue against his lips.

First he had been frozen, but then he had been able to back off.

"My Dad . . . my Dad . . . my Dad . . . in the car. He's waiting." He had turned and couldn't remember getting down the steps or running up the sidewalk.

But why think about Miss Mallow? It was summer, and she was hundreds of miles away at her home in Indiana. Maybe that's why he could think of paying Miss Mallow's price. Except he wasn't quite sure what that price was—not completely.

Rock jerked and then began thrusting his legs as though galloping in his sleep. Ham put a hand on him. The nightmare stopped. The dog lifted his head, opened his eyes, sighed, and lay back down again.

Well, Miss Mallow was out, even though he was sure she would have been good for the money. So who else was there? Rob? Why not Rob!

He reached up for a grape leaf and put it into his mouth. Well, he didn't know. Rob could be crotchety. Like the time he and Mort had been shooting chipmunks with the bb gun they owned between them.

He had come angrily out of his remodeled boathouse with his bright eyes flashing and his pink skin turning red and his white hair seeming to bristle with a rage that had suddenly been ignited when they wounded a chipmunk which had been coming to the stoop for crumbs.

"I'll whip you both so goddamned hard you'll stand at the table for a month!"

Then he had picked up the wounded chipmunk and disappeared back in the boathouse with it. It had been weeks before he'd talk to them, and it had been a month before either of them had gone back to sit in the straight chair by his tiny table while he leaned back in an easy chair and told stories "of the olden days."

But the thing of the chipmunk had passed, and it was many an evening's delight to carry warm food from their house to his—because, as his mother put it, "he's got nobody, poor man"—and then hear how, during his youth, the mudhens put such solid flocks on the water even the river backed up. And how the wolves lived as far south as this place where the boathouse and the other cottages now stood.

People said he was close to a hundred years old, but Ham thought he looked more like perhaps eighty. He could get around as well as anyone else, except that Ham or Mort usually took his pail up the hill to the pump for water.

If there was anything he couldn't abide more than shooting his chipmunks, it was dirt. They always had to take off their shoes before going into the boathouse. Inside everything was immaculate, and the pots and pans hanging from nails in the wall shone as brightly as his shiny face, his snow white and always shiny hair, his sparkling and always shiny blue eyes.

It wasn't until last year that Ham had discovered Rob's last name was MacQuarrie and that he came from somewhere in Scotland while still a very small boy.

"I don't remember the place," he would say, "but I think sometimes I can smell it, especially when the leaves are burning and there's a mist on the river."

Ham lay back then on the cool ground, wondering if he could confide in the old man, and in so doing, get help. Rob had some kind of pension. Perhaps he'd be willing to advance the money, and perhaps he'd be satisfied to get it back in whatever kind of payments might be managed.

Ham knew Rob had a sister somewhere. In the west, he thought. Maybe that was where the money was coming from. So perhaps it would be a small thing to the old man, only a little thing, and he would understand. It might be worth a try.

Still there was the matter of the sparrows. That hadn't been settled, and Ham wasn't quite ready to embark upon any other kind of venture until the thing of the sparrows was finished and filed away.

Abruptly then, he made up his mind. Instead of waiting all day for his father, he'd force the issue. Why not?

He crawled from the arbor and stood up. Rock followed

[30

him down the dusty road, and when he wouldn't go back, Ham threw a stone, careful to aim it to one side of the dog. Rock tucked his mop of a tail between his legs, hung his head, and backed off a few steps. One more stone, carefully thrown off to the side, and Rock turned and went slowly up the slope, toward the cottage.

In town Ham viewed his father's equipment lot from the end of the block for signs of any unusual activity. There was none. His father sat beneath a huge black and yellow umbrella advertising overalls, working on papers he had placed on a barrel head around which he'd wound his long legs.

He turned and started toward the lumberyard. Halfway there he met Old Oscar. "Did ya hear, Ham? Did ya hear?" When the boy shrugged, Old Oscar went on. "Someone threw a whole bagful of birds into Van's house, and they had to get the Volunteer Fire Department to help get them out!" Old Oscar laughed. "That guy ought to get a medal." He laughed again, and then proceeded on uptown. Ham could hear him repeating: "A medal. That's what. A medal."

Well, it was even worse than he thought. Perhaps he should go back to the river to permit tempers to cool, to allow Mr. Van Stylehausen the chance to invent any cover stories he might need.

It would be a miserable day, though, not knowing. Waiting could be worse than any whipping. He went doggedly on then, coming closer and closer to the lumberyard.

The sun was getting high, and it was hot. The stretches of sidewalk between the weed patches burned through the callouses on his feet. He went into the road, moved once to get out of the way of a new Model A Ford, and then going back to the center of the road, plodded on.

It was like a western movie he had seen more than a year ago when the whole family had driven the ten miles to Beaver Dam. He remembered the gunman. He too had come down the middle of the road. He too hadn't known what lay in store for him. But he had walked, alone and unafraid, through the dust under a hot sun.

The drama gripped him. He was the gunman. Six feet tall.

Wearing leather chaps. Two guns of confidence hard against his hips.

Ham narrowed his eyes, lengthened his stride, moved with as much determination and purpose as all of his twelve years and all of his five feet could summon—on step by step down the hot, dusty road.

In front of the lumber company office, he turned abruptly and stood with legs spread, hands on his hips.

Mr. Van Stylehausen's huge face appeared in the office window. It jolted Ham's aplomb. For a moment his courage hopped like a drop of water on a hot stove, never knowing which way to go. Then his resolve melted and his eyes flicked from side to side, as though looking for an avenue of escape.

But he was frozen there by the face. Only when it disappeared could he breathe. So once more he tried to steel himself, but it wasn't necessary. Mr. Van Stylehausen stepped through the door, gave him a quick sharp look, and then after turning to lock the office, went on down the street in the direction of his home.

Not a word. No gesture. Just that one look through the window, then the quick, sharp look when he stepped through the door. Nothing else.

Ham felt his knees trembling. Then he was trembling all over. He turned and broke into a trot. He ran until the trembling stopped—past Jumpy Jones's place, on past the depot, the granary, the feed mill—to the gravel road.

Somehow it was over. He knew that.

Five

HAM DID NOT go to Rob that day, but roamed the river banks trying to find reasons why he should not take advantage of a friendship which—considering all the water carrying—was not exactly a one-way-thing of taking all the time.

That night he went to his cot as soon as it was dark and lay, elbow crooked so his head was braced and raised on a palm, listening. And of all things, the one that always amazed him most was that the world did not stop turning because he had problems.

It seemed difficult to understand that his predicament was not enough to keep a raccoon from coming to catch a frog, a fox from killing a rabbit, a walleyed pike from scooping up a crayfish . . .

When he could bring himself to examine briefly, but piercingly, his own finite river bank sphere of life, he sometimes momentarily understood that come heaven or hell the owl would swoop down on the mouse, the bat collect insects out of the air, the nighthawks make their muffled thunder . . . and all things continue their relentless paths. Neither heartache, sickness, death, drought—or his sin—would give pause to these proceedings.

So he fell asleep still troubled, and when he awakened in the morning he was still tired because his loneliness had come to haunt his dreams. If anything, he was a little angry that everything still stood in its place.

His cot was in the corner where it had always been. Mort's

cot was far across the porch in the other corner. His overalls were draped over the straight back chair. There was sun
and shadow.

Even his mother's usual solicitude, as she hung over him at
breakfast, only annoyed him. Nothing had changed, as he had
somehow hoped, almost expected, it should.

The flowers on the table—nasturtiums. The worn place in
the linoleum in front of the sink. The curtains, moving when
someone passed. Butter warm already and melting on his
bread. Milk, yellow with cream, running in the same rivulets
across the gray face of oatmeal. Rock whining at the door to
be let in. Mort stepping heavily, bumping chairs, making
mouth sounds while he ate, slamming the screen door when
he went out.

How could the time of crisis be so rapidly approaching and
the world continue to drag its heels through breakfast, toward
dinner, under the same unassuming sun?

He pushed Rock away when he went out the door, and
the dog looked bewildered. He declined Mort's invitation to a
game of hitting sticks, which they called cricket, and with an
angry shake of his head, went down the hill, each step a
furious barefooted assault on the unyielding earth.

Halfway between his house and Rob's shack, he dropped so
his back was against a basswood dripping with tiny, yellow
flowers which already, though the day was young, were
buzzing with bees.

He neither smelled the fragrance nor was aware of the insistent hum, but only sprawled there, wrapped up in his own
wrath, until Rob—still straight, still tall, still gleaming—saw
him and walked over.

The Old Man stood for a few seconds as though gauging
the mood of his young friend, then said quietly: "I think it's
a good day to go fishing."

Ham's head jerked. He hadn't even been aware of the Old
Man. "Fishing? Fishing!" The words just came out, but then
he recovered, sat upright, and tried to rearrange his face.

"Why not? I'm hungry for a meal. So, would you row for
me?"

He and Mort did, sometimes, row for the Old Man because they liked being with him and because Doc Shallock had said he didn't think it in the best interests of longevity for the Old Man to be rowing himself—"not when you've got boys around to do it."

Almost involuntarily Ham nodded. Then, remembering his manners somewhat, he said, "I guess so." But still he sat, as though in rising he might have to lift the whole dreadful weight of his overburdened conscience.

When Rob turned away he got up, and taking his cane poles from the nails driven into the side of the house, he walked to the gravel shore and put them in the Old Man's green rowboat.

They went downstream, and the rowing was easy until they came to where the Big Pike River spread into Big Pike Lake and the thrust of the current was diffused. Still Ham rowed on until they were nearly at the lake's exact center, where a submerged bar put forth long tails of greenery and where northern pike and walleyes sometimes came to stalk minnows.

"Want to tell me what's bothering you?" Rob finally asked when the hooks had been baited with minnows and the corks were riding the ripples.

Ham turned his head to look at the old man, but then quickly turned back to watch the bobbers. He felt suddenly that the Old Man had no right to know, or even ask the question. He remained silent.

"It isn't as if we've never talked about your troubles," Rob urged.

And what Rob said was true, because both Ham and Mort had, over the years, sat in the immaculate sanctuary that was Old Rob's boathouse and told him things they never could have told their parents.

Following whippings, or almost any punishment, both boys had gravitated to Rob's front stoop to be invited in, treated to butter bread and lemonade, laced ever so lightly with rum.

Then, whether it was the rum or the Old Man's assurance

that, given time, the whole gray world would once more look rosy, they always went away at peace, if not with the world, then at least with themselves.

So Ham felt both anger and resistance melt, and the need to tell someone suddenly became more necessary than the need to hide within himself the thing he had done.

Still he began cautiously: "What religion are you?"

Momentarily Rob was speechless, but in an instant he recovered. "Methodist, I guess. It's been a long time, but yes, I suppose you would say I'm a Methodist."

Ham was silent now, as though considering just how much he, a Catholic, was privileged to confess to a Methodist. But a look at Rob reassured him.

"Well, I stole some money," he blurted.

Rob lifted a pole, let the minnow swing in for examination, and then put it back out.

"Well, that could be serious," he finally said, "and then again it might not be."

"It's serious."

"Well, tell me."

So Ham did. He told the Old Man, haltingly at first, about how, as was his duty, he had been taking up the Sunday collection in church when a stranger in a Palm Beach suit had dropped a ten-dollar bill in the wicker offering basket.

Ham had seen the stranger even before he entered. The church doors had been standing wide, and from the altar where he'd been lighting candles, he had seen the gleam of the car as it pulled up and parked.

He watched the man take the keys from the car, step on the running board, get down and come in, and even then he had wondered how much he would put in the collection basket.

It was a sort of Sunday morning game and made the Mass go faster. He did it so often that at last he knew the banker was always good for a dime, but the poor lady who had sung in the choir until her voice began to crack was always good for a dollar.

He knew that although Mrs. Van Stylehausen tried to make

a lot of change sound like a fortune, Mrs. Jumpy Jones, wife of the bootlegger, always gave a dollar. He knew, even without looking anymore, that Doc Shallock would give fifty cents, and Miss Mallow, when she was in town, invariably put in a nickel and a dime.

Ham had guessed the stranger would be good for a dollar, but then when he put in ten dollars, Ham had stopped right there in front of the entire congregation to stare. Doc Shallock, sitting nearby, had coughed, so he had recovered enough to get on with the collection.

Then it happened. While in the vestibule, circling to the other pews, he had stopped, snatched up the ten dollar bill, and lifting his red cassock, slipped it into a pocket. The boy paused in the telling.

"But, why the ten dollars?" Rob asked.

So Ham had tried to tell him about the bike, the shiny bike, which rain or shine stood out in front of Solomon Sinkman's junkyard with the sign: For Sale—Ten Dollars.

He had touched the bicycle a hundred times, once he had even gotten onto the seat, felt the rubber handle bar grips beneath his fingers. He had put his feet to the pedals, leaned forward, imagined himself speeding down the River Road Hill.

"I know, I know," Rob interrupted him. "I wanted a bike myself one time."

For a moment Ham was unable to continue. He couldn't believe an adult might understand how he had felt about that bicycle. It didn't seem possible anyone else might know how week after week, and then month after month, he had looked at it hoping no one would buy it—dreaming about a hundred different miracles that would put ten dollars in his pocket.

Ham hesitated in the telling. Rob turned to him. "That can't be all?"

If it only had been, Ham thought.

"Well?" Rob said.

So Ham told him that now he had sinned he could not receive Communion until he confessed the sin. He told him he would have to confess to Father Zamanski who recognized every kid's voice, and even if he didn't, would probably insist on restitution before giving him absolution so he could go to Communion again.

"I've missed three Sundays. My parents are getting suspicious. Three times I've told them it's because I broke my fast, drank water after midnight. Pretty soon they aren't going to believe me."

"What's this fast thing?" Rob asked.

"We can't eat or drink anything after midnight if we are going to Communion."

What he didn't tell Rob was how he had thought about stealing the ten dollars from his father's wallet to give it back to the church, hoping that, in the confessional, stealing from a mere man instead of the church would be recognized as a sin of lesser magnitude and win him absolution without restitution.

And what he didn't tell him was how Father Zamanski had pounded him over the head with a missal the morning he'd caught him drinking what wine was left in a cruet. How he had been made to kneel three hours the Christmas day he'd fallen asleep during the sermon at midnight mass and slipped to the sacristy floor right in front of God and everybody.

What he didn't tell him was that during the school year, when they lived in town, he had to ring the six-o'clock-in-the-morning Angelus because the priest had caught him riding the bell rope right up into the belfry to turn the bell over.

And, of course, he couldn't tell him about the sermon a visiting priest, Father John St. John, had given about a man who regularly rifled church boxes during the Middle Ages, and how the man was visited by the Devil and had been taken cursing and frothing to spend a life in chains in an insane asylum.

And he couldn't, of course, tell him what the depths of his mother's sorrow might be if she found out, or to what heights of rage his father might rise.

Nor could he tell him how he had seen the moon put the cross of Christ on his porch screen as an omen, or about the nightmares from which he'd awaken groaning, or the nights

[38

he hadn't slept at all because his mind was searching, searching for some solution.

All he could tell him was that he had stolen ten dollars from the church and that if he didn't get it back so he might confess his sin and return to Communion, he was in the most serious trouble that had come his way in twelve years.

So he stopped talking and looked at Rob. "What about the bike? Won't Sol take it back?" Rob asked.

"I tried. Mr. Sinkman just laughed. Then someone stole it from where I had it hidden in a shed near the Greenville Gravel Pit."

A bobber went under. Rob lifted the pole, waited, and then set the hook. Soon a three pound northern pike was flopping on the floor boards of the boat. Ham put it in a gunny sack, put the sack over the side, and tied the mouth to an oarlock.

"Well, then," Rob resumed the conversation, "what you need immediately is ten dollars."

Ham nodded. Rob waited. Then Ham said: "That's about it."

Rob coughed. "Knowing your father," he said, "I would think you'd better get that ten dollars and get it back in the basket, and then make your peace with that priest."

"He'd half-kill me, my father would," Ham said.

"I know."

"The priest might too."

"You really think so?"

Ham nodded.

"Well, I'll tell you," Rob said. "I'm going to ride to town day after tomorrow with your Dad, and while I'm there I'm going to the bank and draw out ten dollars. Then when you get a chance—anytime—you just pay me back."

Ham couldn't look at Rob. Not because he was elated or because tears had started into his eyes or even because he was grateful. He couldn't look at him because he didn't have anything to say, because sometimes a night can last so long that morning doesn't seem real and it takes at least until noon to get used to it. So he only looked at the corks riding the little ripples, hoping one would go under so there'd be something to do.

Six

W HILE THE O LD M AN and the boy sat fishing, the wind changed, came out of the north and went around to the south. At once they began catching fish, and there was little time to talk more about the ten dollars. Even if there had been, it was not necessary now because the problem would subsequently be solved.

When they had five northern pike and one walleyed pike, the Old Man put up his poles.

"I'm sorry, Ham," he said, "but I have a pressing need to go to the toilet. Do you think you can row me to Indian Island?"

The boy wrapped the lines around his poles, stowed them, and then while the Old Man pulled up the stern anchor, he lifted the bow weight.

He had been rowing a few minutes when Rob held up a hand for the boy to stop. "I'm afraid we aren't going to make it," he said. "I just can't eat fried onions, and at my age I ought to know it."

"But what?"

"Put out an anchor."

Ham went to the bow and dropped the anchor, and by the time he returned, the old man had his trousers down and was getting ready to hang over the side. But when he did the boat teetered dangerously and he slid back in.

"Try to balance the boat," Rob instructed. "Lean on the gunwale."

Ham did, but it was like a mosquito trying to teeter-totter

with an elephant. Rob slid back into the boat. A spasm of pain crossed his face and he clutched at his middle.

"Well, what are we going to do?" Rob said, when the spasm of pain passed. Ham turned to look toward the island. It was at least ten minutes away.

Another spasm of pain took the old man. "We should have brought a pail," he said, when he could talk again.

"How about the minnow bucket?" Ham asked.

"It'd never work. Too tiny."

Once again the Old Man grimaced, and then he grunted: "It won't wait."

Then Ham had an inspiration. "Why don't you go over the side? Take your clothes off?"

Rob thought for a moment. "You know," he said, "maybe you've got something there."

The boat rocked precariously as the Old Man undressed. When he was naked, Ham saw that he was almost covered with silken white hairs that curled, and where his belly ended there was a drift of hair, like a small drift of snow. He averted his eyes, but had to look back when the boat began to teeter.

Under the boy's gaze the Old Man's face darkened and all the skin of his body showed faintly red through the white hairs. Ham tried to keep his gaze averted, but there was something fascinating about the silkiness, and Ham couldn't help but wonder how he kept so much hair so clean.

The Old Man went over the stern. If he had tried to go over a side he would have tipped the boat. When he was in the water he let himself down. When the water was to his neck, his feet touched bottom.

"I can just touch," Rob said, more comfortable now that he was submerged.

Gradually then he worked his way around to the side of the boat where the gunwale was lower than at the stern and he could brace comfortably. Then he did his job, but instead of everything coming in a neat package to sink or go floating away, it came to the surface to encircle the Old Man's neck in a brown slick.

Rob's pale blue eyes misted over, and the pink veins that delicately traced their way through the white field turned red.

"My God," he groaned.

Ham was horrified. To see such an immaculate Old Man literally wearing a collar of excrement so numbed his thought processes that there wasn't even a signal from his brain to make his stomach sick. If Rob had been his enemy and he had planned some humiliation, he wouldn't have been able to come up with a more imaginative denigration.

It was the absolute, the ultimate insult to a man who scrubbed his pots and pans so you could see your face in them, whose floor was immaculate as most women's tables, whose finger nails were always pink as the inside of a clam shell, with half-moons showing white as a first frost.

"My God," Robert MacQuarrie groaned again.

He tried moving. Hanging to the gunwale he circled all the way around the boat, but the feces followed like filings to a magnet. Then he looked up at the boy as though Ham, dry and clean and above it all, might help.

Ham just shook his head. Rob tried to say something, but it was obvious that he couldn't, so he only stood, and the boy could see the veins of the Old Man's nose redden and turn pale, redden and turn pale, as the nostrils dilated and then collapsed, dilated and collapsed.

Finally Ham broke the silence with a whisper: "Maybe if you ducked."

Rob's brow wrinkled, but then he held his nose, went under and the slick closed over him. When he came back up, his hair and face were streaked and the collar was still around his neck.

In desperation he worked his way to the stern, lifted out so he was laying across the back board, and then, grunting, squirmed his way aboard. In lifting the white hairs had strained the scum so that now, sitting there naked, he was covered with his own excrement.

Ham sat dumbfounded, until the Old Man said: "Row!"

The boy grasped the oars, and in his bewilderment, one oar came from the oar lock, and falling to the water, started to float away. He made a grab for it, seated it again in the lock, and then bowing his back, put all his eighty pounds into moving the boat.

Rob sat huddled, his arms locked across his chest, and his legs crossed tightly.

Ham rowed twenty strokes without taking a breath. Then the air exploded from his lungs. He breathed heavily, gasped for another lungful of air, and then rowed again. But he had to breathe, so he slowed his stroke and managed to synchronize his breathing with his rowing.

Gradually the exercise took its share of blood and his brain began to put the episode into more realistic perspective. Perhaps it would all end well on Indian Island. But he didn't dare look up at the Old Man, so he kept his eyes on his feet where they were braced against a crossboard to give him leverage, and more thrust to every stroke.

But he never slacked off, and before they came to the island, he felt that the air he was taking into his lungs was hot and that his arms were coming loose at the shoulders.

Then the boat grated on gravel, but Ham kept rowing until the Old Man said: "Stop!"

Rob got out at the end of the boat into knee-deep water. He waded chest deep and then ducked a dozen times. Then he came back to shore and finding pockets of sand began methodically to scrub himself. Wherever he scrubbed, he turned bright red. Ham couldn't watch. He got up from the boat seat, wandered ashore to walk back among the trees. Then he slouched to the ground, utterly exhausted.

Gradually the tiny blood vessel which had been throbbing in his neck quieted. He heard a muted bird song, the sound of water on the gravel shore, a rude heron squawking somewhere . . . and he dozed.

The Old Man standing over him was enough to awaken Ham and bring him to a sitting position. The boy looked into his face. It was set. It was like a piece of pink rock.

Rob was dressed, so the boy got up. Neither spoke a word. They walked to the boat and the Old Man got in. Ham shoved off and jumped in. When he was back at the oars, he swung the bow so it was aimed toward the river and began methodically to head for home.

All the way not a word was exchanged, and then more than a half-hour later, when the boat was beached beneath the big willows, Rob got up, and while Ham held the boat, he got out. He went straight to his shack without taking his fish poles and disappeared inside.

Ham took out the poles, let what minnows were left back into the river, and then swung the wet bag of fish ashore. They were all alive, so one by one he eased them back into the current and watched as they swam slowly, disappearing into the brown water.

Then he took Rob's poles and laid them quietly alongside his shack. He put his own poles on the nails in his house, and then put his back against the basswood.

If he could have but said something to show the Old Man how sorry he was—any single, simple, thing.

Maybe it wasn't too late. Perhaps a pail of fresh water. He could go in and offer to go to the pump. And perhaps in some way he could put it across to the Old Man that he would never speak of it—that no one else would ever know.

He braced his back against the basswood trunk and pushed erect. At the door he knocked gently, but there was no answer. He knocked harder, and the door swung a little way, so he pushed it open.

Rob was in his high-backed easy chair, his head against the pillow he had sewn into position. He waited for the Old Man to speak, and then when he didn't, Ham said: "I thought you might like a cold drink. I could go for some water."

When Rob didn't answer, Ham took a step forward to see if he was asleep. His eyes were wide, and the eyeballs were moving wildly in his head.

For a moment, the boy said nothing. Then he whispered: "What is it, Rob? What's the matter?"

But the Old Man's lips did not move, nor did he acknowledge Ham's presence in any way except to look wildly from left to right.

"What's wrong? What's happened!" The boy shouted the words. Still Rob sat like a statue.

"Rob!" Ham shouted, suddenly terrified. "My God, Rob! Talk to me! What's the matter?"

But if there was anything on the Old Man's face it was only a look of hurt in his eyes.

Ham tried once more: "Rob!"

Then he turned and raced for the house, and at the stoop he fell over Rock, who was sleeping there, and his head put a dent in the screen door.

The next half-hour was like a bad dream that can follow a boy right down to awakening and then come again when he falls back asleep.

It never seemed to end, and people gathered to stare at the Old Man sitting there. Finally two men lowered him onto a blanket on the floor. It was twenty minutes or more before his father and Doctor Jacob Shallock came, and then they had trouble getting the pick-up truck between the trees so they could back it up to the door.

His mother had seen to it that a cot mattress was on the rusty bed of the old truck that looked like it had been used for hauling gravel. It was she who brought out blankets to put over the Old Man.

Then Doc Shallock had climbed in beside Rob and put a stethoscope to the Old Man's chest. Ham stood alongside, looking for some sign on the doctor's weather-beaten face. But Doc Shallock only compressed his lips, folded the stethoscope and put it into his side coat pocket.

Then he jumped down, and turning to Ham's father, who had been one of the four to carry the Old Man from the shack, said: "He might last to the hospital, but with a stroke like that he might last another five years. Let's hope he dies."

Ham was close enough to see Rob's eyes roll. He had heard! Ham was sure he had heard! The boy was furious. What kind of a doctor would want a man to die?

"Drive slow," Doc said to the man at the wheel. "Speed can't make any difference now, so don't bounce him."

Slowly the truck chugged up the hill, through the narrow place of trees, and Ham ran alongside. When the driver came to the road, he increased his speed. Still Ham followed, running swiftly, as if it was necessary that the Old Man see him, know that he was still there.

At the curve a blanket blew out, but the truck did not stop. Dust billowed behind to close around the boy. The truck drew ahead. He stopped running. On the way back he picked up the blanket, started up the hill with it, and then crushed it into a ball and threw it back where the blackbirds were cheering.

Seven

THAT NIGHT June bugs thumped the screen, but the drone of mosquitos had subsided to a whine, and the chorus of frogs broken off to solo efforts. Though officially summer would not arrive until tomorrow, it had been hot since school let out almost a month ago, and it was a rare night that sleepers didn't perspire until the earlier hours of morning.

Ham lay withered, not only by the heat, but by the catastrophic turn of events. He was not yet programmed to accept tragedy when it struck without warning, any more than he might shrug off a lightning bolt if it struck his house.

He lay for a long time, staring at the spot of light that seeped under the door from the kitchen where his mother and father sat around the kerosene lamp. When the light finally went out, he turned on his other side and looked through the leaves to where the sky of stars was a broken brilliance.

Mercifully then, the vicissitudes of what must have been the longest day of his life gathered, it seemed, to an exhausting focus and he slept soundly, never dreaming, never awakening, not until the sun was up.

Carl Gremminger told him then that Rob had died during the night. The Gremmingers had a phone, and so he learned of it while standing in the cool milk house at the hill farm, waiting for the farmer to fill the lard pail he had been carrying.

Then after he had given Mr. Gremminger the nickel, he followed the cow path back, and he was surprised that he had not even enough sorrow left to evoke a single tear.

Rob was pretty much with him during the next several days, but finally his own troubles beckoned for entrance and he had no way but to let them in. It was impossible to avoid going to church on Sunday, and once at the altar, he had devised no way to dodge Communion.

Of course he might go with the sin on his soul, but to receive the Sacrament while not in the state of grace was a sacrilege and even sufficient grounds, he assumed, for excommunication. It would be as bad, or perhaps even worse, than a priest taking a wife.

But this Sunday he was trapped. Three Sundays in a row he had excused himself by saying he had broken his fast. It wouldn't work again. It was like standing on a hill seeing a storm coming and having no place to hide.

First there were the bells of the offertory, marking the progress of the Mass. Then the bells of consecration, shaking him like wind can a thin reed. Then came the first bell of Communion, and before the bell could ring a second time he jumped up, genuflected, and ducked out into the sacristy.

Without looking back he headed for the basement, and then, though he didn't have to go, he lifted his cassock, unbuttoned his pants, and made a few token squirts into the toilet bowl.

After Mass he explained to Father Zamanski that he couldn't hold it, that he was afraid he was going to have an accident. The priest's fishy, pale eyes told him he was a liar.

He told the same story to his parents while they drove from town, along the River Road, back to the cottage. And what could they say?

So Sunday went. The heat hung on and on Monday Ham still had no clue as to how he might raise the ten dollars. The Van Stylehausen fifty cents was in a tin can. The tin can was under some rocks in his hiding place where the vines arched in arbors on the cedars.

He went to check it. It was still there. Then he climbed the slope to the crest of the gravel pit and lay in the skimpy shade of a scraggly ironwood. While he was there a huge snapping turtle moved ponderously up the slope, and while he watched she went slipping and sliding over the crest, scattering stones in her descent, all the way to the bottom.

Ham sat up. Turtles were worth money. But he didn't hurry down because he knew the turtle would be a long while in the pit. She had come to lay eggs, which was a laborious thing which might last through the day.

Sometimes his father unhinged a turtle, separating the many kinds of meats, and his mother made a thick soup with carrots, peas, potatoes, and celery. But if he took a turtle home he would not be paid. He was expected to catch and clean fish for the table, and someday when he could hunt, he would offer the day's kill as a cooperating member of the family.

The turtle had walked across the pit floor to where an island of grass was beginning to grow since the trucks had stopped coming.

Ham got up and slid down after the turtle. When he approached, the turtle retracted her head, but then when Ham stopped, she put it out again to twist and turn and blink. When nothing happened, the turtle continued scooping out a hole in which to lay her eggs.

She moistened the soil, and using only her hind legs in a swimming motion, quickly widened what would be an egg pouch in the sand and gravel, but never made the opening larger than was necessary to get her one foot through. The eggs would be round as ping-pong balls and rubbery. She would cover them, and then sometime during the summer, depending upon the heat of the sun, tiny replicas of herself would claw their way to the surface and head instinctively for water.

While he watched, rocks rattled again. He looked up. A second turtle was coming down the slope. Both were huge and almost as round as the wheels on the Model T. Black, corrugated, and moss covered, with leeches still stuck, but dying in the hot sun.

Turtles had always fascinated Ham. He and Mort had

stabled painted turtles and raced them one summer. Often he found a smaller turtle with his initials—one of a score or more he had marked.

But the little painted turtles (muds, he called them) were not good to eat. Only the snappers yielded edible meat, and what's more, it was legal to catch and sell them because they had predator classification—preyed on fish and water birds or even muskrats—though they preferred carrion.

But who would buy them? Jumpy Jones? There was always a sign in Jumpy's window: TURTLE SOUP FREE FRIDAYS. It helped him sell his home brew, his moonshine.

Jumpy bought his turtles from men who hooked them out of the marsh mud in winter, after they'd gone below to hibernate. Then he kept them in his coal bin, and Ham had heard people who'd been in the basement say they didn't know which smelled worse, the fermenting beer or the coal bin full of turtles.

Well, it was worth a chance. The second turtle was busy digging by now, and the first was already laying round, white, rubbery eggs. But perhaps he should wait until they had laid their eggs. So he sat in the hot sun in the bottom of the treeless gravel pit—knees pulled up, arms wrapped around them, head bent, sweat glistening on his forehead—watching the reptilian throwbacks do what turtles have been doing since long before there were any men to interfere.

The first turtle finished and carefully covered the hole. Then, dragging its shell across the area to camouflage it, she started her long trek back to the cool river.

Ham intercepted her, and when she bit down savagely on a stick, he grabbed her tail and flipped her on her back. He didn't wait, but dragging the turtle by the tail went to where the second turtle was still digging.

He put out the stick, and the second turtle grabbed it. He flipped the reptile as he had the first, and then dragging both on their backs labored up the side of the pit and out to the dusty River Road.

It was no easy thing. The turtles twisted and turned, and their rind-hard beaks grabbed onto any passing thing—bush and bunch of grass, sticks, and stones. Then when he was on the road, eggs began rolling out of the turtle which hadn't had a chance to lay hers. He kicked them into the roadside grass and started toward town.

The short tails, however, offered little leeway, and he had to walk in a bent over position to keep from lifting the snappers partially off the ground.

At the top of the first hill, he stopped and waited. The turtles kept him busy. They clawed the roadbed straining to get away. A car came by with a half-dozen kids hanging out the backseat. Ham hurried off into the ditch, and the kids shouted and laughed.

Well, he couldn't drag them all the way to town with only their tails to hold to, so he turned them loose, and went wire hunting. He found a loose piece under an old fence, and by twisting and turning, he made himself two eight-foot lengths.

Then he rounded up the turtles. One of them had wandered almost half the distance back along the road to the river, and the other had gone off into a field, perhaps to relieve herself of what eggs were still waiting to be laid.

First to one and then to the other's tail, he twisted the wire. Then he made loops for hand holds at the other end. Then he flipped the turtles again and was on his way—the huge, black saucers digging dust trails, their necks arching and legs flailing.

After a quarter-mile, the wire was cutting his palms so he had to stop and pad the loops with folded burdock leaves.

Another quarter-mile and the outraged turtles, probably exhausted, became submissive. They tucked in their heads and let their legs go limp, and behind each lifted a little trail of dust. He passed the city limits sign, came off the dust road onto the gravel, and his reptilian cargo slid more easily over the stones.

At the tracks he had to stop. A train, pouring black smoke from its engine chimney and steam from its hard underbelly, came clanging by. The turtles arched their necks and flipped themselves upright. Perhaps some people looking out the windows of the coaches wondered about a boy out walking such strange pets.

The turtles took off in opposite directions when the train stopped, one coach still blocking the crossing, and he stood, arms spread, between them. People waved and laughed, and one man shoved up a window and, hanging his head out, shouted: "First time I saw a boy with a turtle by the tail."

The tiger-turtle play on words was lost on Ham because he had never heard the expression. He waited with a weary look on his dusty, sweat-streaked face, and then when the train started again, he flipped the turtles on their backs. When he came to the next intersection, he turned up the street toward Jumpy Jones's place.

The few people he passed smiled and walked far off onto lawns to avoid him. A gang of several small children, first amazed and then amused, crowded around and began to taunt him. He ignored them until they closed in, and then dropping one wire he began swinging the other turtle around along the ground in the style of a hammer hurler. He scattered kids in every direction.

When he came to Jumpy Jones's place he went around to the back door. Mrs. Jones, a tidy little woman with a crippled left arm, was on the back steps, threading the strings out of string beans. She looked up and smiled. Ham felt immediately at ease. She knew him, of course, from church, and now she asked: "Hammond, what can I do for you?"

"Could I see Jumpy, I mean Mr. Jones?"

She got up and went in, and he heard her call: "Harold? Hammond Drumm would like to see you."

She didn't come back out, and Ham waited. In a few minutes Jumpy came through the door, and he was, as usual, in a dirty undershirt. He smelled as he perpetually did, of moonshine, and now he squinted as though his eyes wouldn't work unless he did.

"What you got?" he asked.

"Two snappers. Want to buy them?"

Jumpy pushed strings of brown hair back from his forehead as though they were obstructing his vision, although they didn't even come down as far as his eyebrows.

"Well I don't know," he said, coming down another step and leaning to get a better look. "They're sure big."

"As big as I've ever seen," Ham said.

"If I hadn't just paid my bills. And then too, I got a few turtles left. I don't know. Maybe there isn't any money in the till. How much do you want?"

"Fifty cents apiece," Ham blurted. He wondered why he hadn't said a dollar as he had intended. They were worth that much, probably more. Turtle hunters who barreled them and shipped the barrels to New York got much more.

"Let me go see," Jumpy said, going back in.

While he was gone, a couple kids his age came along and began bothering the turtles. Ham told them to beat it.

"Make us," they said in unison.

Ham threatened with an end of the barbed wire. The boys backed off.

Jumpy came back out onto the small porch. "All I can give you is fifty cents for the both of them," he said.

Ham shook his head. "No."

"Well," Jumpy said, "I'll give you fifty cents and a pint of moon, and maybe you can sell the moon."

Ham reflected a moment and then said: "I don't want the moon."

Jumpy pulled up the end of his dirty undershirt to wipe the sweat from his face. "Well, take it or leave it," Jumpy said irritably, "but if you don't want it, get those damn turtles out of here."

Ham looked at the turtles which by now had gouged deep holes in the dirt by the steps in their persistent, strong-clawed effort to get away.

"I'll take it," he said.

Jumpy handed him a fifty cent piece. "Wait," he said, going back inside. When he came back he handed Ham a brown paper sack with a pint of moonshine in it.

Ham turned over the wire leads to Jumpy and pattered away down the sidewalk without looking back.

He wished he hadn't taken the moonshine, but now that he

had it, he might as well try to sell it to someone. Old Oscar might buy it.

He went to the square, but Old Oscar wasn't on his bench. He hurried to the feed store, but Oscar wasn't there. Then he headed for the park, and even before he got there, he could see Old Oscar under a huge oak which shaded the bandstand.

"Want to buy a pint of moon?" Ham asked when Oscar sat up.

"Sure," said Oscar, digging into a pocket. "How much?"

"Fifty cents," Ham said.

Oscar pulled out a quarter. "It's all I got. I'll buy half."

"But I got nothing to pour it into," Ham said.

"That's all right. I'll just drink it right now." He handed Ham the quarter and took the sack. He brought forth the bottle and made an imaginary line halfway down with a broken thumb nail.

"Okay?" Old Oscar asked.

"Okay," Ham said.

Oscar put the bottle to his lips and in three gulps half emptied it. He handed the bottle and sack back to Ham and then lay back down. Ham put the cork back into the bottle and the bottle back into the sack.

He started away and then turned back. He didn't want the moonshine, so Oscar might as well have it. But Old Oscar was already snoring, lying loose like a pile of rags, and no amount of prodding would awaken him.

Ham felt like throwing the moonshine away, but kept it, thinking perhaps he'd meet someone on the way out of town who would buy it. He did meet several people, but he knew without asking that none of them would buy the moon.

Well, he had seventy-five cents. Added to the Van Stylehausen half-dollar, that made a dollar and a quarter. He had eight dollars and seventy-five cents to go. It was a beginning, but where in Greenville would he get the rest when grown men were mowing lawns for whatever people might pay them, where in Greenville where times were so bad the curtains on the bank went up only mornings and the door was always locked during the afternoon?

He trotted on the hot sidewalk, but slowed when the sidewalk ended and there were only stones. He thought about Old Oscar, and wondered what it was that made Old Oscar drink. His father said that it was to forget—a woman, a crime, a sin.

He looked down at the brown bag in his right hand. He had tasted beer and disliked it. He had liked the altar wine until Father Zamanski switched from sweet to sour wine. But moonshine?

He took the bottle out of the bag. It looked harmless enough. It was amber, like the sunshine when there was a gauze of clouds.

At the Creek Crossing he turned off the road and went down to where the stream curled off into the shade before making a straight and rocky run to the marsh. He sat in the shade and uncorked the bottle. He smelled it, and it brought tears to his eyes.

He waited until the tears dried, then he lifted the bottle and sipped a little. He nearly strangled. When he could breathe, he put the bottle next to a rock and leaned over for a mouthful of creek water.

Then he sat back to contemplate the bottle. He looked at it for a long time, and then he took it to the creek and, holding it down, tilted it so water could run in. When it was full he shook it and went back into the shade.

Then he sipped. It burned a little, but it didn't taste bad. He took a swallow and it was like a streak of warm sunshine all the way into his stomach. He took another and felt the sunshine spread and spread—out and up and even to the roots of his hair.

He took another swallow. The glen he knew so well became a fairy place of misty greens.

Still another swallow, and he sat up. He knew now that he could go straight to Father Zamanski and tell him how it was with him, God, and the church. He could tell his father. He'd find Lydia. He'd ask Mr. Van Stylehausen if he wanted any more sparrows. He'd kiss Miss Mallow right back, just as hard as she had kissed him, and then he'd leave her sitting. He'd build a monument to Rob . . .

The last thing he remembered before stumbling back to the road was the empty bottle bright and shining on the current of the creek. He remembered it dipping and lifting and sliding easily around rocks. He remembered it riding high and beautiful as a silver duck, a shaft of solid sunshine, a chalice in the altar spotlight. . . .

His father, on his way home from work, found him in the dust unconscious and covered with his own vomit.

Eight

THAT WAS a black night. Except for the brief sparkle of fireflies (which Ham never saw) clouds closed over the sky to shut out the stars. Ham awakened around midnight to be sick again, and he heard his mother: "In the pail, in the pail . . . the pail . . . the pail . . ." Like an echo.

Then he awakened again shortly before dawn, and his mother was still sitting there, but he didn't know it until he felt her cool hand on his warm forehead. He tried to lift himself, and then he heard her sob softly. Then they wept quietly—together.

The next time he awakened it was to a gray day. He had no idea what time it was, and though he listened for clues, there were none.

His stomach churned. His head ached. Then he remembered the bottle riding high and shining down the creek, and he wondered how he had gotten home and into bed.

He tried to sit up, but the porch floor tilted. He gagged, but only a thick mucus came into his mouth and he managed to swallow it. A slop pail was beside his bed. When he saw it, he gagged again.

"You awake, Ham?" His mother had come on tiptoe. He only nodded. "Can you sit up?" He swung his legs out, steadied himself with his hands to the cot, and sat erect. The tree limbs beyond the screen went in and out of focus. The floor tilted. The wall came close, went back. But he hung on.

"I've got some soup for you," his mother said.

The thought of food made him gag again. His mother picked a rag off the floor and wiped his chin.

"You've got to try to eat," she said. "Something."

Shakily he reached for his overalls, and hitching up his shorts from where they'd slid down around his thighs, he held to the chair, lifted himself, and dressed.

He walked gingerly then to the kitchen where the soup was waiting. At first he had to look away from it lest he be sick again. Then he sat down in front of it and picked up a spoon. The spoon trembled. Soup spilled. He got some into his mouth.

Gradually the chicken soup (more golden and rich for being a day old) settled his stomach. Slowly his head cleared.

"Why did you do it, Hammond?" his mother asked.

"I never meant to," he said, looking up. Tears glistened in her black eyes. She blinked, and they rolled down her smooth cheeks on either side of her straight nose. Ham looked away. Tears came into his eyes.

"Your father is furious. I don't know what he'll do."

Ham's stomach started churning again.

"What's troubling you, Ham? Can't you tell me? Ever since school let out you've been a different boy, a stranger."

Here was his chance. He recognized it. Now he could blurt it all out. Tell her everything. With one sweep, wipe the slate clean—the lies . . . everything.

He almost did. But he made the mistake of looking at her and knew that he couldn't add to her sorrow. The way she felt. About church and God. He couldn't. Not add it to all that had already happened. He couldn't. Maybe someday when it was all over. But not now.

When he didn't answer she leaned over and put her fingers in his hair. Now he couldn't hold back the tears, so he got up from the table and hurried outside.

He stood for a moment to brush away the tears, and then he saw Mort coming up from the river. He started away toward the marsh, but Mort saw him and ran. Rock was with him, and he came to leap joyfully, almost knocking him down.

"Dad said you were drunk," Mort blurted with glee. "I saw

him carry you in and wash you up. You were white as a ghost. You looked dead, and you stunk like Jumpy Jones."

Ham turned. Suddenly he was savage. "Beat it!" he said.

Mort came closer. "I don't have to beat it! Not for no dumb drunk! That's what Dad said you were: 'A drunken bum!' He said he found you laying right in the middle of the road, drunk, and said that he'd never thought he'd see the day that a son of his would lay drunk in the road!"

Ham clenched his fists. Any control he might have had was now stretched thin like a wire ready to snap.

He turned to glare at Mort. The look only triggered more abuse. "Drunken bum! Drunken bum! Puke all over yourself! Drunken bum!"

Ham took a quick step and swung. He hit Mort squarely on the nose with all the force of his stringy eighty pounds. Blood gushed forth at once. When Mort saw it, his astonishment swelled to a crescendo of wails. He ran to the house, blood welling down over his chin to stain his overall bib.

"My God, my God, my God!" Ham breathed the words, and his voice was like the whisper of poplar leaves, astonished at the wind. He started running, down the outhouse path, around the outhouse, and to the fence. He tried to go over, got hung up, pulled away, and tore his overalls. Then he dropped to his knees and scuttled beneath the lower wire. He ran again, all the way to the marsh and into the water where the rushes were thickest. There he threw himself on an old muskrat house.

He lay huddled for a long time, and a muskrat swam close to eye him. A huge carp swam lazily by, and a great blue heron dropped down a few feet away, saw him, and with a startled squawk lumbered into uncertain, precarious flight.

Twice he heard his mother call, but he did not answer. The decaying vegetation gave off heat, so he clung close to it and was screened by the new cattails that were already pointing green fingers that would turn brown and fluff away come winter.

He fell asleep and awakened, fell asleep and came awake again . . . he didn't know how many times because even the waking moments had a dream-like, cotton candy consistency.

Then when he opened his eyes, the gray sky had darkened and a single star shone briefly before the clouds covered it again.

Still he waited. Some mosquitos came, and he let them bite him, refusing to brush them away. Close at hand then, he heard his father: "Ham! Hammond! You in there?" But he did not reply.

"Ham! I know you're in there, so come out now if you know what's good for you!"

Ham lifted his head, but he did not get up.

"You're only making things worse. The longer you hide, the worse it has to be."

That was the truth. Ham knew it. He didn't have a chance. There was no hiding—anywhere. No running. No escaping. He tried to get up, but found his legs so cramped he slumped back down to the soggy mound of decaying rushes. He tried again, made it, and then slowly sloshed through the water.

"It's time you ate something," his father said.

Ham was surprised. He had expected to be immediately and painfully punished. His father started up the hill. He trailed, head bent.

At the supper table he kept his eyes on his plate and tried to force the food down, but the beans were like little stones in his throat.

His mother left the table to take her dishes to the sink. Mort got up and scraped his plate into the garbage pail and put it atop his mother's. Then he eyed Ham, and gingerly fingered his swollen, red nose.

"You through, Ham?" his father asked. Ham nodded. "Then wash up. Put on your Sunday things."

The boy's face had been expressionless, but now it showed surprise. He dipped water from the pail into the wash basin and began to scrub his face.

"Down to the river," his father said, coming over to hand him a towel. He went down to the river, shucked off his overalls, shirt, and shorts and scrubbed. He put the towel around his middle and went back up the hill and into the house.

When he was dressed his father was standing at the door. He said: "Come on." Ham turned to his mother as if for help. She only shook her head sadly.

He followed his father out to the car and got in. His father put the gas lever down and the spark lever up and went around to crank. When the engine roared, his father shouted: "Put down the spark." He reached over to put down the spark. Then his father shouted again. "Put up the gas." The roar diminished.

The car started slowly down the hill and then picked up speed. Night had come again, and the jiggling headlights lifted to the leaves, danced to the thickets, the stone piles lining the road.

Several banded nighthawks swished away, just feet in front of the wheels. Several cottontails panicked and ran ahead of the car before darting off into the ditch. Bugs squashed against the windshield and spread their lives in green, starry stains.

The car came off the dusty River Road onto the gravel. The village limits sign shown briefly white, and then the car bumped across the railroad tracks. It went up Railroad Street to go past Jumpy Jones's place, and Ham heard the blare of music: *Yes sir, that's my baby. No sir, don't mean maybe* ... It faded.

All the way up Main Street, then a right turn to North Main. Then just past the church, and in front of the rectory they stopped.

When his father told him to get out of the car, his legs refused to move. From the sidewalk his father called: "Ham! Are you coming?"

The boy stepped onto the fender, stumbled, and went over to his knees on the grass. The grass was cool. It felt yielding beneath his fingers. He could smell freshness, as if it had been recently mowed. He would have liked to lie on it, press himself into it, be swallowed up by it, go down and down until he became a part of it, and never have to get up.

Mr. Drumm was clearing his throat again. He felt his father's hand on the shoulder of the thick, woolen suit that was his winter and summer best. He got up, and following behind, went around on the narrow walk to the side entrance of the rectory.

Miss Biddie Floyd, the housekeeper, let them in. She took them through a dining room with a table on which dinner dishes still stood, and then at a pair of dark, forbidding sliding doors, she knocked gently. Ham heard a newspaper rustle. Then Father Zamanski's voice: "Is it Mr. Drumm?"

"Yes, Father, it is."

"Well, let him in then."

It seemed like magic that the doors parted when Miss Floyd put a hand to each. They stepped inside, and Ham heard the doors click shut behind them.

Father Zamanski was in a huge, black leather chair, behind a newspaper. Slowly he lowered the paper to look over the top. Ham got the quick, cold feeling that it was like seeing a lizard come out of its lair. The priest folded the paper and put it down. Then he picked up a long-stemmed, thin pipe and filled it with tobacco.

"Good evening, Mathew," the priest said. He ignored Ham. "Have a chair." Mr. Drumm sat down on a straight back chair, pulled out his corncob pipe, and when Father Zamanski proffered the canister, he filled it. Ham stood between them.

"Business picking up any?" the priest asked.

Ham stole a look at Father Zamanski out of the corner of an eye. He always felt the priest was made of parchment, maybe because of the dull, gray color of his skin, or the pallor of his eyes, or the way the little veins shown through along the tops of both hands.

Ham's father lighted his corncob, and then answered: "Some business, but not much."

"But it will pick up. It will. You watch. They'll elect a Democrat," Father Zamanski said. He sent a cloud of smoke toward a white Christ on a huge black cross on the wall.

"Maybe you're right," Mathew said. "Hoover sure isn't doing anything."

Ham was beginning to tremble. Now he could smell the incense, a smell which he suspected permeated the person of all priests. For a panicky instant he thought about retreat, back through the sliding doors, out to where the grass was cool and he could roll until the fresh smell of it had become a part of the sweaty wool suit.

His eyes galloped wildly from side to side—to the holy water font with a white, winged angel guarding it, to the picture of Christ, heart exposed and blood dripping.

But how far would he get, and where, in the first place, could he go? His rigid shoulders slumped. His head hung an inch lower.

Father Zamanski was leaning forward now, pointing with the stem of his pipe. "But let me tell you, Mathew, we asked for it. Every bit of it. And, it's not unlike the fall of Rome, because there's no escaping justice—not in this world or the next.

"Just think," he went on, emphasizing with the stem of his pipe, "how we have sinned. So now we have to pay for it, for a decade, nearly two decades of sin."

Ham felt his knees getting weaker. He didn't know if he could hold out. Sweat made his head itch, but he was afraid to scratch it.

"Think back, Mathew," the priest went on. "Think back how it started with the girls cutting their hair. Then the short dresses. The music, the jazz! The moonshine, gangsters! Nobody safe in the streets. People killing one another for a few dollars, for a drink. The movies. The permissiveness. The scandalous parties. Sex, even in the schools. Let me tell you, Mathew, it had to come! It is God's justice! God's children were spitting in His face. They had to pay! No generation has been so immoral. Even the sanctity of marriage, the family, is being threatened."

Mathew nodded, not once, but after every ejaculation, after every sentence.

Ham could feel his muscles go soft. He was afraid that, like noodles, they might fold. He would collapse then, right on the red rug with the blue fringe.

Both men were quiet, and both puffed solemnly on their pipes. The room took on a blue haze, and Ham's eyes began to smart. When he lifted a hand to rub them, Father Zamanski turned to him. "Your father tells me," he began, "that you're having troubles."

Ham couldn't look at the priest, so he looked over his shoulder at a scraggly fern in an enormous green jardiniere. When he didn't answer, his father reached across and nudged him in the ribs with the stem of his pipe.

"Yes, Father," he said in a barely audible vioce.

"Want to tell me about it?" the priest asked.

What could he say? The two men waited. Somewhere a clock was ticking. The pipe stem again. "I don't know," he mumbled. "Things just seem to go wrong."

As though he couldn't contain himself, Mathew Drumm said loudly: "Wrong? Wrong is hardly the word!"

Father Zamanski leaned back, made a church steeple of his fingers and then said quietly. "Maybe it is because you have deserted your God. You know we all need Him and I haven't been seeing you take Communion."

Then the priest smiled but if it was meant to be a smile of encouragement it failed dismally. There could be no warmth, no compassion in the thin, bloodless lips, and Ham had heard one of the back pew cynics once say the priest was so stringy because any fat on his bones would have been considered a luxury.

The priest was talking again: "I'll tell you Hammond, there's none of us so big we can get along without God, and there's none of us so little that He won't help us. But we've got to do *our* part." As if it took effort, he came down hard on the "our."

Mathew Drumm nodded approval, and perhaps encouraged by his support (though it isn't likely Father Zamanski needed any support), the priest continued: "If we don't do *our* part, if we are lax, then we are lost—lost as Lucifer. Maybe yours is the sin of Lucifer—the sin of pride. Perhaps you feel it is no longer necessary to fall to your knees . . ."

Ham thought if the torture didn't end soon, that would happen—he would fall to his knees. And once on his knees, he would fall to his face. He didn't know how he could hold out.

[64

But if there was any mercy in either Father Zamanski or Mathew Drumm, perhaps this was the way they thought it should be dispensed: By bringing a boy right up tight to the hot reality of hell so he would henceforth be chastened.

"You wouldn't want to burn in hell forever and forever?" Father Zamanski asked. Ham shook his head.

"Speak up," Mathew Drumm prompted.

"No, Father."

The walls began pulsing in and out. He grabbed his upper lip between his teeth and bit down hard so the reality of pain would keep him from collapsing.

The priest turned to Mathew Drumm. "Would you mind waiting in the dining room for a moment. I'd like to be alone with the boy."

When his father had closed the sliding doors, the priest told him to kneel. Then he came over, and spreading his hands over his head, began to pray in Latin. After the prayer he put his fingers lightly to the boy's temple and then increased the pressure.

"So the Holy Ghost may go from this holy servant of Christ to you," he said, pressing harder and harder on the boy's temples.

Ham swayed, but he was held so tightly between the priest's bony fingers he couldn't fall. Then he felt the pressure relax, heard the priest move back to his chair.

"You can get up."

Ham put both hands to the floor and bracing, pushed himself up to where he could get a grip on the chair his father had been sitting on. Then he got to his feet.

"Mathew," the priest called. "You can come in now." Ham heard the doors slither open. He hung onto the chair because he had come to the end of his endurance. Perhaps the priest saw it, because he said: "You can go now, Hammond. But Mathew, I want to talk to you."

The boy started dizzily toward the door. "Wait in the car," his father said.

He never knew how he managed the sliding doors or how he made it across the dining room and got outside. But the air revived him, and he could see the shadow of the cross high on the church steeple.

He walked slowly, opened the back door of the Model T, and got in. Then, curling tightly as a fetus, he lay on the back seat and let go of the world.

Nine

His confrontation with the priest had had such nightmarish overtones that he could not relate it to reality, so the next morning his mind filed it in that place where youthful minds have the capacity for filing bad dreams.

But he was wary enough of his father to stay on his cot until he heard the Model T leave, and then he went to the kitchen where his mother went through enough motherly motions to convince him that she loved him very much—if not enough to stand up to the wrath of his father.

So by the time he got outside, his mutilated ego was somewhat repaired, and when Mort came bristling in imitation of his father, he found an adversary on which he could further hone himself.

"What happened last night?" Mort started off. "Dad take you to the sheriff?"

Ham started to say "no," checked himself, and said: "Yeah, he took me to the sheriff."

Mort, drawing his mouth into a straight line like his father did when he was being righteous, asked: "What for? For drinking moonshine?"

Ham nodded. "For drinking moonshine." And then gilding the lily, he added: "And for selling moonshine to Old Oscar."

Mort couldn't hide his surprise. Then he relaxed back into being an eleven-year-old boy. "What are they going to do to you?"

"Jail I expect," Ham said, "or at least the boy's reformatory."

Ham had suddenly gained the upper hand. He was crushing Mort. Tears gathered in the younger boy's eyes.

"They can't send you to jail for something like that. You didn't mean to do it," Mort's voice quavered.

"Oh, no?" Ham said. "What makes you think they can't? Look at Old Oscar. He's been in jail dozens of times, and all he ever does is get drunk."

Ham snipped off a grass blade and chewed it importantly. He could even picture himself behind bars with the family in the prison corridor with presents for him—all weeping. He had to make it solid, so he said: "I suppose the Goeztke kid was a grown man? He was just a kid, and you know where he is. He's behind bars in the reformatory!"

Mort protested: "But he was a lot older than you, and anyway, he almost killed Old Lady Metz by beating her with a hammer."

Ham argued: "The law is the law. When you break a law, you get it. It doesn't make any difference what law or even how old you are."

He had convinced Mort. His brother sank to the ground and began weeping. Ham felt he had gone far enough. He had accomplished what he had set out to accomplish, so now he went over and put a hand on Mort's head. "But don't worry," he said, "because I'm not going to let them get me."

Mort looked up through his tears. "But what can you do? How are you going to keep them from getting you?"

Ham thought about it. There were intriguing possibilities. "Maybe I'll run away," he said.

"They'd catch you," Mort said. "They always catch the criminal—I mean," he quickly tried to correct himself, "they always get the man they're after."

Ham had an inspiration. "I'd die before I'd go to jail," he said. "I'd probably kill myself."

Mort started rubbing his eyes and laughing with relief. "Now I know you're kidding, because if you killed yourself you would go to hell."

Ham put his shoulders back and struck a pose. "Maybe

I'd meet a lot of interesting people down there." He had heard it somewhere.

Mort got to his feet. "Cut it out, Ham! It's even a sin to talk like that!"

There was that word again. It made him pause and think. No matter what his intentions, not matter how he tried, he kept jumping from the back of one sin right onto the back of another.

But this was too good to let go of, so Ham picked it up again: "How come you're so sure I wouldn't kill myself to stay out of jail?"

Mort *was* sure of himself. "Because it would hurt. Because you are scared to. And because you'd go to hell for it."

Ham snorted. He was losing his advantage. "I been hurt plenty of times, and I ain't scared of nothing, and maybe jail is even worse than hell!"

The grin left Mort's face. "You better look out! God's listening!"

Ham began wearying. He wanted to back off, drop it, but a perverse something deep down prodded him on: "Well, you started this whole thing, and now you gotta know that I'm not scared of anything, not even . . ." he had meant to say "hell," but he played it safe and said, ". . . not even jail!"

Mort sensed that Ham was backtracking, easing himself out of an untenuous place. So now he pushed what he considered *his* advantage: "You're just a big BS-er!"

Ham felt the urge to clout his brother, but the recent bloody nose deterred him. So he stalled. "You think I'm a BS-er? You think I wouldn't kill myself?"

"How would you do it?" Mort laughed, "Stab yourself with a pin?"

Ham was suddenly furious. "All right, smart guy. All right, smart guy. What if I swam right out there," he pointed to the middle of the river, "and dived down and grabbed a rock and hung on until I was dead."

Mort was jumping in circles around Ham. He knew he had him on the run. "You couldn't stay down. When you needed to breathe, you'd come popping up just like a cork."

That did it, and Ham swung at Mort, but the boy ducked. "That's what you think!" Ham shouted. "Well, I'll just show you!"

Mort howled: "Show me! Show me! Ham's gonna show me!"

Ham ran to the house and came back in his swimming trunks. In the interim his anger had cooled. But so long as he had his trunks on, he figured he might get some relief from the heat. On the gravel edge of the river, he tested the water with a toe.

"What kind of flowers you want on your coffin?" Mort said, coming up behind Ham.

Ham turned. "If it was your coffin, I'd put skunk cabbage on it."

It was Mort's cue to start up again: "Skunk cabbage would be too good for you. I'd get some thistles."

Ham turned angrily. "You shut up, you damn kid! You just shut up!"

"I don't have to shut up. And anyway, I'm not a BS-er like you. You're nothing but a big mouth. Yeah, all mouth! Nothing but mouth! Not even any arms or legs or any body— only mouth!"

Ham waded knee deep and turned. "I'll show you! I'll show you!" He plunged in and swam beyond his depth. Then he dove and got a fistful of mud. When the fire in his lungs was no longer bearable, he popped to the surface gasping.

He could hear Mort howling from the shore: "Big mouth BS-er! Big mouth BS-er! Hot air. Nothing but hot air!"

Ham swam in circles. When he was breathing more easily, he dove again. On the shore, Mort kept jumping and howling. But when, after twenty or thirty seconds, Ham didn't pop back to the surface, his howling subsided. Finally, after a minute, when there was still no sign of his brother, he went to the water's edge and shouted: "Ham!" Then he screamed: "Ham!"

He searched the surface for some sign, but just as it hid so many mysteries, so now it hid his brother.

"Ham! Ham. Haaa . . ." his voice trailed off. There was nothing out there. Just water, slowly moving water, rippled a little by a breeze, shining in the path of the sun, molten where the willows shaded it.

For half a minute Mort stood transfixed. Then he whirled about, went scrambling up the hill, and screamed: "Mother! Ma! Mother! Ma! Ham's drowned! Ham's dead!"

Mrs. Drumm came running, her long skirts catching at her legs. "What are you saying?" The boy grabbed her dress and pulled her down the hill. Hair pins fell from the bun at the nape of her neck and loose hairs trailed.

"I saw it! I saw it! He went down and didn't come back up!"

Mrs. Drumm stood bewildered at the shore. Then from some well within, a cry of despair: "No. Oh, no. My God, no." She waded in, knee-deep.

"Way out there," Mort said, pointing. "Way out there!"

"My God! My God!" The woman turned toward shore. "God help us now. Run for help, Mort! Run for help!"

Mort ran up the hill, screaming, and at the first of the two cottages across the hill, he hammered at the door. "Ham's drowned! My brother's drowned!"

His mother came up behind him as a man and woman came to the door. "My God, my boy's drowned! Get help! Please get help!"

The man went to a Model T parked alongside the house and cranked it. Then he went off recklessly down the road, heading for the Gremminger farm to use the telephone.

Mrs. Drumm and the boy went back to the hill, but they did not go down to the river. They sat on the hilltop, the boy wrapped in his mother's arms, and they did not weep, but only watched the river, as though by some miracle, Ham would come popping back out of it.

Farmers came first. They had picked up the message on the party line. They launched boats and searched the river's surface. Then in the distance there was the thin wail of a siren. The Greenville Volunteer Fire Department truck came careening, and behind it were two county traffic officers on their motorcycles. Then within fifteen minutes the River Road was lost in a high column of dust.

A drowning, tragic though it might be, was an event. Illogical as it might seem, a depression-trodden people could feel perverse pleasure, because someone had it worse. And there was always time to lock a storefront, put down a saw, and leave the horses standing at the end of a field to witness— even a dog fight.

Sheriff Omar Deene and several deputies, a half-dozen town constables—all the law in the area converged on the Big Pike River. Within half an hour traffic was jammed as far as a mile back and people from Jason, Oak Creek, Paxton, Random— all the towns around—were walking to the scene of the search.

The river hill alongside the Drumm home swarmed with people, and Hammond Drumm, who wasn't dead at all, shivered in his hiding place, wondering how, during this summer of his sin, he could possibly extricate himself from a predicament for which there was absolutely no good explanation.

He had meant only to scare Mort, make him sorry, put him in his place. So when he dived the second time, he swam the short distance under water to the wooden pier and popped up inside its coffin-like interior, where there was an ample pocket of air.

Several times he had been on the verge of popping back out, but then he had experienced a special sort of satisfaction in all the sudden concern for his safety. And he had waited too long, because then, like crows coming to carrion, they flocked to the river and he was suddenly so surrounded that escape seemed altogether untenable.

Through a thin separation in the boards of the pier, he had seen it all happen, seen the drama unfold. There had been something morbidly thrilling in his mother's despair, and then when the farmers had come, it seemed too late.

Now, to arise as it were from the dead would not only

be completely illogical, but completely anticlimactic, and he hadn't the courage to demolish his role, to become an anti-hero.

So he watched, his teeth chattering sometimes and his flesh pimpled with the dreadfulness of standing witness to his own death. Then, from time to time—when one of the fishers tending the grappling hooks lifted loads that turned out to be tangles of coontail, or waterlogged boards, or sections of bed spring, or rusted pails—he felt his heart quicken, too, as a murmur ran through the crowd.

It was like something out of a movie. Through the cracks he saw Father Zamanski put his hand on his mother's elbow and lead her through the crowd up to the house. He saw his father tending lines in the stern of their rowboat, as it threaded its way back and forth among all the other boats which were plying the river.

There was Mort, knee-deep in the river, his face white. There were the children playing, as though they'd come to a county fair. There was the ebb and flow of the crowd as it pushed back and forth—shifting in color and pattern all the way from the shore to the crest of the hill.

In his hiding place, except for the sliver of light from the crack, it was dark. The air was stale, fishy. Boots and shoes drummed close to his ears as people walked on and off the pier. The boards below the waterline were slimy. The boards above the waterline were white, dry, flaky. Gradually his legs became numb. He moved them to restore circulation.

At noon some folks sat in family groups and opened picnic baskets. The sight of sandwiches made him hungry. And always there was the creak of oars, and in the sunlight the sight of sweat streaking the faces of the straining men.

Boats came to shore, grated on the gravel, and new crews took over. The search went on interminably, and Ham was tempted to submerge, swim out a ways, and then pop up right among the boats. He wondered what would happen? Would it be like a firecracker tossed unexpectedly among the milling people on the hill, or would everyone be so angry they'd only row away in disgust and leave him to swim back to shore alone.

He quickly abandoned the idea. It was too humiliating even to contemplate. His legs were numb again, trembling now. He moved quietly toward the shoreward side of his inverted tomb. Here the water was shallow enough so he could sit and still keep his head above the surface. He drew his knees up to his chest, and in the water, wrapped his arms around them. But he could generate little warmth, and though the day was hot and the temperature beneath the pier high, he shivered, more with apprehension than cold.

His life in these past weeks had surely been a headlong and catastrophic series of tragic events. He couldn't believe so much could happen in so short a time. And now he wondered if he'd ever drift again on smooth waters, down the river, and with Rock as his companion, float to the islands to explore or only to lie on a deserted beach and watch the wind move the clouds.

He leaned his head against the side of the pier and napped briefly, but the funereal whisperings of oars in the water and people talking softly along the shore wouldn't let him forget his predicament.

At last he got up and walked back to where he could peer out. The crowd was becoming shadowy. People were drifting over the hill, away. There were the sounds of car engines. Now, in the gloaming, people whispered. Now with night coming on, there came too the feeling that this death of his was a tangible, final thing. That there was no hope.

Boats grated on the gravel and bumped against the sides of his hiding place. Boots thumped on the pier. Through the crack, Ham could see a single star far out over the water.

Along the shore, kerosene lanterns had been lighted. Flashlights dipped and lifted their beams, made white paths on the green grass, streaked quickly and cuttingly across the canopy of willows, hurried like white night birds across the water to lift away and disappear. But always now the lights moved up the hill. Then the last boat was moored, and he heard his father's voice:

"There's just no use. We might as well wait until morning. Perhaps the current . . ." He couldn't understand what else he said.

Then at last there were no lights except in the house on the hill, but the stars were bright enough to silhouette the willows and their long, weeping branches.

Close at hand, a fish splashed, and the sound startled Ham. He heard the insistent inquiry of a black-capped night heron seeking a night camp, and finally the answer, an invitation from the big oaks.

They were all sounds which had once fascinated him as he stretched waiting for sleep, safe and at peace with himself, God, and all the world.

A few mosquitos had felt him out and crawled through the crack. He brushed them away with numb fingers. He knew, too, that some bloodsuckers had latched on. There were at least two gorging themselves on his right thigh, and one on the calf of his left leg.

In the daytime, leeches held no horrors for him. Mort and he sometimes invited their attention. They waded the marshy spots where they knew the suckers were plentiful, and after getting an assortment of all sizes attached to each leg, they would come forth to show any (especially girls) who might want to be horrified. Then they sat with salt shakers to sprinkle their legs and watch the suckers squirm and detach themselves, and curled tightly, die in the grass.

But here in the dark there was something unnatural about these leathery attachments, something suggestive of death. Ham pulled at one to dislodge it, but it slipped easily through his fingers. He dug a thumb nail into one and thought he felt a tiny spot of warmth as it lost the blood it was sucking.

Ham forgot the leeches and pressed his eyes to the crack. The stars were bright enough now to see the river moving like thick molasses, looking lazy in the night, as if it had no desire to go anywhere, especially not to a place where it must lose its identity to the sea.

His thoughts turned to the house on the hill, and he let

them dwell on the soft, safe, warm smell of his baby sister in her crib. Then he thought of his mother and her agony, and how she had called out: "Oh, God!" Involuntarily he sobbed, and then he wept silently. He had to go to her. There was no other way. In the end he'd have to go up the hill, into the house. He had to.

So he held his nose and submerged, swam a few strokes and popped to the surface. Then he started up the hill, on all fours at first because he couldn't walk, and finally he lifted himself so he might look through the window.

All four kerosene lamps were burning, and he could see his mother at the kitchen table, her head down on her folded arms—a rosary wrapped around her fingers.

His father's back was to him, but directly in front of Mr. Drumm and looking right out the window was Father Zamanski. Sheriff Deene was off to one side, a notebook in one hand and a pencil in the other. Mort was in a chair against the wall.

Ham thought the priest must surely see him. He was looking directly into his eyes. Ham averted his eyes, even though he understood that in the bright room the priest could not possibly see outside. He would wait, wait until the priest and the sheriff left. He would hide once more until they went away. But then his mother lifted her head, and when he saw the anguish on her face, he got to his feet and went to the door.

He crept in quietly as light. No one heard the screen door open or close. His mother saw him first. She was looking directly through him as though he wasn't there. He wondered why she didn't move, didn't say something, let him stand there dripping and numb in front of the door, tails of the two leeches still waving wildly on his legs.

His father and the priest were talking, but though he heard their voices, he could take no meaning from their words. The sheriff interrupted to ask a question. Still his mother didn't move.

He wanted to go to her, but he couldn't. He just stood

there, hunched over—wet, shivering, almost hysterical with fright.

Then Mort saw him, screamed, and ran toward the porch. Suddenly his mother cried out too, and it was like the voice of a startled bird in the night. The men looked at her, and then followed her eyes to where the boy was standing.

Ham tried to fold further in on himself. But his mother was up and running. She came across the room, folded him into her arms, wrapped him in the warmth and sweetness of her hair, her face, her breasts.

What happened then never was clear to Ham. Except that the sheriff's voice was raised above all the others in an oath. If there were prayers of thanksgiving or questions, he never could remember. All he knew was that when they all converged upon him, his mother told them to stay back.

How she held them off he didn't know, because she was such a small woman among such big men. Perhaps she did it with her big, black eyes, because once he had seen them flashing.

So the men fell back, and still wrapped in her warmth, they walked between them. She took him out onto the porch, helped him out of his swimming trunks, plucked off the leeches, and edged him into bed. Then when the men came through the door, she said:

"Out! Don't you dare. Don't you dare come in here. Don't you dare touch him!" And they obeyed.

He hadn't believed her capable of such ferocity. She was like a mink he had once seen protecting her young from Rock. The dog had fallen back, threatened, though he could have killed the mink with a single bite.

He tried to tell her then what had happened, but she said: "It can wait."

She brought out a lamp, set it on the floor, and then got another blanket. He heard her light the kerosene stove, and then she had a hot water bottle and hot lemonade.

The voices of the men moved out of the house to the hill. Two car engines roared. They settled to a steady, driving tone. Then it was quiet except for the rustling sound of his mother in the chair beside his bed. Then with her perfume of soap in his nostrils, he told her what happened—why he had hidden, and how he had been unable to come out.

She only said. "Shhh. Shhh." And she caressed his brow, lulled him to sleep.

Much later he woke up. The light was still burning, but his mother was gone. He got up quietly and went to the water pail for a drink. His father was asleep on the couch instead of in bed with his mother. He smelled moonshine when he passed his father. When he was about to go back, his mother came out in her long nightgown. She put an arm around his shoulders and walked back with him to his cot.

When he was back in bed she sat beside him again. Then, just before he fell asleep, a rooster crowed from so very, very far away he was surprised he could hear it.

Ten

THROUGHOUT THE NIGHT, with no boats on it, the Big
Pike River ran peaceably. No one would have guessed that,
when it was very young and engaged in its first tortuous
struggle to get to the sea, it had battered across the earth
bruising the land. Now that it was an old river, there was
little evidence that once it had frothed and foamed against
obstructions . . . bulldozing over, under, around, and through
the world's crust. It looked so peaceful, fit its gorge so well,
almost all signs of the struggle had settled beneath pastoral
pastures, croplands, and woodlots slanting down to the water,
and enigmatic swamps.

Ham looked down on it briefly when he came from the
house, but it reminded him too vividly of yesterday, so he
went back over the hill to where the wild grapevines climbed
the fence and the clustering cedars. He crawled into his leafy
cavern and settled down to look out.

He had come upon an advantage. He felt it. Things had
changed. For now, at least, the pressure would be less. It was
a thing of attitude, and even Mort was more solicitous.

On awakening he had been apprehensive, but all doubts
vanished when his father had come to the porch before going
to work and, looking down at him, had said: "Now don't go
falling off any cliffs" (as if there were any cliffs) and "Don't
go shooting yourself" (but, of course, he didn't have a gun)
and "Maybe you should just stay in bed. At least there you'll
be safe."

But there had been no rancor. It had been his father's way of saying there would be no repercussions. Mathew Drumm had even smiled, if you could call a brief show of teeth a smile.

So the morning passed peacefully, and at noon, when the fire whistle at Greenville was a faint, faraway wail, he went to the house. His mother hovered over him while he ate. Mort remained uncommonly quiet.

When he had finished his chili, his mother said: "Why don't you catch some perch? We could use some fish." She smiled down on him. It was her way of saying he was still a valuable part of the family—not only wanted, but needed.

Mort spoke for the first time. "Can I go along?"

Ham looked up at his mother. "I'd rather go alone."

"He'd rather go alone," Mrs. Drumm said to Mort.

So he crossed in the boat and sat on the river bank among a great clustering of black rocks, because it was here the banded yellow perch came for crayfish and caddis.

Using worms for bait, he had nearly enough fish when he heard a stone roll behind him. It startled him, so he poised as though on the verge of leaping into the river.

"Don't do it," a voice with a laugh in it said.

Ham turned around, and a tall man in overalls was standing over him. He had a cane pole over his shoulder and was carrying a pail.

"I didn't mean to startle you," the man said. "Do you mind if I fish here?"

Ham found his voice. "I don't own it. You are welcome as far as I'm concerned."

The man laughed and sat on the rock. He was younger than Ham's father, and taller, and he was lean and leathery. "I suppose you could say I own it," the man said, motioning to the land around. "That is, if anybody can own anything. I'm the farmer from over the hill."

Ham got up as though to leave. "You can stay. You can fish here anytime. Anybody can fish here. I like to see people fish."

Ham sat back down. "I got twenty. That's about enough for a meal for us," he said.

"Well, why don't you help me then?" the farmer asked, and then added: "My name is John. What's yours?"

"It's Hammond, but everybody calls me Ham."

"Hammond what?"

"Drumm."

"You wouldn't be Mathew Drumm's boy?"

Ham nodded. He waited for the man to ask if he was the boy who had fooled everyone into thinking he had drowned, but instead the farmer said: "I bought a Fordson tractor from your father. It was quite a while ago, but it's still running good." The farmer unwound the line on his pole, sat down, and proceeded to fish.

"This could be my last chance for a meal of fish for a while," he said. "I've got a lot of hay down, and then it won't be too long before we'll have to start harvesting. Then there won't be much time for anything else."

(He caught a perch—as yellow along the sides as butter, with dark bands irradiating almost, but not quite, one into the other; high, dark dorsal fin, orange pectoral fins, and bright eyes which turned pearly white as the fish slowly succumbed.)

Ham caught a fish, and he put it into the farmer's pail.

"Sure you don't need them yourself?" John asked.

Ham hefted the gunny sack from a pool between the rocks. "I've got plenty," he said. Then looking up the high bank to the fields, he noted: "There's sure plenty of oats to cut."

The farmer unhooked a perch and tossed it into the pail. In a frenzy of swimming, the fish cast up water to darken the overalls of boy and man and to leave wet spots on the rock. "Not so much oats as you might think," the farmer said. "But it is better than the corn. The gophers and crows about ruined the corn, and then the heat caught the oats. There isn't much straw, all short stemmed. Probably have to cut marsh hay for bedding."

Ham thought about the crows and gophers going down the

corn rows, digging up the seed, nipping off the sprouts.

"I'd give anything to get rid of the gophers," the farmer said. "Ever see so many?"

Now that Ham thought about it, he had to admit he couldn't remember seeing so many before. They were everywhere. He could mark the progress of a dog or any living thing through a field by the warning whistle of gophers which preceded it. The gophers' tiny trails were worn right through to the bare ground, and where there were pebbles, they had been shined white by belly fur.

"I was going to spread poison," the farmer said, "but too many other critters get to it and die."

Ham hated poison because he had seen a dog die of it. The dog's tongue had hung out, and its lips had curled back from its teeth, and its eyes had gone glassy, and its legs had galloped—although he was lying down—until there was no gallop left and the dog had twisted itself cruelly about trying to bite its own stomach.

But Ham could kill a gopher like he could swat a fly. He even took some savage pleasure in watching Rock crack their heads between his teeth like they were long, striped peanuts.

"Maybe I could help you get rid of some of the gophers," Ham offered.

John was quiet, as though thinking about the offer, and then asked: "How?"

Ham lifted a perch, and while he was taking the hook from its jaws, said: "Well, I could drown them out, and my dog could kill them."

John laughed. "It would take a lot of water."

"Well, there's a whole river full," Ham said, returning the laugh.

John looked at the boy. "You're welcome to try, and I'll give you five cents for every gopher tail you bring to the house."

Ham stood up, and gophers shrilled in every direction. He could see a dozen standing at the edge of their holes where the river bank was steep, their paws tucked neatly to their grayish undersides. They stood like sticks, bright eyes betraying them. He sat back down.

"I've got more perch than we'll eat in two meals," the farmer finally said, winding his line around the pole.

Ham wound line around his pole and made the hook fast in a bottom knuckle of cane. When the farmer picked up the pail to leave, Ham asked: "Did you mean that about the gopher tails?"

The farmer smiled. His teeth were square and shiny. The smile put deep wrinkles all over his face. He held out a giant hand. "Want to shake on it?"

Ham's hand disappeared within the farmer's. They shook, and the farmer climbed the bank to a cow path and followed it around the oat field and up the hill. The whistling of gophers preceded him. At the top he turned to wave before dropping over the other side and out of sight.

Sunday came and went. He didn't go to Communion, and no one said anything. Then on the day he had planned to go gopher hunting a surprise visit to Doc Shallock's office was scheduled, and it shook his newfound aplomb.

"Just a check-up," his mother had said, trying to sound comforting. "Your father thinks you should, and the doctor does, too."

So his father, instead of having sandwiches at the yard, came home for a noon dinner, and Ham went back with him. His appointment was for two o'clock. Sweating uncomfortably, he waited in the equipment yard, standing stiffly in shoes, ribbed black stockings, woolen knickers, belted suit coat, and a white shirt limp with perspiration.

While he was waiting, a band of five boys came by. He knew all except one. "A ghost! A ghost! A ghost!" Dyke Halverson, one of the boys, exclaimed, feigning fright. All five hooted.

"I thought you drowned," Piggie Jones said.

"He did. That's his ghost!" Dyke shouted.

The boys formed a semicircle, like half-wild savages

around a victim, and coming close as they dared, began a systematic dissection of Ham's self-esteem, passing the verbal knife from one to another with an adroitness that only boys are cruelly capable of.

Only Mathew Drumm's huge frame in the narrow doorway of the tiny, square office saved Ham from lashing out with the attack that was expected of him. At once the semicircle of boys collapsed, and they faded down the street in a giggling, whispering huddle.

When the little hand on the big Bank Clock neared two, he started slowly down the maple and elm shaded street to walk the half-block to where Doc Shallock had his combination dwelling and office. Never having been in the doctor's office, he knocked several times, and when there was no answer, he opened the door a little way to peer in.

Mrs. Shallock, in a white dress, was at a desk. She had heard the knock, and anticipating it was the Drumm boy, called out: "Come in, Hammond. Your turn is soon."

There were two other people in the office, which smelled of antiseptic odors that Ham had no names for. "Have a chair," Mrs. Shallock pointed, and Ham sat down, stiffly.

There were two other people in the office—an elderly man he knew only vaguely, and Mrs. Theisen, a young widow. From behind a door in back of the desk at which Mrs. Shallock sat, Ham could hear the low, booming voice of her husband. Then, quite abruptly, the door opened and the Dresden boy, visibly shaken, squirted out. Before Mrs. Shallock could give him an appointment slip, he had gone through the heavy front door and out onto the street. Mrs. Shallock shook her head and then, making a note on the paper in front of her, said to no one in particular: "Well, I'll just have to call his parents."

Note written, Mrs. Shallock lifted her head. "Mrs. Theisen, you're next." The pretty, black-haired widow went through the door, but her perfume lingered behind, and it disturbed Ham to discover that the odor should so stimulate him he had to wriggle in his chair to make adjustments.

Still he was uncomfortable, so he concentrated on a fly, but it had designs on another fly, so he tried looking out the window where an oriole, bright as an orange, was bug hunting among the thick, hanging leaves of a large elm.

But Mrs. Theisen's laughter came through the door, and he was vaguely disturbed. Miss Mallow had laughed like that, low in her throat. He had heard it again when he and two other boys had crept in the dark up under a car in which they knew two lovers had parked. He had even heard his mother laugh like that—once, from out of a darkened bedroom.

Mrs. Shallock must have heard it, too, because Ham could see that she was disturbed. Three times she started up out of her chair as though to go through the door, but each time the booming voice of her husband stayed her.

Mrs. Theisen must have been in the office twenty minutes before she came out, and even Ham couldn't help but notice how her face was flushed and how her eyes were so bright they sparkled.

When she handed Mrs. Shallock the note from the doctor, she sighed. "You don't have to come back," the woman at the desk said curtly, on reading the note.

Mrs. Theisen's half-smile faded. "I don't?" she asked, with obvious disappointment.

"No you don't!" Mrs. Shallock said.

"Oh," Mrs. Theisen said, in a defeated sort of way, and then she went through the door leaving a trace of perfume behind.

The man went in and was back out in five minutes. Then it was Ham's turn. He went slowly across the room, opened the door reluctantly, and then increased his speed when he heard the doctor's voice: "Come on, Ham! We haven't got all day!"

The door closed, and more sharp, medicinal smells enveloped him. "Down to your underwear," the doctor said. When the boy didn't move, the doctor said: "Take your clothes off." Ham looked at Doctor Shallock in disbelief, and then abruptly he wondered if it had also been necessary for the widow to undress.

When Ham began fumbling with his clothes, Doc Shallock stepped forward to help him. Ham stepped back, and hurriedly tugging and unbuttoning, wriggled out of his clothes and dropped them in a heap on the floor. When he was down to his white cotton shorts he hesitated and looked at the doctor. "That's enough for now, Ham. Just jump up. Sit on this table." A piece of newspaper had been laid on the table. He sat on it. And then, for the first time, he looked around.

In one corner, hanging from the ceiling, was the entire grinning skeleton of a man. He had to tear his eyes away from it only to have them come squarely to focus on a brilliant picture of a life-size man with all his insides showing, and though he had seen the entrails of countless animals and birds, it had never quite occurred to him that beneath his own skin there were also what he had come to call in lesser creatures "their guts."

The doctor's voice interrupted his preoccupation with the furnishings of the office: "I said, do you feel that?"

For the first time he realized the doctor had been scraping the soles of his feet with a bright, metal instrument. Ham nodded. "Speak up," the doctor said.

"I feel it," he said.

"Well, it's amazing that you do with the callouses you've got on your feet. Don't you ever wear shoes?"

Ham nodded. "Sometimes."

"Let your legs just hang now," the doctor ordered. Then he was striking the boy with what looked like a little rubber hammer just below the knee. Suddenly, and without warning, Ham saw his leg leap to life, come up in a quick kick he had neither planned nor anticipated.

"Hmmph. Good."

The boy was mystified. In quick succession then, the doctor was looking down his throat, feeling his neck, looking up his nostrils and down his ear canals with a light. He made him lie down, probed his belly, thumped his back and chest.

Sitting up again he made him find his nose with a forefinger with his eyes closed. Then he helped him off the high table and made him walk a crack in the floor which was stained by concoctions of what mysterious ingredients Ham couldn't even guess.

All the while Ham's eyes returned to the skeleton. The double row of teeth and the empty eye sockets particularly fascinated him. Then, without his willing it, his eyes traveled

[86

to the vivid picture of the man, stripped bare of skin in front to expose curling lengths of intestine, a bright red liver and heart—and what all else Ham, in his bewilderment, couldn't identify.

Suddenly then he wondered if women looked the same as men—inside, that is. Or whether by virtue of being women they were less gutty, and the vaginal passage (which he knew about from a first-hand description by one High Pockets Garrity) led to more subdued innards, having a smoother, skin-like quality with which one might equate such an essence as that of womanhood.

He didn't really think so, though, because Garrity had implied that they were as much like men as the insides of a rabbit were like the insides of a dog. Then, sitting there in a snow house they had built with only a candle on a snow shelf to give light, Garrity had said: "And don't get it into your head that they pee strawberry soda and poop cold cream, because they don't!"

At the time it had given him a sense, if not of importance, then of an almost cruel acceptance of a manhood fact that Dorothy Rowan didn't, in fact, smell anything like the perfume she doused herself with before coming to school.

Then suddenly he wondered about the black-haired, amber-skinned widow who had preceded him into the doctor's office, and if she was in fact like the picture on the wall, what was there to laugh about?

Those sex fantasies that had found time to compete with his outdoor world suddenly went down in dust, and it shocked him to think that his approaching nubility was probably a fraud—still, how could so many people be fooled into getting married?

He had almost forgotten about Doc Shallock while his mind raced along neck and neck with the gutsy reality of the female hoax upon the world of men. Then he was told for the third time:

"I said, Ham, to drop your shorts!"

Drop his shorts? He cringed.

"Come on now, Ham. If you don't, I will."

Gingerly he lowered the brief cotton shorts.

"All the way, down to your knees."

He pushed them to his knees, and then horror of horrors, Doc Shallock reached between his legs. His penis retreated in shock, almost to disappear in his belly. Then gently searching fingers probed upward toward his pelvis.

Doc Shallock laughed. "All right. Turn around."

Ham was glad to.

"Now bend over." Ham bent a little way. "Farther. Way over." He bent a little more. "Down, down," Doc was saying. Ham bent.

Then he felt the doctor's hand on one shoulder gripping him. "Now this will hurt, but only for a second. Then it will be over."

The rude intrusion came as such a shock that a scream started in his throat, but when it came out, it was only a long, low whimper. He tried to get away, but the doctor had him.

"Hold still or you'll hurt yourself. I'm almost through."

But he couldn't hold still. He pressed forward, but when the doctor's hand on his shoulder brought him sharply back, the air came out of his lungs in a long, "Ahhhhhhh!"

"There! Now was that so bad?"

He stood up. The doctor was snapping a rubber glove off his right hand. He had never seen him put it on. He looked up into the doctor's face, and then he hobbled around to put the table between them.

"Now get dressed. I've got other patients waiting."

While he dressed, the doctor asked him the date of his birth and whether he'd ever been really sick. Then he put the clipboard down and concluded:

"I think all you've got is imaginitis. It's something that's hard to cure, but you won't die of it, and people usually outgrow it. But, never mind, I'll talk to your father about it."

Then quite suddenly Ham was back out on the street walking toward the equipment yard, feeling, perhaps, like a virgin who has just been ravished.

"You can walk home, if you want to," his father said, standing in the doorway of the tiny office.

At the edge of the gravel road he took off his shoes and stockings, and only when the dust started to come up between his toes did he feel that at last he had his feet back on the ground.

Eleven

THE VISIT to the doctor's office, though rudely embarrassing, could be relegated to the inoperative file, along with such things as a headache, which, if not to be forgotten, could at least be ignored because it was over, done with, fait accompli.

Besides, there were other things, and Ham knew if he now possessed an edge of advantage, it was at best temporary. The basic problem of getting back into the good graces of the church was still very much a fact, and the ten-dollar bill was as important now as before his parents had been made dramatically aware that his mere presence, no matter how irritating at times, was important to them.

Still, he was not unappreciative of the lull, and he was vaguely aware that even boys had to come by some minutes or days during which to recuperate, else they would never be fortified enough to go on.

So he offered no great objections when his gopher hunt was again postponed and on the following day, he was taken to Greenville to buy new shoes. Nor did he put on a long face when told he'd have to wear them fifteen minutes a day so they'd be broken in by the time school started.

He could even manage a self-hypnotic hum that afternoon while polishing more than an acre of farm equipment—tractors and mowers, hay rakes and loaders, cultivators and planters— until the sun danced like red fire from their shiny surfaces.

Then when Sunday came they went to church at Jason instead of Greenville. The week before people had stared. He had been embarrassed the whole time he'd been serving mass. Then on the way out he'd heard whispers and subdued laughter, and he guessed they were talking about how he'd fooled everyone into thinking he'd drowned.

He expected it was his mother who'd finally prevailed on Mathew Drumm to go to Jason. But his father, believing a man must face up to life, bristled all the six miles cross-country and even during the mass.

Then, to make things more comfortable, his mother skipped Communion with him. On the way home the scowl disappeared from his father's face, and breakfast was an almost pleasant affair, except for Mort's insistence that he be permitted to go along on the gopher hunt.

When he got up to leave the table, his mother said, "Why don't you take Mort gopher hunting? After all, he is your brother."

Ham hesitated. He didn't want Mort cutting in on the profits, but perhaps he could find some way of getting around that, and hauling water up the steep banks was hard work. Most important, the pressure seemed to be off. Things were going *for* him. He wanted to keep it that way, so he said, "Okay, if he wants to."

So two pails went into the green boat, and when Rock had taken his position in the bow and Mort was on the middle seat, Ham shoved off. Then each boy took an oar, but they had to correct course constantly because the bow was down and the boat wanted to come around and run with the current.

They went upstream and threw an anchor out among a pile of shore rocks. Across the river on Hanser's Point, cars were being parked beneath the oaks, and women were putting picnic baskets on rough-hewn tables in the shade.

Old Hanser, whose two boys ran the farm now that he was too crippled, rented the oak grove for three dollars a Sunday to groups who wanted to picnic there.

Both boys climbed the steep slope, and gray, grizzled Rock followed. When they were in the oats, they unbuttoned the front of their overalls and jetted yellow streams on the golden grain. Rock lifted a leg briefly and then got on with the hunt.

[91

By the time the boys had finished, the dog was poised over a gopher hole.

"He's got one," Ham said. "Let's go."

So they went to the boat for the pails, filled them from the river, and started up the bank. But full pails were too heavy, so each boy had to spill a little to make it to the top.

Mort poured first. He spilled a little, got the angle, and then water ran down the hole swift and smooth as roof rain down a drain spout. When Mort's pail was empty, Ham moved above the hole and began to pour. When the pail was half empty, water in the hole began to gurgle. Then before he'd emptied his pail, the hole filled and overflowed.

Rock's nose was inches from the hole. Once he snapped at a bubble. Then in a series of gurgles the water receded.

"He's coming," Mort said.

Ham poured quickly to refill the hole. The gopher, eyes shining and hide glistening, stuck its head out. Rock snapped, but the gopher ducked back. Ham poured again, and the gopher popped out. The dog's teeth crunched down on the bright eyes and the slicked head, and the boys heard the bones crack in one single sound like a hickory nut shattering between the steel edges of a nutcracker.

Instantly dead, except for its tail, which twitched at the end of the dog's muzzle, the gopher made no sound. Rock let the striped rodent drop to the ground, looked up for the boys' approval, got a pat on the head from both, and then surveyed the slope for another victim.

He hunted entirely by sight, and on spotting a gopher, rushed it to its hole and then stood with expectancy showing in the tilt of his ears and the rigid, upright angle of his tail.

Twice the boys had to lug water, and then the gopher darted out a back door, but Rock was on it before it could slither down a neighbor's long corridor.

The dog's excitement was passed on to the boys, and they were lavish with praise for their pet's prowess. Then Ham picked up the two dead gophers and went up the hill to the fence line. He marked a post by putting a stone on top it, and laid the two gophers at the base.

Their luck didn't hold on the next hole, and after four pailfuls had gone gurgling away, they gave up. It took some tugging to get Rock away and interested in another victim, but they managed.

The next hole more than made up for the one on which they hadn't scored. After Rock had snapped up the rodent, four more gophers, so young their eyes had barely opened, came bubbling out. The dog didn't quite know what to do with the sudden surplus, so the boys thumped the tiny creatures with their pails until they were dead.

Ham felt a twinge of remorse when he laid the four immature gophers alongside the adults at the base of the post, but he stifled it quickly by counting tails. They had thirty-five cents already and they hadn't worked much more than half an hour.

Their next victim came easy. The water had hardly started down the hole when the gopher shot out and into the air as though catapulted by a sling shot. Rock, fast as a fox, snapped the animal right out of the air, shook his head when the gopher bit his nose, and then dropped it lifeless to the dry, brown grass.

"Let's rest a minute," Mort said.

So they moved out of the searing sun into the shade of a solitary hawthorne tree. Rock, after waiting at a fresh gopher hole for a few minutes, joined them. For a while the dog lay with his head high, listening to the whistling gophers, but then he rolled over on his side and stretched out.

Across the river the picnic was proceeding. A concertina played a polka, and children ran shouting among the trees. From time to time adults moved from the tables down to the river bank to look across to where the boys were resting.

"I hate picnics," Mort observed.

"Me, too," Ham agreed.

"People must be nuts to drag all that stuff outside to eat when it's so much easier to do it right in the house," Mort said.

"Yeah," Ham agreed, "unless you're hunting or fishing what's the sense to it?"

The day had become almost unbearably hot. When the boys got back up, they avoided stepping on stones lest they burn even their calloused feet. Before resuming the gopher hunt, they followed the dog down the bank and into the river, never bothering to take off any clothes, and when they came back out they were refreshed.

There weren't as many gophers above ground now that the sun was almost directly overhead. But there were enough, and Rock was soon poised over a hole.

The rodent came out on the third pail of water and sailed right through Rock's jaws to land on his head. There it clung until Ham made a grab, got the gopher by the tail, and with a wild swing heaved it into the air. Rock stood head high, ears cocked, watching the animal tumble end over end to land in the river. Then he ran down the bank and swam toward where the rodent was streaking for shore, its tiny tail straight behind like a rudder.

In the water Rock reared to get a line on his quarry, and then with powerful strokes, swam to meet the gopher. When the dog opened its jaws to chomp down on the rodent, it slipped past the long, white teeth and was again perched on the dog's head.

Rock shook his huge head, but the gopher was dug in and rode all the way to shore. With a convulsive shudder, the dog dislodged the animal which dived with a sharp squeak for safety among a jumble of boulders. The dog clawed at the rocks, and the gopher whistled in fear, but the dog had chased gophers among the rocks before, and he quickly gave up.

When the dog came back, Mort said: "That was something. Let's try it again."

So when the next gopher came popping out, Mort held Rock back. Ham grabbed the little animal and sent it sailing into the river. The dog had broken away from Mort, and his jaws closed with a snap just inches from Ham's wrist. Then the dog swung his head to follow the high, arcing flight of the rodent, and when it hit the water he was down the bank and after it.

This time, however, the dog kept an eye on the gopher

as the pair came nose to nose and snapped it into his mouth before it had a chance to climb to his head. When Rock's paws touched gravel, he gave the gopher an extra bite to insure its demise, and then dropped it.

Twice more the boys managed to get gophers out into the current for Rock to catch. Then their father's voice, like a foghorn floating across the water, bellowed for their return.

"Must be past dinner time," Ham said. "We'd better hurry." He counted the gophers. There were eleven. "Fifty-five cents," he said to himself. He covered the bodies with oat straw so the crows wouldn't find them, and then clambering down the bank, he preceded Mort into the boat and with an oar, pushed the craft out into the current.

The stream seemed swifter, and they had to battle, each at an oar, to keep from being swept past their landing. Even before landing they saw their father standing in the midst of a group of women. When they came up the hill, one of the women pointed and said: "Those are the boys!"

"I've never seen anything so cruel in all my life," another woman said.

The boys stopped in astonishment. "They kept throwing live gophers into the water so the dog could swim them down. I think the Humane Society should be notified."

Ham and Mort both put their heads down and tried to scuttle on by the group. "Just a minute," their father commanded. The boys stopped. "Were you throwing gophers into the river for the dog to retrieve?"

Reluctantly, both boys nodded.

"Were the gophers alive?"

Both boys looked at each other. Finally Ham said: "Well, yes, sir. I guess they were."

One of the women gasped. "See! It's just as I told you. Don't these boys realize that these helpless, harmless animals are God's creatures?"

Ham had never really thought about it, but he supposed gophers were also God's creatures. As for being harmless, well they were doing a creditable job of ruining crops and strewing gravel on pasture lands.

"The farmer asked us to help him get rid of the gophers," Ham said.

"Well, that farmer needs to be straightened out," one of the women said. "How anyone could . . ."

Mathew Drumm interrupted. "Go on up to the house," he said, motioning to the boys, but there was no threat. As they trudged up the hill they could hear the women all talking at once. Though Ham couldn't understand their objection to gopher killing, he was beginning to see how there might be some element of torture in the live retrieving method. He was even beginning to feel a little sorry for the gophers when he looked at Mort and saw the face he was making in imitation of a gabbling woman. That corked up what milk of human kindness might have flowed, and he began to laugh. Mort began to giggle, too, and then both boys broke out in uncontrolled, raucous laughter. The women were shocked into silence.

"Get into the house!" their father roared, and the boys dove for the screen door, scrambled through the kitchen past their mother, who was feeding the baby, and threw themselves on their cots so they could watch from the porch.

The women, if anything, had ganged tighter around their father. They were all talking at once and waving their hands, and Mathew Drumm, a good foot taller than any of them, was motioning with his hands like a teacher trying to silence a classroom of noisy kids.

Rock stood off to one side, his head turning left, then right, as though attempting to understand what was going on. Then he lowered his head and began striding toward the group with that off-center walk he used when having designs upon a certain tree. He circled the women, who were oblivious of his presence, and sniffed delicately at each as he went by.

"Oh, no!" Ham said. "Jeeze, no! God, no! Jeeze!" He wanted to scream out at the dog. But he would have been too late, and it isn't likely that Rock would have listened anyway, because he had made up his mind. He had found the woman he wanted.

Ham often thought about it later, wondering especially what

[96

process of elimination Rock had employed to come by the one which smelled just right.

On the porch both boys held their breaths. Out on the green hillside, Rock looked a million miles off into space, artfully lifted his leg, and then the golden stream jetted forth and the white dress darkened and the dog was through before the animal warmth got through to her leg and she turned and then screamed in horror and humiliation.

It was too much for the boys. They roared, stuffed their mouths with pillow slips, turned red, and roared again. Mathew Drumm kicked, and his foot landed, and Rock took off as though someone had put a match to his bushy tail.

Maybe it was only because Mathew Drumm wanted to get away from the women, but anyway, he took out after the dog, and about every tenth step he got close enough to swing wildly with his right foot.

The women scattered like leaves going up the hill and then regrouped as they came to where they had three cars parked. On the porch the boys were too exhausted and their sides too sore to laugh anymore.

Twelve

HAM DIDN'T GET a chance until the following morning to cross the river and collect the tails for presentation to the farmer. He had also planned to drown out some more gophers, but when he picked up a pail from beneath the sink, his mother made him put it back.

"There will be no more gopher hunting until your father says so," she said.

Well, his father was at work, so there was no way to get his permission—permission which Ham somehow felt would be forthcoming.

Surprisingly, his father had not been angry about the gopher incident, and instead of punishing them, he had followed his wife around the house chuckling and saying: "You should have seen her face when Rock let go! Honestly, Rose, you would have split."

Mrs. Drumm had smiled, perhaps because she was expected to, but then she had been bold enough to say: "What if it had been me? Just imagine how humiliated I'd have been. I don't think it was funny. Whatever got into that dog?"

Ham wondered about that too. Rock was a meticulously clean dog, in or out of the house. But once he had wet on a cousin who had kicked him. The revenge came later while the girl was sunning herself on a blanket near the river. Rock had come up from behind. The cousin had never come back.

So, though he couldn't drown out more gophers, he could

at least collect from the farmer. But just as he was about to shove the boat into the stream, Rock and Mort jumped aboard, almost upsetting the craft.

"Who asked you to come along?" Ham objected.

"It's just as much my boat as it is yours," Mort countered.

Then the current caught them and they were moving downstream. Ham struggled with the oars, and then said: "Well, if you're coming, help me row."

When they came to the fence post with the rock on it, the gophers were gone. The grass and oats which had covered the carcasses was scattered. Ham poked around and found one tail and two tiny paws.

"Crows got them," Mort said.

Ham snorted. "Crows my eye! Look at Rock!" The big dog was bristling. A rumble trembled the hairs of his chest. He walked stiff-legged, examining the ground with his nose.

Ham slid down the slope to the cow path and followed it until he came to a distinct imprint in the dust. "Badger!" he shouted to Mort, who was still poking around in the oats. "A big devil!"

Mort came down the cow trail to where Ham was kneeling. The track, slightly pigeon-toed and clearly showing the long digging claws, was in the center of the dusty trail.

"Big as a small bear track," Ham marveled.

Mort snorted. "As if you knew what a bear track looked like." Ham ignored the thrust.

Rock was reading the signs. He blew great gusts from his lungs to clear his nose and then sniffed delicately. Then he moved slowly down the trail. But he did not display the tail-flagging glee he exhibited while hounding a rabbit, a squirrel, or even a fox. He moved stiffly with hair bristling.

"Rock is scared," Mort said.

"He should be."

"Why?"

"Badgers are tough."

"But how does he know it's a badger? He's never seen one before."

"Dogs just know."

Mort laughed. "You gotta be nuts. Who ever heard of anybody knowing about something he's never seen."

"He sees with his nose, you dummy!" Ham said.

Mort hooted. "Sees with his nose! You gotta be crazy!"

Ham ignored the invitation to argue as Rock left the cow path and trailed across the pasture which spread a green border between the river and the field of golden oats.

The boys were silent now. In the grass, yet damp from the night, Rock moved faster, and they had to run to stay with him. Cow birds, investigating cow dung pantries, flew out of their way. Grasshoppers, still stupid with early morning lethargy, made short, unenthusiastic hops.

Near the pasture corner, where rocks scavenged from the oat field had been piled, the dog stopped in front of a gapping hole.

"Here's where he lives," Ham announced. Rock put his head a little way into the hole, growled, and backed out.

Ham looked around. From where he stood he could see four holes. He walked around the pile of rocks and discovered two more den entrances. "He's sure a digging fool," Ham said.

"How do you know it's a 'he'?" Mort asked.

"Aw, shut up and go get me a stick."

"Go get your own stick."

Ham walked across the pasture and twisted a long willow wand from a brushy stand at the edge of the marsh.

Rock cocked his head while Ham probed the hole with the stick. "No bottom," he finally said. "This whole corner of the pasture is probably tunneled."

He pulled out the stick and threw it to one side. Rock ran over, and smelling the stick, picked it up and shook it in a show of bravado.

"That dumb dog sure doesn't like the smell of badger," Mort said.

"That's because he knows a badger can tear the guts right out of him," Ham said.

"Aw, you're crazy." Mort laughed, but without conviction.

"Here, Rock, here." Ham went through the motions of digging with his fingers.

The dog growled and then barked. He rushed the hole and backed away. "Get 'em, Rock! Get 'em!" Ham urged.

The dog thrust his head into the hole. Then he began digging, thought better of it, and suddenly chose to ignore the whole thing by looking off into space as though he had never scented a badger and there was no hole.

"He's sure scared," Mort said.

"But he'd tackle that badger if he got mad enough." Ham came to the dog's support.

"Boy, I'd sure like to see that." Mort began to dance excitedly in a circle at the thought of the pair fighting.

"Well, you'll never see it," Ham said, "because even ten men couldn't dig that badger out. A badger can dig fast as a steam shovel—almost."

Rock had moved off to one side and was watching. The brothers sat on the grass. "What'll we do?" Mort asked.

Ham shrugged. "Nothing to do." Boys and dog stretched full length in the sun. Then suddenly the dog jumped to his feet.

"What's gotten into him?" Mort asked.

"Maybe smells a rabbit," Ham said.

The breeze was coming across the oats, and the kernels, heavy and hardening to ripeness, bent in waves like richly golden water. Ham looked at the dog and then looked hard at the field where Rock had centered his attention. Once he thought he saw a patch of gray, but guessed it was the dusty earth bared momentarily when the breeze combed a part in the straw stems.

"This is spooky," Mort said, noting Rock's and Ham's apprehension.

The dog was on his feet advancing slowly toward the field of grain. Ham got to his feet, but he waited. Halfway to the fence the dog stopped. He lifted his head, tasting the air again, and then, turning a little, took a few more steps.

"What is it?" Mort asked.

"How do I know?" Ham's voice was hardly louder than a whisper. "Just hope it isn't a skunk."

Mort's courage returned. Skunks were nothing to be afraid of. Just stay far enough back and pelt them with rocks. Maybe Rock would get messed up, but he'd been skunked up before. It would mean staying outside the house for awhile, but nothing more serious.

Ham moved up behind the dog. Again he thought he caught a glimpse of gray—something squat, scuttling.

"What is it, Rock?" Ham asked the dog.

The dog growled and backed a few steps.

"That ain't no skunk," Ham announced. "And it ain't a mink or a fox or a coon."

Mort managed a nervous laugh, and then trying to be facetious enough to relax the tension, he said: "Maybe it's a bear."

Secretly, Ham hoped it was the badger. Frank Tyson, who tied his own trout flies, had asked Ham to keep his eyes open for a car-killed badger. "I could sure use some badger hairs for my streamer flies, and I'd pay good for a badger."

He got another glimpse of grizzled gray when the oats went over in the breeze, and this time he was sure it wasn't the earth, because he had seen the oat stems part as something proceeded through them.

Mort had seen it too, and now he said: "Maybe we'd better get out of here."

Rock backed off. Now even his belly hairs bristled. Now his ears were as flat as he could lay them, and his tail was tucked tight.

Ham looked for a weapon. There was nothing except the fragile willow and rocks. He took a few steps and picked up a fist-sized stone. While he was straightening up, Rock gave a horrendous roar. A squat bundle of long, gray muscle was humping along the earth straight toward him and the dog. Without thinking, Ham hissed:

"Get 'em!"

Goaded by the hissing command to charge, Rock lunged forward. He came head on at the animal and then leaped clear across as his adversary rolled over on his back, presenting paws armed with long sharp claws.

"It's the badger!" Ham shouted.

The badger, back on its feet, squatted flat, showing two rows of sharp, white teeth. Rock stood spraddle-legged, battle threats rumbling in his throat and his lips turned up and out of the way so his teeth were white in the sun.

Mort was retreating. "Call him off," he pleaded. "Call him off!"

Ham wanted to, but he thought of the price a badger might bring from Frank Tyson, so he hissed again:

"Sic! Sic! Get 'em, Rock!"

The dog shot forward, and there was a flurry of snarls and legs and fur and teeth. Then Rock bounced back and began to edge around for a flank attack. But the badger turned with him, and the white stripe down the narrow head and face wrinkled as he tried to keep his flews free of his teeth.

Ham moved forward, too, with the rock ready. "Get 'em, Rock! Get 'em boy!" The dog charged, and this time the badger's timing was perfect, and he rolled and raked the dog's belly. Rock yelped, grabbed a patch of hair, and then the badger raked him again and the dog fell away with a patch of hide in his mouth.

Now Rock's belly was streaked with red. Foam began bubbling from the badger's jaws. Rock tried to position himself for another attack, but he staggered. The badger charged, but instead of attacking, he went right between boy and dog and hurtled down the den entrance. Ham threw his rock after him, and then ran to bend and look into the hole.

Rock moved slowly. Mort came back. Ham stayed at the hole, reluctant to believe the animal had gotten away. Then he heard Mort's voice.

"His guts are out. Jeeze, his guts are out!"

And, it was true. Rock's intestines were bulging through a hole the badger had raked in his grizzly hide.

"He's dying," Mort howled, tears rushing to his eyes.

Rock gave a few weak wags of his tail and started to lie down. Ham jumped forward and held the dog up.

"We can't let him lay down," Ham said. "If he gets his guts full of dirt he'll die for sure. Quick, give me your shirt."

While Ham held the dog, Mort stripped off his shirt. With Mort's help, Ham wrapped the shirt around the dog's middle, and using the sleeves, tied it tightly up over the back. Then he let Rock lay down. The big dog rolled his eyes, but his tail continued to thump the ground.

"We got to get him to a vet," Ham said. "Go see if there's a fish bag in the boat."

Mort came back with a wet sack. They rolled the dog onto it and sledded him to the boat. The loop of intestine bulged and showed pink-gray through the blood-soaked shirt as each boy took hold of the animal and, lifting, laid him in the boat.

The boat veered left and right as the boys, in their haste, pulled at the oars independently of each other. Long before they reached shore, their shouts had brought a half-dozen people.

A fisherman offered to drive them to Oak Grove where the veterinarian had his office. Ham went along, but at his mother's insistence, Mort stayed behind. With the dog cradled in his arms, Ham had time to reflect once more on how every venture to obtain the ten dollars necessary to erase his sin seemed to end in disaster.

The fisherman, who had said his name was Verne Blocker, helped the boy carry the dog into the small building of concrete blocks.

"He's lost a lot of blood," the veterinarian said, as he and the fisherman carried Rock through a door to the rear of a building lined with cages housing cats and dogs, all of whom protested the arrival of the newly wounded.

Ham followed to watch the men lay Rock on a porcelain-topped table. "He's got spunk, though," the veterinarian said, as the dog's tail wagged.

Ham watched as the veterinarian, whose name he had learned was Marion, rolled up his sleeves. Then as he was cutting away the bloody shirt, he turned to the boy and said: "Best you wait outside."

[104

Ham went through the door and around to the shady side of the garage. Then he slumped to the ground with his back to the wall.

He had never realized until now how much a part of his life the dog had been. Almost as far back as he could remember, the dog had been there—in his dust nest by the stoop, stretched beneath the kitchen sink, running across the hill to put a squirrel up a tree, crawling close to put his head in his lap. . . .

There was the first muskrat, and it had grabbed Rock by the nose and he still had the scar. There was Froedert's cat, and they had gone to court about that, but the dog was exonerated when it was proved the cat was trespassing. There had been scores of rabbits put into stone fences, and wood-piles to be dug out for the family table. There had been any number of skunks and subsequent ammonia baths—and too many fights with other dogs to even remember.

It would be lonely if Rock died. Ham thought of Rob MacQuarrie's death, and then he thought of all the things that had happened to him in this most hectic of all summers— the carp he sold to Nero, the sparrows, the turtles, moonshine, priest—and the day he had hidden under the pier while they dragged for his body.

It weighed on him now—all of it—and he didn't hear the door open and Dr. Marion come out. He only looked up when the veterinarian said: "That's a mighty tough dog you got there, son."

Ham looked up. "You mean he's going to be okay, that he's going to live?"

"Well, the odds are all with him," the doctor said, rolling down his sleeves. "In fact, if infection doesn't set in, he's a cinch to pull through and be as good as new."

Ham got up, was dizzy, and almost fell. The doctor grabbed his arm.

"Hey, not you now," he said, holding his arm.

Ham's vision cleared. "I'm okay."

Dr. Marion led him toward the house. "Maybe you'd better come in and lie down for a while," he said.

Ham shook his head. "No. I'm all right. I feel fine."

They went in together then, and the doctor gave Ham a glass of water. "I don't treat people very often," he said, "but if you still feel whoozy, I've got something that will help."

Ham shook his head.

"Maybe you'd better leave the dog here for tonight," Dr. Marion said.

Ham thought about it. "He'd tear things to pieces. He's never been away overnight before."

The doctor laughed. "Oh, we could take care of that all right."

Ham looked up at the veterinarian. "How much do I owe?" he asked.

"Will you have to pay, or will Mr. Drumm pay it?" Dr. Marion asked.

Ham said: "I don't know."

"If your Dad pays, it's ten dollars. If you have to foot the bill, you come over and talk to me, and I'll find a couple Saturdays of work for you." He held out his hand. Ham took it, and they shook hands.

"But I'd still like to take him home now," Ham said.

"Okay," the doctor said, "but just make sure he doesn't tear the bandages off so he can get at the stitches or we'll all be in trouble."

The fisherman and the veterinarian carried Rock out. He was bound tightly around the middle and taped. His eyes were open, but they had a faraway, dreamy look and he didn't recognize the boy.

"I put him to sleep for a little while," the doctor said. "He's just waking up."

That night they let him have the dog on a blanket next to his cot. Ham slept soundly for several hours and then came awake. He reached for the flashlight beneath his pillow and shined it on the dog. Rock was tearing at the bandages with his teeth. Ham pushed the dog's head back.

It was quiet then, and a screech owl mourned softly. Then Ham could hear the dog tearing at the bandages again. He reached over in the dark and pressed Rock's head down onto the blanket. Then he got up and went into the kitchen where the kerosene lamp burned low. He turned it up a little, and from a cabinet he got a jar of mustard and a shaker of red pepper. Then he went back out onto the porch and with his fingers spread mustard on the bandages and then sprinkled them with pepper.

He took the pepper and mustard back to the kitchen, turned the light back to low, and going onto the porch crawled over the dog to his cot.

Once after that he heard Rock sneeze, heard his teeth click. Then he fell asleep.

Thirteen

SUMMER MOVED ON into August. The heat persisted, and creeks dwindled. Pastures turned brown, and some farmers turned their cattle into the corn. Marshes became scarred mud flats. Leaves began to crisp on the trees. The elderly wilted, but the young hardly noticed, and if they walked into the river more often or followed along on the shady side of a street, they did it in the same unthinking way of an animal.

Rock healed fast, and the bandages came off, but he still humped along as though bound tightly around the middle. Ham spent more time than usual in his retreat among the cedars, but once again he was becoming restless.

Then, as was inevitable, both boys revisited the scene of the fight, the rock pile where the badger had his den. Ham knelt at the hole down which the badger had fled, and in a loud and mocking tone said: "Come on out and fight. Come on, we'll fix you."

But, of course, no badger replied, nor did one so much as show its grizzly muzzle, so they tired of the place and followed the cow path down to where it passed through the edge bogs of the marsh to a forested knoll.

Halfway across the area of bogs, Ham saw a bumblebee disappear into the side of a grassy hummock. He stood quietly while three other bees—fat, black, and yellow—came in for a landing.

Mort stood off to one side of the flight pattern. He scrubbed with a bare toe in the dust of the path and turned up a stone. He let it fly into the side of the hummock. There ensued an angry turmoil of buzzing bees.

One fat bee waddled out onto the grass landing strip and became airborne. Then in quick succession, squadrons of bees were off the ground hunting the invader.

Mort panicked and ran. A bee dove and stung him. The boy slapped the bee from his neck and kept running.

Ham held fast, though every fiber of him wanted to run. He tried not to blink. He kept his eyes open until they filled with tears. Within a few minutes the air had cleared. Ham backed away cautiously.

Finally turning, he asked Mort: "Why did you run?"

"Because I was scared."

"You're just lucky the whole gang didn't take out after you. By now you'd have so many warts, you'd look like a pickle. Next time stand still."

Mort fingered the lump. "Let's burn them out," he said.

"What's the good of it. Now, if they were honey bees . . ." a thought struck Ham.

"What's the matter?" Mort sensed Ham was about to suggest they embark on some adventure.

"I was just thinking," Ham said, "that there's a bee tree on the knoll, and maybe we could raid it."

Fingering the lump on his neck, Mort said: "Count me out."

Ham was, of course, envisioning jars of amber honey that could be taken from door to door in Greenville and turned into cash, enough cash to free him from his sin.

"We could smoke them out," Ham said, fingering the slender shafts of blue and redheaded matches he always carried.

"You can smoke them out if you want to," Mort declared, "but I'm going to stay clear."

The boys came out of the bogs. The cow trail ended on higher ground where the cattle were wont to disperse and graze the wooded knoll.

Ham found the bee tree within minutes. It was a huge, high,

hollow linden—almost punky with age. But the bronze honey bees were still using it in a continual procession through a triangular shaped opening at the base of the tree.

Ham looked for fuel. He gathered fists of dried marsh grass and piled it near the opening. Then he gathered dry sticks. He stayed out of the flight pattern because with these bees there was no preliminary circling, and they were arriving at the rate of four or five a second.

When he had gathered what he assumed was enough fuel, he stood off to one side to watch. Most amazing was the way the incoming bees avoided colliding with those leaving the tree in their search for more flowers to gather materials with which to build the wax comb and make the honey and bee food. He broke a leafy branch from a hazel bush and held it in the flight pattern. The bees went over and under it without hesitation. Then as Mort stepped back, he moved his body right into the flight pattern. Not so much as one bee put a wing to him as they winged around.

Victoriously Ham teased Mort: "Let's see you do it."

"Why? What's the sense to it? You gotta be nuts to do a thing like that!"

"You're scared. You're a coward," Ham said.

"I've just been stung. You haven't."

"Let's smoke 'em out," Ham said. Mort didn't answer.

Kneeling off to one side of the tree trunk, Ham quickly stuffed dry grass and twigs into the aperture. Several bees circled angrily, but before they could find a target, Ham struck a match and flames were leaping up the sides of the tree. He retreated to watch.

Incoming bees hit the circle of heat and swung off. The fire spread from the base of the tree, and then in seconds it began running through the leaf mold in the dry woodlot. The boys took hazel brush branches and began beating the creeping fire in an effort to contain it. Smoke choked them and stung their eyes. The little hairs on their arms curled with the heat and disappeared. Sweat rolled down their faces, which were darkened with soot, and the hot ground burned their bare feet.

"Jeeze! Hurry!" Ham shouted.

"What do you think I'm doing," Mort said.

Because cattle had kept the grass cropped nearly to the bare ground, the boys were able to contain the fire, but only after it had marked out a black circle as big as a couple of houses.

Exhausted, they fell to the ground, but from time to time they had to get up and hurry back to beat out the fire where a spark had gathered enough substance to create a new flame.

Then Mort noticed that the tree was burning. "Look," he shouted, "that whole darn tree is on fire!"

Flames had started up the side of the linden. They rushed in to extinguish them, but the hot ashes on their bare feet made them retreat to unburned ground.

Now there wasn't a bee in sight. The flames climbed, and where the bark was brittle it spurted brightly colored snappings of fire. When the bark ten feet up had been consumed, the flames died, but the punky tree continued to smolder.

"Look, look," Mort exclaimed, moving around so the sun was at his back. Ham looked up, and at a knot hole which had obviously been enlarged to accommodate squirrels, an amber stream of liquid honey began running down the charred tree.

"There goes our honey," Ham said. "There it goes, right into the ashes."

On the still air, the smoldering fire put up a steeple-straight column of thick, gray smoke.

"What are we going to do?" Mort asked.

"Nothing. There's nothing now. The honey will all melt. We can't save the tree. But we gotta stay to see the fire doesn't spread."

When the fire had first started, a couple of cottontails had scuttled away through the dry brush, but then the woodlot had been silent. Now a bluejay came in for a look and went away screaming, and a hawk circled and keened, hoping perhaps that the fire would leave some carcasses for it to feed upon.

The tree trembled. "It's going to tip over. It's going to fall," Ham announced. Both boys made ready to run.

"Rotten clear through," Ham said. "Only a shell. All hollow. Dead."

"Not all dead. Look." Mort pointed to where there was one spray of leaves on a high, canting limb.

The weight of the tree made the burning base settle a little, and sparks flew. Then the linden trembled again.

"Man, the way that tree's acting you'd think it felt the fire," Mort said.

"Maybe it can."

Mort laughed. "You crazy? Trees can't feel."

"How do you know?" Ham asked.

"Because they're trees. They aren't people."

"So I suppose a dog can't feel because it isn't people?"

"But that's different," Mort said.

"Yeah, what's so different about it? A fish feels, doesn't it? A worm feels. It squirms when you put it on a hook."

"Yeah, but they are living," Mort argued.

"You mean trees aren't alive?"

"Well, not like people."

Ham had hit on something. He had never thought of it before, but suddenly now, with the old tree dying before his eyes, it seemed that anything that grew had life, and anything with life didn't want to die.

So, if somewhat illogically, he pursued the premise that trees didn't like to be hurt or to die anymore than people, and he said: "Trees groan, don't they? They crack and rattle, don't they? And they even bleed?"

The thought of a tree bleeding was a little too much for Mort. He scoffed, "Now I know you're nuts. Whoever heard of a tree bleeding?"

"Just cut one and see what happens. It bleeds."

"Aw, that's only sap. That isn't blood."

"All blood isn't red. It doesn't have to be red. What about a grasshopper's blood? It isn't red. And look at the pine trees. Their blood even clots. Look at the maples. Tap one and you get a bucket of syrup. The syrup is their blood." The thought intrigued Ham. "Yeah," he went on with obvious satisfaction, "maybe we're drinking blood everytime we put maple syrup on our pancakes. Maybe we're cannibals."

The big tree, as though to add credence to Ham's suddenly discovered theory, creaked, groaned, and then swayed perilously. The boys jumped back and were poised to run.

"She's gonna go," Ham said.

A mighty shudder ran the length of the tree. It leaned. For an instant it seemed to cling to the very sky for which it had been reaching all its life. Then slowly it began to slant.

The massive trunk picked up momentum, and in its death throes, maimed and killed other trees beneath it. The crash it made on hitting the ground was a resounding tumult of breaking branches. The trunk of the tree bounced a few feet back into the air on hitting, and then settled to the earth which had given it life in the first place, and the dust, ashes, twigs, and leaves clouded around.

The boys stood petrified. They hadn't expected that an inanimate object like a tree could die in such a spectacular fashion. It had been like watching a hundred years suddenly dissolve into an instant of time.

When the debris had settled, all Ham could say was: "Did you see that?" His voice was hushed.

"Yeah," Mort whispered, still breathless.

A crackling in the brush behind them brought both boys to their senses. They turned and saw a man running toward them. He was carrying a shovel.

"Oh, man," Mort whispered to Ham, "now we're in for it."

The boys hardly noticed, but behind the man coming through the bogs were two girls.

"My God, boys, what's going on?" the farmer asked, as he stood in front of them, breathing heavily.

Mort started to run, but then stopped. There was only water in the direction he had planned to flee. Ham stood his ground.

"You could have burned the woods down," the farmer said, angrily. "In this heat you could have set fire to the marsh. It might have run on up into the oats!"

The farmer was the one Ham had fished with, the one named John. He pushed past the boys now and walked across the circle of burned-over ground. Then with effortless strokes he began heaping earth on the smoldering stump and along the fallen trunk.

The few flames winked out. The smoke abated until there were only wisps leaking up through the dirt to spread and thin out to nothing on the still air.

When the farmer came back, Ham stepped forward and forced himself to explain: "We're sorry, but we were trying to smoke out some bees so we could get the honey."

Then he braced himself, waiting for the tirade to begin. But the big farmer spoke softly. "You should have come to me. I'd have helped. It's too dangerous now, and anyway, it's too early to be collecting honey. That's for fall when the combs are full. God, when I think of it, you could have set the whole county on fire."

Ham hung his head. "I'm sorry," he said again, and found it was easy to apologize to this man. Mort kept his back turned, but his ears seemed to twitch, as though waiting for the warning to flee.

Both boys, their eyes big and white in their soot darkened faces, looked like chimney sweeps, those English urchins lowered down the chimneys of London. The farmer smiled. Then he said, more kindly: "Well, there was no harm done. So, if it taught you a lesson, I guess that's worth a lot."

John walked again through the circle of burned-over land and heaped more earth on the trunk and the stump. The two girls, evidently his daughters, had come up and stood watching.

"Well, I've got to get back," the farmer said, shouldering the shovel. "The threshers are coming tomorrow."

He strode out of the woodlot and onto the cow path which led through the bogs. The girls stood looking at the fallen tree. When the farmer was out of hearing, the older girl, who looked as though she might be as much as fourteen, said: "You could have got yourself killed."

"How can a tree kill you?" Ham asked. "All you have to do is jump fast."

The girls, both wearing short, blue cotton dresses, were barefoot like the boys. They were tanned, had dark brown hair, and each had a sprinkling of freckles across the bridge of her nose. They viewed the boys solemnly. Finally the older said: "I think boys are foolish. They are always getting into trouble. I'm glad there are no boys in our family."

Mort came forward grinning. "You don't know what you're missing," he said, all of his cockiness back, now that the danger was over.

"Humph!" the girls snorted in unison.

The farmer had disappeared over the crest of the hill.

"What if a bee had stung you?" the younger girl asked.

Mort turned his neck so they could see the lump. "One did sting me," he said proudly.

"Honestly?" the older girl asked.

"Sure, a big, fat bumblebee," Mort said, displaying the swelling as if it was the purple heart.

"And you didn't cry?" the youngest asked.

"Cry? Cry?" Mort scoffed.

It was Ham's chance. "You sure screamed bloody murder."

Mort made a fist. "You're crazy. I never let out a peep. I just stood there and let them come at me."

"What a liar!" Ham said.

"Who you calling a liar?"

"I'm calling you a liar."

"Step over here and say that," Mort offered.

Ham looked toward the girls. They had lost interest and were starting back along the cow path. The boys trailed after them.

"Bet you never caught any turtles," Mort said, trying to get back on stage.

"Who wants turtles?" the older girl said. "I can think of many more interesting things."

"Bet you never caught a ten-pound pickerel," Ham said.

"Who wants a fish?" the girls said together.

"Wish I had a snake," Mort said.

"What would you do with it?" the older girl asked.

"Bite its head off," Mort said.

"How silly can you get?" the older girl said.

When they had crossed the boggy area and come out onto the pasture, the four walked abreast.

"A badger almost killed our dog over there," Ham pointed.

"I'll just betcha," the younger girl said.

"Well, it did. Ripped his guts out," Ham said.

"You're fibbing," the younger girl said.

They had come alongside a thick arbor of wild grapes in the fence corner. Wild grasses grew up through the tangle of vines. It was the place for a natural parting of their separate ways, but instead of leaving, they stood there.

"What a cozy place," the older girl said, pointing.

Neither boy said anything, but they exchanged glances.

"We could sit in there and be out of the sun," the older girl continued. Then as if to show the boys how comfortable it was, she bent over, and going beneath the vines, sat so she was facing them.

"Why don't you sit over there, Marge?" the older girl prompted the younger one.

"Okay," the younger one said, and crawled into another nook among the vines and sat looking out at the boys.

"You, come here," the older girl said, pointing to Ham. Mesmerized Ham walked over and stood in front of her. "Why don't you go over by Marge," the older girl said to Mort. Both brothers looked again at each other, and then Mort went over.

When Ham was close to her, the older girl whispered: "If you show me, I'll show you." Ham's throat went dry. He wanted to run and he wanted to stay. "Wouldn't you like that?" the girl asked. Ham nodded.

The girl pulled up her dress. To Ham's astonishment she had no pants on, and to his utter amazement he saw a triangle of black hair.

Now, of course, it was impossible to fulfill what amounted to an obligation, because he couldn't let her see that as yet he was completely without even a trace of hair. He swallowed, but the swallow seemed to stick in his throat. He couldn't look away from the girl's long legs, tan to just above the knee and milky white above. On the verge of panicking, he looked to where Mort was. He had crawled in with the younger girl.

"Well!" the older girl said. "Open your pants!"

Ham turned and started away. The older girl jumped up. "Come on, Marge! Let's get out of here, away from these dummies!"

Mort jumped to his feet and backed away. The younger girl got up and followed her sister. Mort tagged along behind them. Ham called: "Mort, let's go home."

"What's your hurry," Mort called back.

"Come on. I'll take the boat and leave you."

"Go ahead. I'll swim."

"Aw, let him go," the older girl said. "He's a poor sport anyway. Let him go."

Mort trailed after the girls, and Ham, regaining his composure, caught up with them.

"Who asked you to come?" the older girl said to Ham.

"This is a free country."

"Not on my father's land it isn't," she said.

"He told me I could walk on his land."

"Well, I'll fix that," the girl said.

Both boys were silent. Mort had his eyes on the younger girl and never noticed the soft platter a cow had left. He stepped into it and some of it splattered on Ham's overalls.

Both girls giggled. When Mort came to another platter he stepped into it with such purpose he sent some splattering as high as Ham's waist. The girls laughed.

Angrily, Ham pushed Mort away from the platter and stomped his foot so forcefully into the green, runny center that some went flying into Mort's face. The girls howled.

And so the battle was joined, the battle of cow manure, and by the time the brothers had liberally smeared each other from head to foot, the girls were already at the edge of the oat field.

Then before they went over the crest to disappear, the older one shouted back, "Pigs!"

And the younger one echoed her, "Yeah, pigs!"

The brothers stood watching the girls until they were out

of sight. Then they turned and slunk down the cow path.

Now there was nothing left for Ham except humiliation. Coupled with his humiliation was embarrassment and a feeling that girls were not the pristine symbols of virtue that his mother had led him to believe they were, that they were as gutty as a rabbit in heat.

But never Lydia. Not Lydia, sitting in the morning sun, combing her long, golden hair.

Then as Ham slipped into the cleansing waters of the river he wondered: Where was Lydia? And would she ever come?

Fourteen

A UGUST MOVED APACE, and though the heat held, the tempo quickened. Owls, mostly silent in summer, whimpered more often. Young mallards quacked more anxiously. Teal gathered a few flocks into small colonies. Martins and swallows gathered on wires, getting ready for their trip south. Dogs seemed more restless, and in the night their barks could be heard from many directions.

But for Ham there was the gift of uneventful, almost peaceful days. He went to church as always, but never received the Sacraments. Father Zamanski largely ignored him, but his father sometimes still bristled, and in his mother's eyes there was an unfathomable sadness.

The matter had not been resolved. He knew that. His own conscience stung him enough. And in the end, probably when vacation-time settled into the routine of school, he would be called to give an account. He could only hope that the day of reckoning could be postponed that long. In the meantime a miracle might happen.

What miracle he didn't know. Perhaps Lydia would bring it, if she came. But the summer was waning, and every morning he looked out the screen before rising from his cot, and the tent was never there.

It was illogical to think, of course, that Lydia's coming might solve anything. Why he clung to such a thread of hope he didn't know. What could she do? How could she help?

When worry overwhelmed him, he found surcease in the

river. It was like going to an old and familiar friend who never ceased to intrigue him with aspects of character he had never suspected. No day on the river was without discovery.

He wondered, of course, why the priest and his parents did not make an issue of his failure to go either to confession or Communion. He guessed it had something to do with his visit to the doctor's office. It was an advantage he hadn't anticipated, even though he knew it couldn't last.

So the pattern of peaceful days moved warmly along to a Friday near the middle of the month. Then like a thrown stone can break the calm of a lake, the chugging of an automobile along the dusty road signaled the beginning of a new adventure, though at the time Ham never knew it.

He was standing on the hill, and he heard the auto. Then an ancient Dodge came over the crest, coughed a few times, and came to a trembling halt inches from a large oak. Jumpy Jones got out and walked over to the boy.

The man was excited. It seemed, according to Jumpy, that as a joke someone had raided his coal bin and turned his turtles free. He had searched Greenville for two days, and here it was Friday and there was no turtle soup on the menu.

Ham could have told Jumpy that the turtles wouldn't stay in Greenville, that they'd come to the condensery ditch, like filings to a magnet, then follow it down to Lost Creek, and so come back, eventually, to Big Pike Lake and Big Pike River.

"It's too late now for turtles," Jumpy said, "but I'll give you two bucks if you get some fish for me."

Ham was immediately wary. He hadn't gone through the fish gambit with Nero for nothing. He wasn't about to step into another trap.

"It's against the law, Jumpy—I mean, Mr. Jones."

"You can call me Jumpy. Everybody does." He scratched his chin, where whiskers grew in sparse patches, and then brushed at the thin, pale, brown hair.

"I'd catch the fish myself," Jumpy went on, "but I don't know how. I never caught a fish."

Ham was tempted, and he thought about the idea of palming some carp off on Jumpy. But he might get caught. People who frequented Jumpy's place on Friday came because the food was especially good. They were discerning people. They'd be sure to know, and quick to tell Jumpy.

"If I don't at least have fresh fish tonight, they'll tear my place apart," Jumpy said.

Ham looked thoughtful, and then tried to be helpful: "Why don't you just lock up for one night?"

Jumpy shook his head. "For years people have been coming. I've got the best Friday night business in the county. They'd break the doors down. They even drive out from Milwaukee. You wouldn't believe it, but I make more on Friday than all the rest of the week put together."

Ham was amazed that Jumpy's place was so popular. "I wish I could help you," he said, "but we might get caught. It isn't legal."

"Maybe if I fished with you. Wouldn't that make it legal? If I sat in the boat with you?"

Ham thought about the two dollars. He thought about God, Father Zamanski, and his father. What's more he had the fifty cents from the sparrows, the fifty cents from the turtles, and the twenty-five cents from the moonshine all in a can in the cedar grove. Two dollars would bring his savings up to three dollars and twenty-five cents.

"What if the fish aren't biting?" Ham asked.

"Don't they always bite?"

Ham wondered how anyone could be so stupid about fish. "Not always," he said. "And anyway, it depends. What kind do you want? Perch? Northerns? Bullheads? It's too hard to get walleyes in the daytime."

"Big ones." Jumpy measured with his hands.

"Then it will have to be northerns; people call them pickerel."

Jumpy nodded vigorously. "That's fine. That would be swell. Let's go."

"We have to get bait first," Ham said.

"How do we do that?"

"With a net," Ham said.

"You got a net?"

Ham nodded.

"Well, let's get going."

"Okay," Ham agreed, but not without misgivings.

Jumpy took a brown paper sack out of the car and followed Ham down the hill into the dirt floor basement of the cottage where the fishing gear was stored. Ham handed Jumpy a pail, then took a fine-mesh seine from its stretching pegs.

Where a boat passage had been cut through marsh rushes, Ham instructed Jumpy on how to hold one side of the net. The he dragged his side slowly forward and around toward solid ground. They lifted, and there were a half-dozen carp measuring about three inches in the net. While they were making another pull, Mort came down. He objected to Ham's warning to get along and mind his own business, but he did go when Jumpy said: "Beat it!"

They collected twenty small carp and shoved off. At first Jumpy sat still and erect. He braced both palms to the stern seat, and his eyebrows went up each time the boat tilted.

"It won't tip," Ham said, seeing his apprehension.

"Feels pretty tippy. I've never been in a boat before." It was incredible to Ham that here was a man who had neither fished nor ever been in a boat. He was wondering how Jumpy had used up his boyhood, when the man took a quart bottle of moonshine from the brown paper sack and pulled the cork with his teeth. Ham watched, fascinated at the way Jumpy's Adam's apple bobbed as he swallowed. But then, as the smell of the moonshine wafted over to him, he felt his insides shake.

At the entrance to Turtle Slough, Ham anchored the boat. Then he baited three poles with carp by inserting the hook just back of and beneath the dorsal fin. The three bobbers skittered about on the water as the bait fish tried to free themselves so they might hide from predators in the coontail moss which lined the entrance to the slough.

"This is nice," Jumpy said, taking another swallow from the bottle. "I can see now why some guys are so nuts to go fishing. This is nice." He smiled, showing a ragged edge of snuff-stained teeth.

Ham wished Jumpy wouldn't drink anymore. It made him sick everytime he opened the bottle.

The boy didn't see the bobber go down when the first fish struck, but he heard the loud popping noise it made when it submerged. He lifted the pole and held it at arm's length to provide all the slack line he could. The fish went almost to the end of the line before stopping. Then Ham knew it was turning the carp in its jaws so it might swallow it head first.

It was nearly a minute before the line began to move again. Ham knew the fish had swallowed the carp. He took up the slack left in the line and then deftly set the hook.

The pike made several frantic rushes, bending the pole perilously close to breaking. But then it surfaced, and thrashing bubbles in every direction, was skidded to the side of the boat. Ham flipped it aboard, took out the hook, and slipped it into the gunny sack.

It was a nice fish, about four pounds, grass green with white bean-shaped spots and needle sharp teeth in a jutting jaw.

Ham hadn't had time to give Jumpy a thought, but now he noticed the man was so excited he was on the verge of falling into the river.

"That's nothing," Ham said, boastfully. "Wait. Maybe we'll get hold of a big one."

Fortified by another gulp from the bottle, Jumpy quieted. "I never saw anything like that in my life. But then when you think of it, I never got out of Cicero until I was twenty-one, and after that it was the mills at Gary—so how could I?"

Ham didn't have time to feel sorry for Jumpy, because another bobber was skittering across the surface. The fish went all the way to the end of the line without stopping. Luckily, however, the hook caught and held, and when the fish felt the steel it came vaulting into the air in a spectacular, writhing leap. It was a big fish with gill covers nearly as large as saucers, and when it crashed back into the water, man and boy were sprayed.

Ham tried to ease up on the pressure, but the hook must have entered the pickerel's jaw at an unusually sensitive spot— perhaps near an eye—and in a surging run toward the middle of the river, it broke the line near the tip of the pole. The bobber skimmed for a distance as the fish continued to drag it along, and then it disappeared when the fish dove.

Ham looked at Jumpy. He was wild-eyed and standing. He was waving the bottle and shouting: "Did you ever! Did you ever! Son-of-a-bitch did you ever!" He became incoherent, and Ham got to his knees to reach over and urge the man back into his seat.

"If you fall in, you'll scare all the fish away."

"If I fall in," Jumpy howled, "I'll drown because I can't swim."

Jumpy sat back down and turned his attention to the bottle. In quick succession then, Ham caught two fish he estimated at five pounds apiece.

"How many you want, Jumpy?" he asked.

"How many we got?"

"Three."

"I mean, how many pounds?"

Ham figured. "Maybe fourteen pounds the way they are. Maybe ten pounds when they are cleaned."

"Ten pounds?" Through the moonshine-fogged brain Jumpy was figuring. "Ten pounds. A quarter pound a serving. Forty servings." He stopped mumbling and looked up at Ham. "Can we get ten more pounds?"

Ham was skeptical, but he nodded. "We might not get any more. You never know." He thought about moving to another location, but decided against it because it would waste time.

So he sat and waited for a strike, and Jumpy, lulled by alcohol, hummed a low dirge and swayed back and forth to the sounds of his sad song.

It took nearly three hours to catch three more fish. One was what Ham called a "snake," a small fish of about two pounds, but the other two went five pounds or more.

"I don't think we can get any more," Ham said.

Jumpy drank the last swallow from the bottle and put it back in the paper sack to carry along home where it would be refilled. Ham hoisted the anchor and pointed the boat for the big willows upstream.

Bucking the current brought beads of sweat to the boy's

brow. The boat wanted to come around, and in trying to correct for the thrust of water, Ham maneuvered a snaky course. Jumpy was half-asleep. He swayed with the boat, and Ham hoped he wouldn't fall in. It would be difficult trying to get him back into the boat.

But they made it safely, and when the bow grated gravel, Jumpy, instead of waiting, stepped over the side in knee-deep water. Then he fell, and Ham had to extend an oar for him to hang on to so he could come erect, sputtering.

The sack of fish was too heavy to carry, so Ham dragged it up the hill, with Jumpy trailing uncertainly behind. At the car, Jumpy went through his pockets, and finding no money, explained to Ham that he could collect tomorrow. Then the man eased in back of the steering wheel, and Ham tried to crank. Twice the engine started, but twice Jumpy killed it by accelerating too swiftly.

"Let me behind the wheel," Ham finally said, "and you crank."

Jumpy got out and went around to the front of the car, and Ham got behind the wheel. On the first turn of the crank it kicked back and got Jumpy under the chin. He collapsed.

Ham got out and, going around the front of the car, helped Jumpy to a sitting position. When the man's eyes finally opened, he shook his head and looked around. "What happened?" he asked.

"The crank kicked you. Right under the chin." Jumpy rubbed his chin.

"Get back in the car," he ordered Ham. The boy got behind the wheel. Jumpy spun the crank again. The car roared. Ham let up on the gas. The car muttered contentedly.

Jumpy came around and Ham got out. The man turned the Dodge, and it took off in starts and stops on down the hill. At the curve, instead of following the road, it went straight ahead and came to a stop with a crash against a tree. There was a tinkle of glass. Ham ran down the road.

"What happened?" Jumpy asked, when Ham came up.

"You forgot to turn. You hit a tree. The windshield is broken." A small piece of glass had cut Jumpy's cheek and now a thin trickle of blood coursed through the patches of sparse whiskers.

"You all right?" the boy asked.

"Sure. Sure. I'm all right."

"But you're bleeding."

"Just a scratch. Say, can you drive?"

"Well, I don't know. A little, maybe. But I'd better not."

"You gotta. We gotta get these fish to town. And in a hurry." Jumpy's voice slurred the words, and then he got out from behind the wheel and slumped to the ground. Ham looked around, as though for help. There was no one. Drunk as he was, Jumpy was pulling at Ham's clothes, pleading with him: "You gotta drive. You gotta. We gotta get those fish to town."

Actually Ham had driven. He had maneuvered the tractors on the equipment yard into place, and he had driven his father's car back and forth along the top of the hill. Perhaps he could. It was only two miles.

Jumpy was back on his feet. Ham got behind the wheel. The man went around and somehow, despite his drunkenness, was able to give the crank a half-turn. The motor caught, came alive, roared. Jumpy came stumbling around to get in along-side Ham.

"Take her away!" Jumpy shouted with enthusiasm.

Ham put the car in reverse and came out of the ditch in kangaroo-like leaps. How he managed to stop without going all the way across into the other ditch amazed even him.

"That was good. That was fine," Jumpy said. "You can do it. You're a good driver." He had a grip on Ham's right arm.

The boy tried to ease the car into gear, but it went off down the road in rabbit-like hops, and then finally, settling into high gear, kicked up a tremendous cloud of dust.

The Dodge wanted to go left, and Ham always over-corrected, so they cut a zigzag course down the dusty road. Gradually, however, Ham began to get the feel of the wheel, and then he felt exhilarated as the breeze came shooting through the broken windshield. He gave it more gas. The car shot up a hill, and there, in the middle of the road, was a wagon piled high with hay.

Ham had a fleeting impression of a pair of high-stepping, frightened horses, of a man standing on the pile of hay pulling back on the reins, and then he shot the Dodge into a farm drive to avoid a collision.

They went right through a flock of white ducks which lifted and scattered like sheets of newspaper in a high wind. Ham wheeled frantically to get the car back up on the road. The Dodge humped through the ditch, hit the road, and they were headed for Greenville again.

The boy lifted himself up to see through the rearview mirror and got a glimpse of the farmer on the hay load, shaking his fist. He got a glimpse of something else too, something white, and he dared turn his head for a look. There was a duck in the back seat.

"Jumpy, throw the duck out," Ham shouted.

"What duck? I don't see no duck."

"In the back seat."

Jumpy turned around, saw the duck, turned to Ham, and said: "We'll keep him. We'll eat him."

"Throw him out. Now!"

Jumpy looked at Ham as though he had lost his mind, but then he turned and, leaning back over the front seat, reached out and got the duck by a leg. He lifted the big, white bird and the wind did the rest. It caught the duck which had spread its wings, and car and bird were separated.

Where the dusty road ended and the gravel began, there was a stop sign, but by now the boy had the car under control. He came to a stop, shifted, and was on his way again. They came to the railroad track without incident and bumped over it, and then when Ham went to put his foot back on the accelerator, he found another foot, Jumpy's, was where his foot ought to be.

"Lift your foot," Ham shouted. But Jumpy, apparently never realizing his foot was on the accelerator, pressed harder. The car shot forward and whipped through an intersection, barely missing a Ford which had already started to cross. Jumpy's foot came down harder.

"Lift your foot," Ham screamed, and he kicked at Jumpy's shin to dislodge the man's foot from the accelerator.

The car whipped through another intersection, and Ham had a glimpse of people watching. He had to get off the street onto one of the town roads where there would be less traffic. At a dog-leg in the road, he almost laid the vehicle over on its side to make the turn, and then there, right in front of him, was a train on the crossing road.

He wheeled the car into a private drive with tires screeching, catapulted across a piece of lawn, taking a clothes line and some clothes with him. Then he was back out, around the house, and into the street, and the clothes were left behind in the road.

Now he was headed for Jumpy's place and still picking up speed. He stood behind the wheel and pulled back on the emergency brake. Tires smoked. He jumped on the brake pedal. The car slowed, but still it moved. Then in desperation he let go the wheel and bending beneath it grabbed Jumpy's foot in both hands and lifted it off the accelerator.

The engine of the car sputtered and died, and then gently the car crossed the sidewalk and nosed to a stop, tight against the side of Jumpy's place.

"You did it! You did it! I knew you could!" Jumpy exclaimed, climbing out.

Ham was trembling, and a few tears slipped down his cheeks. But he brushed the tears away, got out of the car, and taking the fish bag dragged it around to the back stoop. Jumpy was already there on the top step, sleeping with his head in his hands. His tiny wife had come out and was trying to awaken him.

"Jumpy, it's late. People will start coming. You've got to get cleaned up." But Jumpy slept on.

Mrs. Jones went back into the house. When she came back out, she carried a pail of water. She dumped it over Jumpy's head, and he came out of his lethargy like a stung horse which has made the mistake of bedding down on a hornet's nest.

Jumpy shook himself, looked sheepishly at his little woman, and then went inside. Dragging the bag of fish, Ham followed Mrs. Jones through the door. She directed him to the kitchen, a sparkling place of pots and pans and white dishes. The neat, clean kitchen was in such contrast with anything Ham had come to expect of Jumpy that all he could do was stand and look.

Mrs. Jones took the fish, but then when she couldn't lift the bag to the sink, Ham helped her. She emptied the pickerel out, and one was still breathing, so she struck it a sharp blow over the head with a wooden spoon. It stiffened, shivered, and went limp.

Then one by one she took the fish to a square carving block, and standing on a footstool because she was so short, she took a knife which looked to be almost the length of her arm and skillfully filleted the pickerel until it was two long, white strips of clean, fresh fish.

She shoved what was left into a large lard can on the floor and got another. In no time, she had fish slabs piled high on the cutting board.

Ham was just getting over his amazement at her skill with the fish when he had another surprise. Jumpy was back in the kitchen wearing a clean shirt, and his face was washed and his hair parted and matted to his head. The man sat at the table, and Mrs. Jones put a large mug of black coffee in front of him. He drank it in what seemed like a single, long gulp and then got up.

"You all right now?" Mrs. Jones asked.

Jumpy nodded, and then wonders of wonders, he came over and gave her a peck on the cheek.

She pushed him away. "You just get in there," she said, pointing with the knife. "Tony should have been relieved an hour ago, and the girls are starting to come." Jumpy put a hand on Ham's shoulder, closed his fingers only a little, and then went out through the door.

On a huge wood-burning range that was beginning to make the kitchen almost intolerably hot, Mrs. Jones had a deep kettle of lard which was beginning to smoke. She cut the slabs of fish into slender fingers of flesh, put them into a wire basket, salted them and popped the basket into the lard.

"You gotta stay for supper," Mrs. Jones said, wiping perspiration from her rosy, round face with a clean, white rag.

"Oh, I couldn't." Ham knew that if his father found out he had been in Jumpy Jones's Speakeasy, he would get the switching of his life.

"Nobody will ever know you've been here," Mrs. Jones said. "And anyway, you're in my kitchen and you aren't out in the bar."

Ham wanted to stay. It was such a pleasant kitchen. The aroma of good food was comforting. Mrs. Jones herself exuded such a warm friendliness. Her work was so well ordered, so meticulous.

"It's all right," Mrs. Jones reassured him. She had pushed the footstool to the front of the range, and from time to time she stepped on it, lifted the wire basket from the lard, shook the fish around, and then put it slowly back.

There was music now, coming from the direction of the bar. Ham went through the door and out into the hall in the direction of the music. A beaded curtain hung over the doorway. He parted it and peeked.

Jumpy was behind the bar, serving beer to three men on stools. Two girls in short black dresses, long black stockings, and white aprons no larger than a lady's handkerchief were talking to some men at a table. On all the tables stood bottles with lighted candles in them. There were glistening balls hanging from the ceiling, and there was the smell of moonshine, beer, and sweat, all mingling with the intriguing odor of perfume.

The den of iniquity, Ham thought. The den of iniquity which Father Zamanski sometimes talked about. He let the beads fall and went back to the kitchen.

"You like that music?" Mrs. Jones asked. Ham nodded. "It's a new loudspeaker Jumpy invented himself to attach to the radio. If he'd have had his chance, he could have been somebody," Mrs. Jones said, rather sadly, looking at the boy to see if he believed her.

Though she was only as tall as he was, she took him by the arm now and led him to a chair at a small corner table. There was a plate heaped with golden fingers of fish, green-white cabbage slaw, and two white slices of thickly buttered home-made bread.

"Eat," she commanded. "Sit and eat."

He had never tasted anything so delicious. No wonder, he thought, they came from as far as Milwaukee.

The music stopped. Ham could hear the girls laughing. The laughter did something to him, made him tingle. There was something hidden in it, something mysterious—as though the girls were hiding some surprise, and all you had to do to get it was to come looking.

He finished the fish, got up and took his plate to the sink. "That sure was good, Mrs. Jones. Thank you very, very much."

"I'm glad you liked it," Mrs. Jones said, and now her face was almost brick red as she lifted a stove lid and shoved in more wood. Then she took his arm again. "How much does Jumpy owe you?"

Ham looked down at the scrubbed floor. "Oh, that's all right. I kind of wrecked his car, and you gave me supper, and . . ."

Mrs. Jones cut him short. "How much?"

"Well, he said he would give me two dollars."

"Okay, you go into the bar and say I told him to give it to you. I've got to get the rest of these fish on."

Ham parted the beaded curtain. The music had started up again. One of the men was dancing with one of the girls. The other man at the tables was trying to pull the other girl onto his lap, and she was laughing. Jumpy was drinking beer from a tiny glass.

"Hya, Ham," Jumpy called out, just as though he was seeing him for the very first time that day. Then, before Ham could say anything, Jumpy went to the cash register, opened it, and took out two one-dollar bills and handed them to him.

"Thank you, Mr. Jones," Ham said, awed by it all.

"Wanta beer, Ham?"

A sharp voice from the back of the room said: "Jumpy!" Ham turned to see Mrs. Jones looking through the beaded curtain.

Jumpy laughed, nervously. "No, I guess not. I guess you don't want one."

Ham folded the two dollars and put them into his watch pocket. Then he went through the beaded curtain and stopped to put his head into the kitchen. Mrs. Jones said, "You better get home now, Ham. Good-bye."

He said good-bye, went down the hall, away from the music, and outside. The sun was getting low. The old car was still nuzzled up against the peeling paint of the bleached green building. Ham trotted down the street, thinking people sometimes just weren't at all like you thought they were—not at all.

Fifteen

ALL THE NEXT DAY Ham had the feeling he had seen something fine and beautiful in the Jumpy Jones kitchen. It was akin to the feeling he had when he was with Lydia. He couldn't describe, even to himself, what that something was, but he could feel it. He suspected it had to do with the relationship between Jumpy and Mrs. Jones.

As for the episode of the car—well, anything that ended well could be dismissed during this long, hot summer of his sin. So Saturday droned by without incident, but Sunday morning catastrophe in sandals and coarse cassocks stalked the altar of the church.

Two strange priests had come to conduct a retreat for St. Joseph's girls and boys. It was Father Zamanski's gesture, each summer, to make up for the fact that the parish could not afford a Catholic school, and in his words: "To interject into that idle summertime of your children's lives something to spiritually sustain them until school once again requires most of their time and they are too busy for most of the Devil's temptations."

To Father Zamanski, the Devil was a very real personality who lurked about, waiting his chance to lead people into sin. It was also his contention (and he should have known since he heard everyone's confession) that idle hours were not in God's best interests, and that "young people drifting aimlessly across the warm weeks of summer are veritable hothouses wherein the Devil can plant his seeds of evil."

Well, Ham didn't know about that. But he did know that a retreat required that every youngster make a general confession, reviewing for the priest all the sins of his lifetime, and then receive Communion.

What's more, from past experience, he knew about retreat priests and the special training they had in breaking down any resistance a youngster might put forth against being made holy. Though Ham never realized that they were master psychologists, and though the word "brainwashing" hadn't yet become a part of the language, he had, in the past, come under their hypnotic influence. So he had a very lively and breathtaking fear of them, especially in this instance when he was so terribly vulnerable.

Sunday he was still safe (they started work on Monday) and most of the day he sat in his vine-covered corner, wondering how he might armor himself. That night he was a long time falling asleep, and when he did the darkness was suddenly illuminated with nightmares. He came out of one screaming so loudly his mother came with a light and sat by him for a while.

While she was there the moon came up, and then when she left, the moonbeams formed their luminescent cruciform on the screen. Though he knew it for what it was—a perfectly ordinary phenomenon—he could not take his eyes from it, and when he turned over and closed his eyes, the cross was still there, as though branded on his eyelids.

In the morning there were dark circles under his eyes, and he dragged through breakfast, hardly eating. Then he and Mort rode with their father to Greenville for the boys' morning sessions, which were a part of the three-day affair of prayer.

The retreat priests, one tall and gaunt, the other short and enormously wide, wore brown, coarsely woven cassocks, and their bare feet were in sandals. They stood at the door to the church basement and watched as the boys filed past.

Then while the fat priest, a Father Fabian Freud, knelt in prayer, the tall, bird-like priest, who said his name was Mark Flint, took the boys of all ages on an especially elaborate and

[134

well-illustrated verbal tour of the kind of insane asylum they could expect to end up in if they succumbed to the temptation to masturbate.

When the priest began, Ham was mildly titillated by the thought of sitting back among the cool vines, having a sexual fantasy while he softly caressed his penis. But as the imaginary tour through the asylum progressed past raving maniacs shackled to the wall, he felt his penis dwindle, retreat. Then when the priest described how "one man's private parts decayed and fell away from excessive masturbation," his penis shrunk so far into his belly he was sure he'd never be able to retrieve it far enough to go to the toilet if that became necessary.

He was almost physically sick when the priest finally finished and the boys filed out. No one spoke, nor did any boy look at any other boy, and even the heat of the day was not enough to keep Ham from shivering.

That afternoon was given over to meditation and prayer, upstairs in the church proper. It was a three-hour session, with a three-minute break every half-hour during which sinners could come up off their knees and sit back in the pews.

The girls were all on one side of the church and the boys on the other, and Ham never let his eyes stray once. They said the rosary, way-of-the-cross, several litanies, and between periods of meditation read assorted prayers designed for retreats and printed on stiff cards which had been passed out as they entered the church.

At the end of three hours, they lined up for confession. The girls were on one side, where Father Freud was in the confessional with its wicker door and heavy curtains and stale air, and Father Flint was on the other side waiting to wash the boys' souls white.

Ham located himself at the end of the long, restless line. For a brief minute then, he debated the advisability of going through with it. He might have a chance, he thought, of getting absolution from Father Flint merely by promising restitution. And the priest would not recognize his voice. But he might make Ham promise (of his own free will, of course) to bring the issue into the open outside the confessional—make a public admission, and perhaps, involve his father in the restitution negotiations. That, of course, would be suicide, pure and simple.

He just couldn't take the chance. So he looked down the line of restless boys, and when there were no eyes turned his way, he slipped the few feet backward into the vestibule and then hurried out of the dim church into the bright sunlight. He walked around to the back of the brick building to where a blue spruce offered shade and sat with his back against the stones of the foundation.

The real showdown would come, of course, in the morning at Communion time. But, along with some other valuable methods of sidestepping stress and strain, he was learning about meeting an obstacle when the obstacle presented itself. So he usually did a fair job of finding other things to think about. But now, try as he might, even with the church right at his back, he could no longer get a clear picture of the farmer's daughter leaning back and pulling up her blue dress to where a nest of dark hair marked the beginning of her white belly.

He did wonder, though, when his hair would begin to grow, and he hoped it would happen before he was a freshman in high school. Otherwise he wouldn't go out for football or basketball, because to undress in front of his teammates and expose a bald belly—he couldn't do it.

Children's voices interrupted his worries, and he got up and, sauntering around the church, eased himself leisurely into the crowd. Finding Mort, he led him away, and then the two went to their father's machinery yard where they all got into the Model T and went home for supper.

That night the dishes were left unwashed in the sink and the entire family, with the baby sleeping in her mother's arms, went to town for the evening services. At church Ham went around to the rear entrance to the sacristy, and even before he had put on his red cassock and white surplice, the smells—of incense, burning candles, musty rooms where a window had never been opened—began to sicken him. He hoped he wouldn't vomit. It might be a sure sign for all of them, dressing now in their gold-fringed finery, that a devil had come to visit, and they might single him out for such a session of purging as he had only heard about.

But he made it out to the altar, which was streaming with long rivers of blazing candles, out to where the glittering, golden monstrance held the gleaming, white, unleavened Christ.

He couldn't look up at his Christ. It was asking too much. So he kept his eyes on the red carpet, said the prayers by rote, and was surprised to hear his voice clear and purely ringing as a bell when he sang the "O Salutaris Hostia," and the "Tantum Ergo Sacramentum."

It seemed his strength returned at the altar, and there was almost a note of triumph when he said with Father Zamanski: "O Sacrament most holy! O Sacrament divine! All praise and all thanksgiving be every moment Thine."

But if he had gathered a little strength in being swept along by the music and pageantry, it quickly dissolved when he went to his tiny, varnished, round stool to sit for the sermon.

He knew it was going to be an ordeal even before Father Flint began. Then when the priest started talking, though he heard the first few words, they held no meaning for him because edging in across the whites of his eyes to blot out the pupils was a creeping curtain of black, and he knew he was about to faint.

"Lower your head! Lower your head!" He remembered the admonition. His teacher, Miss Mallow, had been forever giving the advice to Audrey Kirks, who was always fainting in school.

Quickly then he pretended to sneeze and let the force of the nasal explosion carry his head down beneath his knees. He held his head there, felt the blood come back, raised it again to find that the priest, the candles, and the other acolytes had come back into focus.

He'd have to hang on, he thought, looking out over the congregation to where his father sat, ramrod straight, and where his mother was leaning her head against the babe's, which she held in her arms.

"There is only one way to God," Father Flint was emphasizing, "and though that be a narrow, a rocky, a treacherous road, we must—from the bottom of our hearts—thank the Father that He gave us Jesus Christ, who, in His infinite mercy, and after thousands of years of waiting, removed all barriers to the kingdom of heaven."

Ham felt he knew what the rest of the sermon was going to be about. In the six or seven years of retreats which he could remember, it varied little. And he was right.

"But even for those of us, who by our prayers and good works," the priest continued, "manage to stay on God's road to heaven, there is still one stopping place, a place which most of us cannot bypass, one last place of penance, one last place where we must be cleansed so that we may be worthy to come into the presence of the Almighty, and that final place is purgatory.

"Unless there is a saint sitting in this church tonight, or standing here at this altar of God, not one of us may attain heaven, gain admittance to the kingdom of God, without first atoning, being purified in the fires of purgatory.

"Fire," the priest went on, "is the great purifying agent which separates the gold from the gross metals, and until we shine like the gold, we cannot go through the gates."

He paused, took a clean, white handkerchief from his sleeve, patted his smooth brow, then continued: "But the fires of purgatory are like a mere pinprick of punishment as compared to the eternal fires of damnation which await us in hell!"

His words literally seemed to sizzle. It was almost as though you could feel the words, even see them like sparks shooting out across the Communion rail to be sprinkled red hot among the congregation.

His piercing black eyes in his gaunt face were brilliant with the fire of his faith. His eloquent and long, bony fingers lent an ethereal quality to each phrase as he motioned to emphasize each word. The bald spot above the fringe of hair shone like a halo. Father Flint was gathering in his sheep with a sermon in which you could smell the flesh burning, see the fires, and hear the wailing and gnashing of teeth as the lost souls tottered over the brink.

It all came to Ham in movie-like flashes of people writhing

among flames, and always, as in the paintings, they were naked.

"You shall go naked," Father Flint said pointedly, "and the agonies of hell which will engulf you defy any mortal's description. The blistering, burning flesh can never be imagined, because no words have been coined to tell of the terror which awaits the damned."

Ham was swept away. He went down into the abyss with the priest, heard the moans. He saw the men, women, and even the children raising their arms through the flames in supplication. Then he went beyond all terror to that place where the mind must balk, and then only a numbness took over.

Then, even as the oratory was still echoing from the choir loft, the priest abruptly changed pace, and in an uncommonly quiet but penetrating voice, he said:

"Now tonight you must all promise me one thing. You must promise me that when you go from this house of God to your own homes, when you have closed the night out behind you, when you have gathered at the kitchen table, you will light a candle. Then I want each of you in turn to put your finger in the flame and let the fire burn you. Then I want you to get on your knees and think on how this fire can burn and burn for time without end every inch of your body. Then ask yourself if such eternal punishment is worth any pleasure the world has to offer, if in obtaining that pleasure you stoop to sin."

The church was silent. The priest stood like a great, gaunt bird of doom, looking far, far beyond the congregation. Then he turned and walked without a sound to the foot of the altar. A vigil light sputtered in the last liquid of its life. A child coughed. A man moved his feet. A woman sighed. And then, instead of singing the resounding "Holy God, We Praise Thy Name," the priests turned, and the acolytes led them from the altar without another word. For Ham it was a devastating climax, and the sudden silence shook him as much as the sermon had.

The Drumms rode their winding way home, and no one spoke. When they were in the kitchen Mathew Drumm lighted a tallow candle, dripped tallow into a saucer, then set the candle solidly upright and placed the saucer on the kitchen table. Then he put his finger into the flame, and Ham thought he heard the flesh crackle, smelled the little hairs burn.

"I just think this is going a little too far," Rose Drumm said, backing away. Ham could see the hint of tears in her eyes. Mathew Drumm took her wrist, but she shook him off, and then she put her finger into the flame.

It was Ham's turn next. He looked at the fire leaping from the thick wick. He looked at his mother. The tears had come from her eyes, were streaking her cheeks. He looked up at the stern, bristling visage of his father. He put out his finger, pulled it back, and then quickly thrust it in and out of the flame.

"Put it in, Ham," his father said.

Ham put his finger in the flame, and the pain ran like a red hot wire up the veins of his wrist.

Mort was weeping. Mathew Drumm pushed him forward. Then the father took his son's hand and forced a finger into the flame. The boy screamed. Tears ran down Mrs. Drumm's face, and she sobbed. Then when her husband turned toward her, she grabbed the baby off the couch and ran with her into the bedroom. Even after the door had slammed, Ham could hear her crying softly: "No. No. No. . . ."

"Now, go to your beds and pray," the father said.

Ham lay a long time on his cot with his clothes on, exploring with his tongue the taut blister on the end of his forefinger. Finally he got up, undressed, and went back to bed—but he didn't pray.

Emotional upheavals are sometimes the strongest of sedatives, and Ham spent an untroubled night. He awakened refreshed in the morning, though he knew a crisis was imminent.

Before Mass the children gathered in the basement where Father Freud led them through the rosary. Ham hid his blister, but peeked surreptitiously at the fingers of his friends. He saw no other blisters. Then they marched by twos, girls first, up into the church.

Father Flint was saying the Mass, and Fathers Zamanski and Freud were his acolytes. Not having to serve Mass was a stroke of luck Ham hadn't anticipated. At Communion time, he lined up with the others, but as the file moved to the rail, he slipped over into the returning column of Communicants and slipped back into a pew.

There were two more days of meditation, prayer, sermons, instructions, intermittent attendance at service, Then on the last night after benediction, just when Ham thought it was all over, he felt his father's hand on his shoulder as they walked to the car, and Mathew Drumm said: "Father Zamanski wants to see you."

His father walked with him along the narrow path of concrete around to the priest's house but left him at the door. He rang the bell, the housekeeper admitted him, and then when the three holy ones came in, she scuttled like a scared rabbit for the kitchen.

The priests seated themselves, forming a semicircle, and when they were settled, Father Flint cleared his throat and began the inquiry: "Father Zamanski tells me you are in danger of losing your faith," the gaunt priest said, narrowing his eyes against the smoke from a long, thin cigar.

Ham kept his eyes on a green circle in the brown carpet until it began to whirl, and then he looked up and over the heads of the priests at the plants by the window.

"Well?" Father Zamanski prodded.

"I don't know," Ham said.

"What do you mean, you don't know?" Father Freud asked.

"I don't think I am," Ham said.

"You don't think you are what?" Father Zamanski asked.

"I don't think I'm losing my faith," Ham said.

"There is reason to believe you might be," Father Flint said.

Ham waited, expecting the priests to be more specific. To be a fallen-away Catholic was to be in worse straits than being a Protestant.

"Do you pray?" Father Flint asked.

Ham could only nod as the nature of the inquisition became more apparent.

"Speak up, boy," Father Freud said.

"Yes, Father, I pray," Ham said.

"Do you pray often?" Father Flint asked.

Ham hesitated, and then because he couldn't lie to, of all people, a priest, he said: "Well, not too often. Not regular prayers like the Hail Mary and the Our Father."

"What do you mean?" Father Zamanski said, leaning forward as though he had scented on something. "Do you mean to say that you have found some better prayers than the Lord's Prayer and the Ave Maria?"

Ham shifted his feet. It might have been easier if they'd let him sit. He didn't know how long he'd be able to stand. "No sir, I mean Father, I don't mean they are better. Just easier."

Father Flint caressed the long, thin, brown cigar with his long, thin, brown fingers. "Just what kind of prayers do you say?" he asked.

"Well, they aren't really prayers," Ham said.

"Well, if they aren't prayers, just what are they?" Father Flint asked.

Ham tried for words but couldn't find any that fit. "Mostly, I suppose, they are just the way I feel about things."

"And how is that?" Father Zamanski asked.

The boy hesitated, put his fingers to his mouth, and then fumbled with a lock of hair which had fallen to his forehead. Finally he said: "I don't know how to explain it, but if I see a bluebird that makes me feel good, then inside I'm glad God made that bluebird, and I thank Him for it." The speech left Ham breathless.

All three priests were silent for what seemed to Ham a considerable time. Then Father Flint asked: "And you consider a prayer like that better than the Ave Maria?"

For the first time Ham took his eyes off the plants and looked at the priests: "Oh, no," he said, "I know it isn't, but it's more . . . well, it's more . . . I don't know, but sometimes I don't understand prayers like the Hail Mary."

Father Flint asked: "But you understand these other prayers. Those prayers like, well, like the one you say when you see a bluebird?"

Ham thought about it, because the subject simply hadn't

occurred to him before. Finally he said: "Maybe it isn't a prayer. I guess I just thought it was."

"Do you say other prayers like that?" Father Freud asked.

Ham searched his mind. "I suppose so," he said.

"Like what?" Father Zamanski tried to pin him down.

Ham squirmed inside. Now he wished he hadn't mentioned the bluebird.

"Speak up, young man," Father Freud said.

"Well, sometimes at night," Ham began slowly, "if I'm scared, I ask God to take care of me. Or if I hear that someone I know is sick, I wish to God that he please won't die." He looked at the priests, waiting for them to say something. When they offered no help, he went on: "And when I'm hot and tired and I get a drink of really cold water, I think about how God put it there for me, and I feel glad about it, and . . ." That was all. He couldn't go on.

Again the priests were silent. Finally Father Freud broke the silence. "You know," he began, with some show of emphasis, "that some of our greatest saints wrote the prayers of the church. They were not only holy men, but highly intelligent men, filled with the spirit of the Holy Ghost."

Ham nodded. "I know," he said.

"But you think your prayers are better?" Father Zamanski asked.

"Oh, no, never," Ham replied. And then, despite his fright and for no reason he could ever explain, he had the heretical feeling that maybe they were—for him, anyway.

Maybe his inquisitors saw the change in the boy, because Father Zamanski changed the subject: "How come I haven't been seeing you receiving Communion as often as you should?"

Ham's hopes got a little lift. Then the priest didn't know that he hadn't received Communion once since school had let out. It was time to bolster his position: "I guess I was just sort of unlucky." The lie had come easy, even if it was to a priest.

"What do you mean 'unlucky'?" Father Flint asked.

"Like breaking my fast and getting sick, or having to leave the altar to go to the toilet in the basement." Now that he was gaining ground, now that he found he could lie as easily to a priest as to anyone else, he had a crazy thought, and gave voice to it: "Like not always feeling worthy." At least that was partially true.

All three priests leaned back in their chairs. Perhaps he had blunted the inquiry. At least they hadn't ruled for excommunication, and this had been a serious consideration, at least in *his* mind, when he was summoned.

"You know your father is worried about you." Father Zamanski picked it up again.

Ham nodded. "Yes, I guess he is."

"Your father is a good man," Father Zamanski went on. "Even in these hard times he gives to the church first, and then considers his corporal needs."

Ham wasn't sure what his father's corporal needs were, but he had a feeling that the crisis was past, that somehow he had survived, and now all he could think of was getting out into the fresh air, away from the clinging smell of incense and cigar smoke.

Yes, it was over. He knew it because Father Flint began a summing up: "If you like your prayers and they give you comfort, I can see no reason why you shouldn't say them. But you must remember, the church is thousands of years older than you are, and infinitely wiser, so you must say her prayers, too, and what's more, you must abide by her laws.

"Just remember," the gaunt priest said, leaning forward like Ham had seen a heron about to spear a frog, "the prayers of the church were not penned in haste or without much meditation. You say them, and you go to the Sacraments, and maybe God will help you stay out of some of the trouble I hear you've been getting into."

Ham nodded and waited.

"You can go now," Father Zamanski said.

Ham turned and walked toward the door. He had a feeling that somehow he had won the encounter. At the door he turned to say good-night. Then Father Flint got up and went out with him. He could feel the tall priest as though he were hovering over him, but he didn't turn his head to look back.

Then, just before he got into the car, the priest put an arm around his shoulder and gave him a surprisingly comforting squeeze, and then he knew he hadn't won at all, because there were no winners or losers in that kind of encounter.

On the way home he huddled in the back seat, watching the moon make every conceivable shape of shadow.

"Thank God. Thank God, for a beautiful, beautiful night," his mother said softly.

It was a prayer he could understand and appreciate.

Sixteen

THE NIGHT FOLLOWING Ham's bout with the priests was charged with the kind of elemental force that can touch off devastating weather, and if no humans were aware of the impending peril, Rock felt it. He paced endlessly from kitchen to porch, his nails clicking on the floor, until finally Mathew Drumm arose and banished him from the house.

Throughout the night, no blade of grass moved, nor did a cricket sound. The sky seemed to settle and press upon the living, and men lay wide-eyed, vaguely disturbed by the oppressive darkness, and children had troubled dreams.

Then in the morning, Ham looked up at brassy skies and wandered off down the trail to the outhouse, with Mort trailing. Both boys stopped to check the tobacco supply in the box nailed to the side wall, and Mort took a pinch. Then they walked out among the reeds and rushes of the marsh and sat where retreating waters had left white traces behind.

Mort put the tobacco in his mouth, chewed reflectively, and then began spitting furiously. "I don't see how they can do it," he said. "It's worse than when we smoke it."

"Then why do you keep trying?" Ham asked.

Mort only shrugged and spit again. For an instant Ham's mind dwelt on the rectory confrontation, but he was becoming more resilient with every new experience and had already regained his equilibrium. But he couldn't stay still, lest things past come creeping back, so he turned to Mort and said: "What'll we do?"

"Well," Mort said, putting a forefinger into his mouth in search of tobacco remnants, "we could go down to Indian Island and dig up a grave. We might find some treasure."

The thought of buried treasure had always intrigued Ham. But he remembered how hard they had dug in the past and how every grave had held the same, only a few bones, sometimes a skull, that their father always made them take back to bury where they'd found them.

"There's no treasure in those graves," Ham said. "The Indians didn't have money, and there was no gold around here for them to bury."

"But we might find some arrowheads," Mort said.

"Who wants arrowheads!" Ham had a shoe box half filled, and though he had spent many an enthralling hour fingering them and wondering how many animals, Indians, or whites they had killed, there just wasn't any market for them, so why—in his circumstances—bother.

Mort was spitting again. "Aghhh. Hope I don't get sick. I chewed Beechnut once. It was kind of sweet, but these cigar clippings. Aghhh!"

Ham dug his toes down through the marsh muck until they found water. He enlarged the hole until there was a small pool. With the little lake made, he looked up. "We could go to Squawk Island and see how many herons are nesting there. Maybe we could get a bundle of feathers and sell them to Mrs. Dressler."

Mrs. Dressler made hats or redecorated old hats other women brought to her. Because she was a divorcee and pretty, most women didn't like her, but they did patronize her because she had a flair for making such ordinary apparel as a man's fedora into what people claimed was the next thing to a Parisian creation.

"Women aren't wearing feathers," Mort said. He had heard it somewhere.

"Oh, yes," Ham countered, "some of them are. I heard mother say that feathers are coming back."

"That's a long, long row down there," Mort said.

"We could take sandwiches."

Mort looked interested. "Maybe we'd get to take a couple of bottles of pop."

Mrs. Drumm gave them egg sandwiches, but the two pop bottles were filled with water.

Rock tried to get into the boat with them, so Ham had to take him to the house. He whined and scratched at the screen, but Ham put both hands over his ears and ran down the hill.

The boat moved easily with the current. There were a few fishermen afloat, and they waved to the boys. Then, long before they got to the island, herons began rising from the high branches of the tall trees, and by the time their boat bumped shore, there was an umbrella of big birds above.

The still air was acrid with ammonia from their droppings. Trees were leafless, barren, reaching ghosts, and every inch of the island was whitewashed. The nests of sticks, crude platforms, were stacked sometimes ten and twelve to a tree, and the young birds, almost ready to take wing, were so crowded in their homes that they had to take turns squatting or be pushed overboard to go wildly flapping to the ground.

"I'm not going ashore," Mort announced.

"Why not?"

"Just smell. You think I want to get whitewashed?"

Ham looked disdainful. "It washes off."

Mort didn't move. "The smell is enough. It makes me sick."

"Boy, are you a coward."

"I'm not a coward. I'm just not a darned fool. I'm going to wait for a good rain. Then when everything is clean, maybe I'll come back."

Ham stepped to the whitewashed stones. The young birds gawked over the sides of the nests at him. Their bright eyes, their long beaks, and their stilted legs gave them a cartoon-like image, as if created, not by any God, but by the brittle, sharp pencil of some sardonic man.

The boy's invasion precipitated a quickening in the traffic pattern of adult birds and guttural squawks from several. At least a dozen fliers, fearful for their young, let loose with streams of digested fish which came splashing on the water, the trees, and the shore. Involuntarily, Ham ducked.

"You better come back," Mort said.

"Why?"

"Well, for one thing, it is going to storm." As if his words were a signal to precipitate the thunder, it came rolling in out of the west. Ham paused to look. There were thunderheads like black castles, with sunshine illuminating their spires.

"It's a long way off," Ham said.

"But we're a long way from home."

"I came this far, and I'm going to get some feathers." Ham walked up off the rocky shore among the trees. Some of the big birds above were dispersing to other shores. They went away gracefully, long necks tucked in, legs straight behind like featherless tails, wide wings beating rhythmically as a ticking clock.

The boy poked around under the trees. There were plenty of feathers, but all were filthy. He picked up a few and carried them to the water. But washing didn't help. They frayed and broke, and when clean, they seemed colorless. He threw them away and stood staring at the tree tops. A close clap of thunder startled him.

Both boys turned. They couldn't believe the storm had come in a matter of a few seconds from the far horizons to where it was high enough to threaten the noontime sun.

"You'd better get in here," Mort said. "You know what the rules are about being out in a storm."

But Ham wasn't ready to go. He crabbed up a tree until he could get a limb hold, and then hoisted himself just below a nest. The gawky, young herons on the stick platform backed away. Then one uncoiled its neck, and in a swift, snake-like motion stabbed at Ham with its stiletto bill.

The boy's head snapped back. He lost his balance, slipped, and fell. He grabbed wildly for branches and managed to slow his fall, but hit the ground hard, and his last glimpse of the world around was focused on the high, black clouds with their shining edges of sun.

By the time he came to, it had started to rain. Mort was prodding him, weeping and saying: "Wake up, Ham! Quit fooling me. Wake up!"

Ham moved his head slowly from side to side. Then the world came back into focus. The almost intolerable heat had gone, and it was cold. The sky wasn't blue, but an angry, wild boil of clouds. Water was being whipped right up out of the lake to join the raindrops in drenching them. The island was enveloped in sound, a roar. He never heard the trees go down, but he saw them, and saw the young herons whisked away like wet rags.

Mort was tugging at him, and as if from a distance, Ham heard his voice: "Get up! You gotta get up! Trees are falling! We've got to get off the island. Get up!"

He leaned forward and tried his hands on the ground. He pushed. Then he stood up, but the wind bent him, and he had to lean to stay on his feet.

Both boys turned their backs on the trees and started toward where the boat was threshing about at the end of its anchor rope like a terrified horse. Ham waded in, grabbed the bow, and pulled the boat toward him. He leaned on the gunwale and fell into the boat. Through the torrent of rain and the threshing of waves he saw Mort's face. He grabbed and pulled the younger boy in with him.

Ham reached for an oar and lifted it. The wind snatched it as if it were a heron feather. Waves broke against the sides of the craft, and their crests spilled in. The boat pitched and bucked and slid off into wave troughs, only to be picked up and tossed into the air, then brought down again, spraying water and foam.

Ham thought for a split second about praying, and in almost the same instant, had the feeling that any prayer would be as ineffective as Mort's wails, which came to him intermittently on stray strands of wind.

Once the boat went so far over that both boys fell over the side and, like wildly crawling crabs, scrambled back in.

"We've got to bail," Ham shouted, but if Mort could hear him, he was beyond comprehending. A can swooshed past Ham. He grabbed it, and lying flat in the water-filled boat, he began whipping water out. The wind took the water, mingled it with the rain and the waves, and flung it up on the island.

The boat, almost level full, dipped forward in a deep trough, then reared back as the following wave lifted it. The anchor rope broke, and the submerged boat, with two boys sitting in water up to their waists and clinging to the gunwales, ran south like a water-logged bird, too drenched to fly, yet too buoyant to sink.

Once Mort tried to get out. Ham reached over, and getting hold of a shoulder, slammed him back into the boat. Once the craft hit the rocks and went spinning slowly around and around. Once Ham thought he saw another boat go skimming past, riding high and fast, but in the watery confusion he couldn't be sure.

Then gradually he understood that if they stayed in the boat they would eventually come to some shore. He crawled forward so that he could get an arm over Mort if he stood again, and then bowed his head away from the wind and waited.

He did not have to wait long. There was a sharp jolt. The boat hesitated. The stern lifted. The wind caught it. Then it upended and the boys were thrown into the water. Ham stood up, and it was only waist deep. He looked for Mort and saw him through the rain, standing a few feet away. He walked toward him, and they wrapped their arms around each other to wait.

They had not long to wait, because the wind had been dying for some time before it overturned their boat. Then in minutes the storm passed, and as if by magic, the washed sky was blue in the wake of the fleeing clouds.

Ham let go of Mort, rubbed the water out of his eyes, and looked around. He recognized Goose Bay. They'd been blown to the far southern end of the lake. Their boat had hit a deadhead, half-submerged, half-waterlogged log.

White caps were still adding foam to the rind of white which had formed along the reedy edge of the marsh. Ham decided to head for the point where a high ridge of trees slanted its crest in a long slope toward the lake. He took Mort's hand, and they started walking. When they came around an outcropping of rushes, they sighted another overturned boat. An outboard was still fixed to the stern transom, and the propeller glistened in the sun.

They walked around the boat and almost immediately bumped into a man lying face down in the water near the edge of an old muskrat house. Ham dropped Mort's hand, and grasping the man's hair, lifted his face clear of water. The man gasped.

"Help me," Ham shouted to Mort.

Together they rolled the man over on his back. Then, keeping his head above water, they floated him to the muskrat house and got his head high enough so it rested on the edge of the pile of rotting vegetation. The man's breathing became more regular. Finally he opened his eyes.

"It's all right, Mister," Ham said. They helped the man crawl up higher on the old reed house. He lay for a long time while the boys stood in the water alongside him. Finally he lifted his head and looked around.

"Boy, that was something," the man finally said.

"Maybe we'd better try for shore," Ham said.

The man, bigger around than the rain barrel which stood under the downspout at home, put a hand on each of the youngsters' shoulders. The weight pushed both boys into the muck, and they had to struggle to keep from falling.

Gradually then, the man slipped off the muskrat house and came erect. Walking for him was a chore because he sank so far into the muddy bottom. Each time he would lean on a boy to pull a leg out for another step. It took them a long time, and when they reached the shore the tail end of the storm was already disappearing over the horizon and the sun was as white hot as before the rain came.

When they reached high ground, all three lay down to let the ferocity of the storm recede in their minds and to regain energy for the trip up the hill. After a while the man spoke: "Where you boys from?"

"Greenville," Ham answered.

"I'm from Oak Grove. I own this farm and several others right along here. My car is on the ridge road. I'll take you home."

Ham felt relieved. At least they wouldn't have to walk the eight or nine miles back. They could always come back and pick up the boat.

While they were climbing the ridge toward the car, the fat man said: "Sure lucky for you kids I found you. You might have drowned."

Ham looked startled. He opened his mouth as though to protest, but then closed it, not being able to find anything to say. Perhaps he had misunderstood the man, Ham thought.

Both boys got into the back seat and the man drove off. Several times they had to stop and move branches from the rutted tracks, and once they had to drive out into the woods to get around a tree which was down across the road.

The automobile was an expensive and shiny piece of machinery. Ham hadn't thought to look before they got in, but he guessed it was a Packard. The man himself was not dressed in overalls like most fishermen, but wore pearl gray trousers and a white shirt with gold embroidery on the pockets, both of which were now torn and streaked with mud.

So maybe this was the miracle he had been waiting for. Up until the time that the hum of the tires and the steady drone of the powerful motor had assured him that he really was safe at last, Ham had completely forgotten that there was a past—so compelling had been the present. But now, once again, he was looking for some angle. Maybe he had found it, and this man would be the angel to drop a ten-dollar bill into his pocket.

They had helped him, probably saved his life. He was floating face down when they found him. He was much too huge to have gotten out of the marsh by himself. So maybe he did owe them something, and maybe he would reward them. Why not?

Ham even speculated on the rhetoric which might precede the awards. If the man asked what he could do to repay them for helping him, what should he say? Come right out and ask

[153

for ten dollars? Might as well. Why not? It had been going on far, far too long. Get it over with now, for once and for all.

Perhaps it wasn't the thing to do. Certainly he had been taught to be more humble, less opportunistic. But was there time left to play the hero?

So all the way to Greenville, Ham waited for some mention of a reward, and although the man talked continually, it was mostly about the ferocity of the storm, about seeing other fishermen's boats being swamped. Over and over he said: "that wind must have been hitting more than a hundred miles an hour because it almost lifted me . . ."

The boys learned, too, that the man's name was Martin Grosslire, and that he was a member of the legislature down at the state capitol in Madison, and that he might even "get to be governor at the next election."

In Greenville the man parked the car in front of Jumpy Jones's place. "You kids wait right here in the car," he said, "and I'll buy you some soda pop."

Ham wanted to get home to let his mother know he was safe. It had been a terrible storm. She would be worried. All along the road they had seen the destruction. Barns and trees down. Some homes without roofs. But they waited, and in five minutes the man came out with two bottles of orange pop. He smelled of moonshine. His face was vividly red, and his little eyes were shining like glass marbles dropped in the sun.

"Now don't go," the fat man said, "because I'll be right back, and I'll take you home." He crossed the street and went through a door with gold lettering proclaiming it as the home of the Greenville *Gazette*.

The soda was cold. It loosened their throats and their stomachs. It started saliva flowing again, helped them breathe easier.

When they had drained the soda, Hyatt Langley came out with the senator, and the two of them went into Jumpy's place. Hyatt owned and ran the Greenville *Gazette*. He was thin as a straw, and he walked as though he was always bracing forward into a high wind.

The boys waited, but Ham was becoming increasingly

irritated. Finally the pair came out. Both men now smelled like moonshine, and Hyatt was bent over farther than usual.

"You kids are sure lucky," Hyatt said, as he opened the car door and motioned them to get out. "I want to get your pictures. This is a good story."

The boys got out and they stood on either side of Martin Grosslire, who put a hand on each. Hyatt focused and then shot the picture.

"Don't you want another?" Mr. Grosslire asked.

"Nope. I never miss," Hyatt laughed.

The two men went back up the steps to Jumpy Jones's place. At the door Mr. Grosslire turned and said: "You kids better get on home. Your folks might be worried."

When the pair disappeared, the boys looked at each other. "Son-of-a-bitch!" Mort said, and swinging his pop bottle, he threw it up against the concrete foundation of Jumpy Jones's place. The bottle shattered into a curb full of diamonds. Ham threw his bottle, but it did not break. Then both boys started at a dog trot off down the street.

It was a long, hot, dusty two miles back. They walked between fields of corn which had been flattened, between woodlots with trees strewn to the ground, past barns without roofs, past machine sheds which had been reduced to kindling.

At one farm a man and a woman were searching the roadside for cattle which had strayed when a falling tree took a fence out. At another farm, the farmer was driving a team of horses roped to the dead body of another horse. They saw some dead birds, one dead chicken.

Quite suddenly then, as if on some secret mutual signal, they both began hurrying. As the sight of wreckage became commonplace, it must suddenly have occurred to them that perhaps their own home had not escaped the storm. Their feet put spurts of dust kicking quickly into the air. Then below the last hill they began running.

Except for limbs and leaves, however, the river knoll showed little effects of the storm. Before they topped the rise, they would see the roof of their own river cottage. Both slowed their pace.

When they topped the hill so they could look over the other side, they saw their mother on the river bank. She was looking downstream in the direction they had rowed what seemed like days, instead of only hours, before.

When they called out to her she turned, but stood as though not believing it was them. Ham called: "We're okay. We're home."

She lifted her skirts then and came running up the hill. She almost fell on reaching them, then regained her balance, and tiny as she was, swept them both into her arms.

"Oh, thank God! Thank God! Thank God, you're safe. We were so worried."

She smothered them, and then, as if remembering, she asked: "Did you see your father?"

When they both shook their heads "no," she said, "He's out looking for you now. Were you in town?"

When they nodded their heads "yes," she said: "Maybe he's heard that you are safe."

But their father hadn't heard, and when he arrived a half-hour later, the relief on his face was something the boys had never seen there before. The almost-grim visage shattered like the surface of a pond touched by a wind, and for a moment both boys thought he was going to weep.

But he reassembled himself, put his features back sternly together, and then he said. "I have to go. There are so many that haven't been found."

They walked awkwardly with him to the car, like he was some stranger they had only just met. Then they were waving shyly as his car moved down the hill onto the dusty road.

As soon as he was gone, their mother had her arms around their shoulders again, and together they moved toward the cottage.

Seventeen

THAT NIGHT a white face floated through Ham's dreams. It stared with pale, dead fish eyes, and the hair went away from the round head like the thin tendrils of vines spreading on the water. The blue, bloated lips never moved—the lips never smiled, and the fishy eyes never blinked.

Ham awakened from the dream with a start. He was wet with sweat, so he got up to go to the kitchen and get a towel to dry himself.

It was almost daylight, and as he was about to turn back toward the porch, his father came in looking haggard, his clothes awry, his hat in his hand.

"It was terrible," his father said. "It was terrible. Now go back to bed."

But Ham couldn't sleep. Morning came slowly, lighting up the leaves of the oaks outside first, then coming onto the porch, and finally sneaking rays into the kitchen.

At breakfast he learned that the dead in the county would probably go over the twenty mark, and that nobody had any idea how many had been injured. Teams were still searching for the missing, and his father had been with the searchers throughout the night. Now over a cup of coffee, he said he was going back to help.

"You boys sure were lucky Senator Grosslire came along when he did," he said. "You would surely have drowned if he hadn't helped you."

At first Ham was too surprised to say anything. He looked

over at Mort, whose head had snapped up out of the cereal bowl. Gradually their part in the rescue of Senator Grosslire had been relegated to a role hardly worth mentioning as the magnitude of the storm had been unfolded for them on the kitchen radio. But now Ham spoke up: "But we were the ones who pulled him out of the water. He didn't help us! We helped him!"

Rose Drumm turned from the sink where she'd been washing dishes. "But how could you pull a man like Mr. Grosslire out of the water? He must weigh close to three hundred pounds."

"But we did!" both boys said in unison.

Ham explained: "We floated him. Like a boat full of water. It was easy. We just skidded him through the water to a muskrat house."

"I just can't believe," their mother said, "that a man like Mr. Grosslire would make up a story like that. Perhaps Father just heard it wrong."

"I heard it right, Rose," Mathew Drumm said. "And probably in the confusion of the storm the boys thought they were helping the senator. Don't you think that might be the case?" he asked, looking directly at Ham.

"No it isn't," Ham said, looking right back, directly into the stern eyes. "He was laying on his face. We turned him over. He was unconscious. We floated him to a muskrat house."

"Now, Ham," the father said, "that's a likely story."

His father didn't believe him. He believed Senator Grosslire, but he wouldn't believe him, his own son. He looked to his mother for help. She just bent her head slightly toward one shoulder in her typical gesture of helplessness.

"I've got to go now. I promised I'd help. We've got several more barn ruins and a couple of houses to dig into to see if there are any bodies we missed." He went out the door, and the way he slammed it, the boys knew the discussion had ended so far as he was concerned.

Ham picked up the betrayal and carried it from the breakfast table back to his grapevine corner, and there he chewed on it. Mort came crawling in among the cedars once, and all he said was: "The dirty son-of-a-bitch!" And then he crawled back out again.

That night Mathew Drumm took the whole family on a tour of back roads and on a ride through Greenville so they could see how the high winds had leveled barns and homes, laid low whole sections of woods, put down poles and wires, killed horses and cows. They went slowly past the Jannsen Furniture Store and Funeral Parlor, where a crowd had gathered and where they could see a line of coffins through the front window.

On the way back home Mathew Drumm stopped at the Greenville *Gazette* office to pick up a paper which had come out a day early because of the storm. Then Ham saw why his father was so certain Senator Grosslire had rescued them. There was the proof, in black and white:

PROMINENT STATESMAN SAVES LOCAL YOUTHS

There was a four column picture beneath the headline. It was a picture of Senator Grosslire standing like a mountain of flesh between two skinny boys.

Rose Drumm read the story aloud while they drove: "Senator Grosslire Tuesday rescued two Greenville youths from drowning in the waters of Big Pike Lake when he saw their boat overturn during the storm which wrecked havoc in Pemberton County, taking the lives of at least twenty people.

"The Senator, who has been actively campaigning for the governor's seat in the November elections, said he carried the two boys to safety before joining others in the rescue work which involved bringing hundreds to where they could get medical attention.

"The storm, which hit shortly before noon, caused an estimated five million dollars in damage to crops, buildings and utility installations. The files indicate it was one of the worst storms to hit Pemberton County in sixty-two years, since the Century Tornado (called that because it killed one hundred) came sweeping out of the west . . ."

Ham got the paper later that evening, and edging into the circle of light from the kerosene lamp, looked at the picture. Then he saw their names beneath it: "Hammond and Mortimer

Drumm. Rescued by Senator Martin Grosslire, candidate for governor." Mort looked over Ham's shoulder. He was reading, too, and after he had read it, Ham heard him say: "That fat shit!"

And for Mortimer that was the end of it. He could drop it. He had a convenient way of filing irritable experiences and thoughts in a back recess of his mind where eventually they were forgotten.

But it was never that easy for Ham. Perhaps if he could have talked to someone. But who? His mother would be sympathetic but hardly understanding, always leaning in the direction her husband indicated. And his father? Forget it. And who else, looking at the picture of two skinny, runty kids standing on each side of a three-hundred-pound man, would believe that they had been the rescuers and not the rescued? No one would believe it.

Except perhaps Lydia? But Lydia wasn't there. And if she had been, it wasn't likely he'd even have told her the story because it wouldn't have been necessary to talk about it. There would have been other, quieter concerns.

But he wasn't about to let it pass. Rummaging through his things he found a school tablet and pencil, and sitting at the table, began composing a letter:

"Dear Editor:

"Your story about my brother and me being rescued by Mr. Grosslire is not right. The fact is that my brother and I found Mr. Grosslire flat on his face in the water, and we turned him over. Then we dragged him to a muskrat house and got his head up out of the water. When we had his head up in the air, he began to breathe better . . ."

Ham felt someone looking over his shoulder. He turned and looked up. His father was reading the letter.

"You can't send that, Hammond. All you can make is trouble," his father said, reaching down and picking up the paper.

Ham jumped to his feet. His eyes flashed defiance. "What I wrote is the truth!"

It was the first time he had openly defied his father. He

waited for Mathew Drumm's hand to strike him. But instead his father crumpled the paper and threw it across the room.

"Even if you are right," his father said firmly, "you are not going to write that letter. Senator Grosslire is on the Highway Committee. Highway Committees buy mowers, graders, tractors—all kinds of equipment. I sell mowers, graders, and tractors, and if I don't, you don't eat. You're not going to write that letter."

It came clear in a flash then. Like the sun can suddenly stab into the darkness of a root cellar when the trapdoor is lifted, the truth stabbed into his mind. Even as he was trapped by people like Miss Mallow, Mr. Van Stylehausen, Father Zamanski—even as Old Oscar was trapped by the moonshine he drank—even as his mother was trapped by his father—so, too, Mathew Drumm was trapped by men like Senator Grosslire, and by only the Lord knew how many others.

He put the pencil down, got up, and went over and picked up the crumpled paper. He smoothed it out, folded it, and then tore it into many pieces. He went to the garbage pail beneath the sink and let the pieces of paper fall like tiny white birds down with the coffee grounds, the frying pan grease, the plate scrapings—and then he walked past his father and out onto the porch to lie down with his clothes on.

And they called him Honest Mathew Drumm. Everybody did. Anywhere you went in the county, they said Mathew Drumm's word was enough. No need for a signature. Not even a handshake. But now he knew. Even his father was trapped, like Rob MacQuarrie had been trapped by his pension, like Father Zamanski was probably trapped by the Pope, like Mort was trapped by him, Ham—like everybody everywhere was trapped by something or somebody.

Perhaps he could sleep that night because he had come to the realization that the rest of the world was as troubled as he was—maybe even more. He could sleep because he had come to understand that there were burdens to be carried other than his own.

But by morning this common communion of misfortune, though valid, had lost its impact, and his ego got out front

[161

once more, so he decided that the least he could do was have a talk with Hyatt Langley.

There were new cuts across the road, especially at the Creek Crossing where the torrents of rain must have put water right up over the top. The grass in the ditches was all flat, pointing downhill in the direction the water had taken. In several places where trees had fallen across the road, the middles had been sawed out of the trunks, and the tops lay on one side and the stump sections on the other.

Much of the storm damage had been cleared up, but here and there lumber from a barn was still scattered across a field. One house without a roof didn't even have a canvas to keep out the rain. Some wires which had come down had been coiled and were still hanging on the poles.

Ham left the sidewalk at the railroad tracks and walked the rails. At the first crossing, he turned back onto the sidewalk and was soon in front of the gray brick building which housed the Greenville *Gazette*.

But now that he was here, he was afraid to go in. He stood for a moment, and then walked slowly up the street. In front of the feed store he said hello to Old Oscar, who looked surprisingly alert, and then turned and came back.

When he was once again in front of the newspaper office, Hyatt came out.

"Hya, Ham," he said. "I was about to come out and look you up. This is lucky. Senator Grosslire is on his way over, and the wire services have been asking for a picture of you shaking hands and thanking the senator for saving your life."

Ham stood flabbergasted.

Hyatt rambled on. "Where's Mort? We'll need him."

Gradually Ham got out from beneath the torrent of words. He didn't know who or what the wire services were, but he couldn't see himself shaking hands with the senator and thanking him for saving his life.

"I'm supposed to get home," Ham lied.

"It'll only take a minute. Here comes the senator now."

Ham looked up the street. The car shone so in the sun that it was enough to send a dog off yelping. It came sharply to a halt at the curb. Hyatt went forward to open the door.

Senator Grosslire squeezed out of the car like toothpaste from a tube and deposited his bulk between the curb and the walk. The effort left him breathless. He shook himself, as if to rearrange his clothing. Gradually then the redness in his face drained down into his perpetually red neck.

Ham had half-turned, as though to start running, but the senator had already started forward. "My boy," he said, "there'll always be a special invitation for you to come to the capitol after I'm elected governor. Bet on that, you and your father will never be forgotten."

Ham wondered why, all of a sudden, his brother hadn't been mentioned. How come the senator had specifically mentioned his father? Was he trying to make a point? Was it a threat? A threat aimed at his father, if he, Ham, didn't keep his counsel about the truth of the Big Pike Lake matter?

Ham didn't know. All he knew was that he was helpless to do anything about the senator's lie. That nothing he could say would change anything. That the only thing for him to do was to forget the whole incident.

"I hear," the senator said, lumbering toward the boy, "that Mr. Langley here wants a picture of us for the wire services. Would you accommodate us, my boy?"

He was reaching out, evidently with the intention of putting an arm around Ham's shoulder. It was more than the boy could endure. He turned and started trotting toward the tracks. Just as he was about to turn off onto the railroad right-of-way, he heard Hyatt's voice:

"Ungrateful kid!"

Eighteen

SOMEDAY, PERHAPS, Ham would learn to look on the Grosslire incident as a lesson in living, but that night it seemed he could not, and the skies were one with the boy because they wept. But where the rain had come violently, if briefly, with the storm, this was a gentle, steady wetting that the scorched earth accepted gratefully. There was a comforting rhythm of drops, without wind, thunder, or lightning, and the water went mercifully to roots, creamed mud bars where crustaceans were waiting to be revived, saturated potholes where frogs were buried, and crept back into marshes among dying reeds and rushes.

It soaked shingles, laying them back flat on roofs. It gathered in boats, and cracked decks healed. It wet the grateful owl, and the mouse washed in it. It brought a vigor to brown pastures, to a land dying of thirst, and men sat up to listen, and grateful once more, put their arms around their women and fell into peaceful sleep.

Ham lay listening, afraid it might stop. Then it seemed night was over in moments and he awakened to a wonderfully pearl-gray morning, with no blazing sun to burn through a boy's eyeballs into his brain. And he soaked his feelings in the freshness.

He ate breakfast hurriedly, and then calling Rock, went down the hill to stand under the willows. While the dog waited patiently, he stood watching the rain speckle the river, saw silver strands of water run the length of the weeping willow branches. At his feet tiny streams gathered mud from the banks, and then washed themselves clear as they crossed the gravel to join the river.

Finally he motioned the dog into the boat which had been retrieved from Goose Bay following the storm. Then, pushing off, he sat idle at the oars while the current carried him past Turtle Slough and around the bend to where he could see Indian, Squawk, and the other islands.

It began to rain harder, and Rock came down from his high position in the bow to curl up on the boat bottom. Ham took the oars, and where a pasture peninsula came jutting out, he pointed the boat toward land and rowed hard, slamming the bow high aground. He got out and dragged the boat until only the stern touched the water, and then with a heave, he turned it over.

He crawled beneath the overturned boat, and Rock crawled in beside him. The heat from their bodies made it a comfortable shelter.

Rain drummed steadily on the boat bottom. Ham stretched out and the dog stretched out beside him. There was enough bend to the gunwale so he could see out, and in the tiny bay were a last few white flowers in an inlet that had been covered with water lilies. And along the inlet edges there were still a few yellow spatterdock among green pads, though most had shriveled and were pricked shut like prunes.

Frogs, up from imprisonment, were on the march. Some hopped into the sides of the boat, and several came beneath. Ham tickled them with a grass straw until they hopped out again.

Now the cattails, still so slender and waiting, would grow as plump and brown as hot dogs on the ends of roasting sticks. Now the wild grapes all along the fence would come plump with juice instead of drying on the vine. Now the corn would get milk to turn hard with its store of energy.

Ham put his head on his outstretched arm. He could see a rock that the rain had washed so silver threads shined, and beyond, a flock of teal, new to wing, circled a half-dozen times before coming down in the old water lily field. On the water they ducked, joyfully running pearls off their oily feathers.

Heat from the boy and dog lying so closely together made them both drowsy. Then they slept, but Rock whined sometimes, and his paws twitched in a running motion as if in pursuit or running rabbits or the Oak Hill fox.

Ham dreamed he was back home, and his father had his arms around his mother, and there was no sadness in her eyes. And Old Oscar sat out front of the seed store in a new suit, and with a fresh shave. And he was walking up the street, picking up ten-dollar bills which he took to place before the altar, and Father Zamanski came smiling out of the sacristy.

He came down a sidestreet where Miss Mallow was surrounded by men. Jumpy Jones was serving sodas instead of moonshine, and his hair was combed. He saw Martin Grosslire in a white linen suit in front of cheering people to whom he had just told the story of how two boys had saved his life.

He saw Lydia, and the frightened look which sometimes came into her eyes was gone. She wore a high-necked blouse and a clean skirt and shoes. And when she got into the old stake truck, it turned into a shiny, new Buick.

And Old Rob was on the stoop of his shack, whittling a new balsa bobber and looking way over the heads of everybody, farther away than anybody can ever really look.

Even Rock kept going and coming in his dream in which all badgers were friendly, and gophers, like linked sausages, kept going around and around in some kind of friendly animal game.

And Ham knew he was dreaming, but he tried hard not to wake up. He let the missionary priests come up the walk so close he could see the snowy white cassocks which had replaced the coarse brown ones they always wore.

Then he was in the church, and the Virgin Mary came down off her side altar, and walking over to the cross, threw a robe over Jesus's nakedness.

But then there was a fiery candle, and he put his finger in the flame, and he came awake with such a start he rammed his head into the boat-bottom boards. Rock came awake and looked startled. Then when Ham lay back down, the dog stretched and yawned.

Ham looked out. The teal were no longer sporting in the water, but had come up on a half-sunken log. Some were down flat, with their heads tucked back and their bills thrust beneath their wings, and others were standing on one fragile leg.

The rain had stopped, and wind was scattering the clouds to let the sun through. But the heat did not return, and when Rock crawled from beneath the boat to go cock a leg at a tuft of grass, Ham followed and likewise relieved himself.

They walked inland then, and frogs jumped in all directions. Where there was a small pile of rocks, Ham gathered wood, and using his handkerchief because the fuel was wet, lighted it to start the fire. Then he placed a flat stone in the middle of the flames and went off to chase frogs.

He knew about frogs, so he always brought his cupped hand down in the direction the frog was facing, because they couldn't change direction before he could catch them.

Rock had helped catch frogs before. So he began pouncing on the amphibians, holding to earth until Ham could grab their slippery legs. Each time he caught a frog, he would hold it by the hind legs and rap its head briskly against a stone so it was instantly dead, and the long toes would stiffen and quiver.

When he had fifteen, he cut the legs from the bodies and with his pocket knife peeled the skin from the legs. Then he built the fire up with more wood. After it burned down, he swept the stone he had put among the embers with a twig until it was clean of ashes and then laid the legs of clean muscle on his hot stove.

The legs kicked and quivered, but then lay quiet and turned pale brown. He turned them with his knife, then lifted each to a lily pad he had brought up from the water's edge, and sat down to eat.

He tossed the slender bones to Rock who swallowed them whole. The flesh had a flavor so delicate he wished he had some salt to bring it out.

[167

Frog legs gone, he wiped his hands on his overalls and walked back to sit on the overturned boat. The sun was getting low, and now he waited to see the window diamonds in the east, so far away the houses were invisible, but he knew they were there because all their windows shot up shafts of diamond-bright light.

The earth was drying slowly, and insects were beginning to move. There were armored dragonflies, sometimes standing still on vibrating wings and sometimes flying a little way backward. There were black, shiny crickets coming out from under stones. There were flies, tiny as pinpoints, whirling in tornado-like storms. There were bees, and three monarch butterflies, and one white moth.

On the ground there were slugs now, moist and pallid as a dead animal's eyes, and snails with horns as harmless as wet noodles. And there were some ants hurrying to repair storm damage, and one pink nightworm, waving its head blindly like a small snake.

A few feet beyond, in the water, were so many things Ham never knew what men called them all. Tiny shrimp, worms encased in sticks and stones, miniature dragons, high water striders, horse-like creatures with feelers instead of manes—multitudes for the fish to feed upon.

He sat with the dog at his feet until the west was putting flares of pink high above a necklace of horizon clouds. Then as night began to subdue the evening celebration, and the window diamonds miles across the lake blinked out, he tipped the boat back, and straining, slid it into the river.

When he turned upstream, herons were already calling out. So he bent to his task, and the current burbled about the bow, which was down because the dog wouldn't sit in the stern. The effort built up bubbles which were gathered up by the whorls from the oars and passed swiftly astern to the wavering wake.

His arms were tired by the time he grounded the boat beneath the willows. He held the bow hard against the bank by bracing with the oars until Rock jumped out. Then with a lighter bow, he drove the boat ashore, and when he stepped to the gravel he took the anchor with him and made the rope taut.

Except for a plate for him, the supper table had been cleared. Mr. Drumm was going over business accounts under the largest of the kerosene lamps at one end of the kitchen table. Mort was stretched on the floor trying to build a fort of finger-sized logs cut from brush willows which grew along the river. The baby was in her crib, and in the shadows by the sink his mother moved quietly at her work.

"The ham and cabbage is cold," his mother said, "and I've already cleaned the stove."

"I like it cold." He was hungry. The frog legs had been like nothing. He ate noisily while his father told his mother that Mr. Van Stylehausen's insurance claim for damages done by sparrows to his house had been denied.

"You mean they won't pay anything?" his mother asked.

"Nothing."

"But how did the sparrows get into the house in the first place?"

Ham waited. He couldn't chew.

"Van Stylehausen seems to think it was a fellow who used to work for him," his father was saying.

Ham resumed chewing.

"But how?"

"Put them in a paper sack and threw them right through the front door."

Rose Drumm shook her head. "I never! But why?"

"Well, it was some fellow off the freights. Ambrose gave him a job, and then the fellow started drinking and almost set the lumber on fire one night, so he fired him."

Ham stopped chewing again. He felt sorry for the man they were accusing.

"Where's the man now?" Rose Drumm asked.

"Probably a thousand miles from here."

Ham felt better. He started chewing again. Out of the corner of his eye Ham could see his mother suppress a laugh. "It must have been something," she said.

"It was from what I hear," Mr. Drumm said. "They don't

even know to this day if they got all the birds. They still come popping out of closets, out of furnace pipes. That house was a mess."

Ham picked up his plate. They didn't know. His parents didn't know he had done it. He went into the shadows where the garbage pail stood. He scraped it carefully with his fork. Then he put it on the sink, and with the dipper, poured a little water over it so food remnants wouldn't dry on.

As he went by his mother she put a hand to his head. He stopped. Her fingers were warm down along the back of his neck. Now he felt just a little guilty. He moved on, stopped to bend over the sleeping baby, then walked past his father out onto the dark porch.

Nineteen

NEXT MORNING was sunny and pleasant. Ham came away from breakfast to do his morning chores with the feeling that all accounts would be squared in the end, and that even his difficulty with the church would be resolved.

He took the slop pail from beneath the sink, brought it to the marsh, and gave it a swing so the garbage went out in an arc to come down on the water among the reeds.

Then he watched as the brightly painted turtles, that had learned about this morning mission, paddled over to eat. He watched the tiny fishes that had first scattered like a gust of chaff put their school back together as one or another picked up a coffee grain, rejected it, picked up a bread crumb and swallowed it.

A school of golden carp, each hardly larger than a man's hand, swam over. They found a few peas, the red shreds of a tomato, the half of a potato which had been left on a plate, and they even ate the coffee grounds.

After the garbage pail had been scrubbed and put back in its place beneath the sink, he took the two water pails to the pump platform. After pumping off enough water to insure a cool stream, he hung each bucket to the large spout, and then riding the long handle of the pump, filled the pails.

He straightened the old army blanket on his cot. Then with a dust mop, he caught up what his mother called the little dust devils and took the mop outside to shake it in the fresh breeze.

By then there were potato peels and carrot ends for the brush pile where a rabbit lived. There was the heart of the cabbage, which was destined for the evening stew, and he salted it lightly and took it with him to eat at his leisure.

Outside he headed for the cedar arbor. He stood for a while looking and listening, and then getting to his knees crawled back to where the sun didn't shine.

He was in a reflective mood, and while he ate the cabbage heart, he wondered why Mrs. Jones put up with Jumpy? Where Old Oscar slept in winter when the park was covered with snow? What Farmer John's wife looked like? Whether Senator Grosslire had any children, and did they know what kind of man he was? Would Miss Mallow try to kiss him again? Had his father ever, ever kissed his mother? Was Rob in heaven or in hell? And how would he be able to endure it if he had to go to hell? Or even purgatory? And had Father Zamanski ever been a boy? Would Rock, who was getting old, die pretty soon? Was Mr. Van Stylehausen sorry about the starched collars and cuffs his wife made him wear? Where was Lydia? Yes, indeed, where was Lydia? Why did Widow Theisen so obviously enjoy being examined by Doc Shallock? Was it sinful to kill, even gophers?

Inevitably his mind drifted to the encounter with the daughters of Farmer John. In his mind's eye he saw the fourteen-year-old lie back and expose herself, and he tried to fantasize. What was it like? He felt a pressure in his overalls. Angrily he got to his knees. Not today, he told himself. It would spoil everything. He crawled out of the arbor.

Back out in the sunlight he got to his feet and drifted through the gravel pit, up the slope to the Gremminger farm yard. On the way a Rhode Island Red chicken came out of the thistles along a fence line, trailing four fluffy chicks. They'd hardly be feathered by frost time, Ham thought.

Along a southern slope he could see Mr. Gremminger driving a team of bays harnessed to what was already an old fashioned hay rake. He heard the clash of metal each time Mr. Gremminger lifted the rake by pressing a lever with his foot to release a roll of hay where it might be forked onto a waiting wagon.

Already horses were becoming obsolete. Ham had heard some say that in ten years the horse would be as rare as the otters, who only sometimes still visited his river. He thought it a sad thing, though tractors and cars excited him.

He stopped at the gate and stooped to pick some blue-black gooseberries, and then, not seeing anyone in the Gremminger yard, he drifted back along the lane, back through the gravel pit, and on to the shores of the river.

Then he hiked up to the Gremminger rock pile, which formed a pier of stones right out into the river. Here he rested. Then he went on to Schwantes' Slough, and sitting with his back to a hickory on a knoll, watched the ducks down on the water. Noon came, and he didn't go to the house for lunch. Instead he followed the river even further south.

Sometimes he just walked. Other times he sat dreaming beneath a tree. Once he took a short nap where clover was ripe and bumblebees droned. The afternoon grew old, and perhaps he aged a little with it.

Only when the sun was setting did he direct his steps toward home. Supper was finished when he came into the kitchen. The stew was still warm. His mother asked where he'd been. He said he had only been exploring. Supper finished he went directly to his cot on the porch. He sat for a long time with his clothes on, looking out where stars sprinkled light through the trees like fireflies.

Then he undressed and crawled beneath the army blanket. Gradually his reverie drifted on to dreams. Then sleep eased over him, and he sighed, turned on his side, and was all but gone when a streak of light, flashing but for a single instant, brought him wide awake and up on an elbow.

There were more lights flashing. Then he heard a car's engine. He leaned to look. Either someone was drunk and had driven off the road to cruise the fields, or, or—maybe the pearl divers were back!

Ham had given up hope of seeing the pearl divers that summer. Other years they'd pitched their tent in June and had been gone by the first of August.

The car engine was silent, and Ham could hear car doors banging. He could hear people talking, but they were too far away to understand, nor could he distinguish one voice from the other.

He leaned against the screen with his forehead and strained so hard to hear he could almost feel his ears extend themselves. The car's headlights were still on. From time to time someone passed in front of them. Then he heard what could only be the sounds of stakes being pounded into the ground. Ham thought it must be the pearl divers, and he wondered if Lydia was with them.

She never went pearl diving, but stayed in camp and did the cooking, aired the blankets, or just sat in the sun combing her long, golden hair.

On first seeing her, Ham decided there was nothing more beautiful. He had never changed his mind, though his mother had said that her hair was probably golden because she put peroxide in it and that her lips were red because she put lipstick on them.

There had been considerable discussion when they seemed to drop out of nowhere three years ago, and Mathew Drumm had summed her up so all his family would know, by saying: "A woman who flaunts her body like that is an instrument of the Devil."

It hadn't made sense to Ham then, and it didn't now. And then one day he had seen his father back of the outhouse in the bushes, watching through the leaves. Lydia had washed her hair, and she had her blouse off and was combing it in long, slow strokes, with only a towel around her shoulders. He had felt so embarrassed for his father that he had backed quietly away, and sneaking back down the hill, sat under the willows to think about it.

He had been angry, too, angry that his father should be spying. The very fact that a man should hide to watch her diminished Lydia, and it diminished his father, too.

Ham had never been embarrassed in Lydia's presence. All

[174

he knew was that each time he was with Lydia he was more comfortable than with anyone else. He didn't know why, because he did not feel comfortable around other women, especially not the girls in his class at school.

And it was strange because he did not even know where Lydia came from, or where she went each year when they broke camp. All he could gather from her talk was that during the summer they drifted from river to river, opening the big, black clams to search the pale, pink flesh for pearls.

But if Ham liked Lydia, he almost hated the men she traveled with. He never stayed in camp when they were around, but from his grapevine corner he had heard them curse her, and he had heard her curse them right back. And amazingly, somehow, her cursing didn't matter.

It didn't even embarrass him when she bent forward over the fire and he could see her breasts beneath her blouse, round and firm looking as the little melons in the field beside the path. Once she had been sitting on the chopping block, and he had been sitting on the ground in front of her. Her legs had been spread, and he had seen all the way up her thigh, and she hadn't had any underwear on, but he hadn't panicked—only averted his eyes.

She had quickly put her knees together and said: "I'm sorry, Ham," like she was excusing herself for spilling coffee from a cup she was handing him.

It was the only time and place that he drank coffee. It was forbidden at home. She sweetened it so none of the bitter taste was left, and they talked about the blackbirds and the river and the teal which had a nest back of the outhouse the two men had made of tarpaper. Sometimes he brought her wild flowers because he liked to hear her low, excited exclamation, and once he brought his Indian arrowheads to show her.

That first year his father had said they were nothing but a trio of filthy gypsies, and he bought locks for the cellar door, and even bought a chain and a lock for the boat.

"They'd steal the fillings right out of your teeth if they got the chance," his father had said.

Ham just hadn't listened. But then that first year they had

left without giving the farmer his camping fee, and they had to pay double before they could get in the next summer.

So Ham took to fantasizing, and had himself convinced that she was a sister trying to keep two wayward brothers out of trouble and full of food.

The car lights blinked out. There were no further sounds from the camp. Ham lay back on his pillow. But he did not sleep for a long time, and when he did it was to dream of a girl with golden hair.

In the morning Ham hurried through breakfast and his chores with only a passing glance at the sadness in his mother's eyes. Then he went to the grapevine corner, where he might watch without being seen.

The two men were wading in the marsh, pushing a scow they must have brought along on their stake truck. The trail they had made the previous summer was pretty well over-grown, and a few late-nesting blackbirds lifted to protest the intrusion. When the water got knee-deep, the men got into the boat and poked with poles at the bogs which blocked their way. Eventually they came to the current and were carried away with it.

Ham sat and waited. A woman came out of the tent as soon as the voices of the men had faded. Only for a moment he wasn't sure. Then when she put a coffee cup next to the chopping block, sat on the scarred chunk, and began combing her hair, Ham knew it was Lydia.

For a long time Ham only watched. From time to time the woman stopped brushing to take a sip of coffee. She must have been humming, because he could sometimes hear thin strains of music that seemed to get lost among bird sounds, but then lifted a little, only to spread again on the breeze like the pale smoke of the breakfast fire.

Finally she finished and threw the dregs from her cup into the fire. Then she went into the tent. When she came out she had a small trench shovel. She began digging a little ditch around the tent so the water would be carried away in the event of rain.

Ham parted the grapevines and crawled under the fence.

When he walked up she stopped digging, stood erect, and tossed the hair from her eyes with a gesture of her head. Then she said: "My old friend! How are you, Ham?"

Ham smiled. "You're late this year."

Lydia laughed, and that made Ham laugh, though he didn't know why.

"We ran into a little trouble. Those guys can get into more trouble . . . but tell me, what have you been doing?"

"Same old thing," Ham said.

"I see you've added some inches, but how come so thin? You haven't been sick?"

Ham shook his head. "No, I've been fine." Now he felt no need to tell her about his sin and the grief it was giving him. Somehow, it didn't seem to matter very much now when he was talking to her. He had a sort of feeling that she would pass it off like yesterday's headache, and that he could do the same.

The woman bent as though to start digging, and Ham stepped forward. "Let me do that, please."

Lydia laughed again, and Ham smiled. She handed him the shovel and went to sit on the chopping block. While Ham neatly trenched around the tent, she hummed, and Ham thought it was a sad tune, but it didn't make him feel sad. It was a sort of lullaby, but a lullaby with a lilt to it.

When he'd finished trenching, Ham cleaned the shovel with a handful of grass and then took some ashes from an old campfire and shined it before handing it back.

She kept her knees properly together, set the shovel aside, and proceeded to clean her nails.

Looking up she asked brightly: "Like some coffee?"

Ham nodded, and she disappeared through the tent flaps. She came back out with the fire blackened pot, two cups, and a brown bag of sugar.

"Start up the fire," she said.

Ham picked some kindling from the small pile, stirred the coals, and put on the wood. The sticks turned black before bursting into flame. Lydia put the pot on a flat stone so an edge projected out over the fire.

"The teal nest here this year?" Lydia asked.

"No," Ham said, "they didn't come back."

"Any duck nests around?"

"There were," Ham said, "but they're all hatched and the young are flying already."

As if on cue, a formation of eight mallards appeared over the marsh, banked hard left, and then speared down. Fifty feet above the water, they broke their flock like seeds scattering, and on cupped wings, silken undersides glistening, they splashed legs first into a pothole.

"Did you ever?" Lydia exclaimed. "Did you ever see anything quite so pretty in your life?"

Ham thought about it. He had always known how beautiful ducks were when they came in to land, but he had never thought to speak of it, to share it.

It was exciting to hear her put it into words, to single out a thing like ducks landing or a sun setting. When she put words to a thing like that it was sort of like putting a frame around the picture so a boy, or anybody, could stand off and consider it, see it sharply, aside from everything else crowding around.

Steam was coming from the coffeepot spout, so Lydia knelt, and using the hem of her blouse as a pot holder, poured the coffee into tin cups. She poured sugar from the brown bag into both, then picked up a splinter and stirred.

Ham had always wanted to ask her what her last name was, and about her relationship to the two men, and he had an inclination to do so now. But he squelched the urge. Things were too good.

They sat for a long time, sipping coffee and watching a stilted killdeer race and stop, cry out plaintively, race and stop. She lighted a cigarette and held the match until it almost burned her fingers. Then she flung the match away and laughed as though she had just fooled someone.

"Do you smoke?" she asked.

Ham said: "Not really. Sometimes my brother and I roll a cigarette and take a puff or two."

"I don't suppose it's good for a person," she said, inhaling deeply. "But I'm afraid so many of the things we like aren't."

Ham felt he knew what she meant, but he knew she wasn't

moralizing, only filling in the quiet moments with the softness of her voice.

He liked the way she puckered her lips when she blew out smoke. It made it look like fun. Then he looked from her lips to her eyes, made himself look at her part by part.

The eyes were gray, and though Ham never knew it, perhaps too small and too close together. Her nose was a little too wide, and perhaps a little too flat, but to the boy it seemed perfect. But as his eyes strayed to her chin, his concentration fell apart, and he knew he couldn't consider her feature by feature because it was all of her in one piece which counted, and for that Ham had no description, nor did he need or want one.

"How long you going to stay?" he asked.

She shrugged. "Who knows?"

Ham wondered how it would be to have to move from place to place. The only moving they did was from the town house to the river house, and that would have ended if anybody would have had the money to buy the river house.

But perhaps she had a winter home. Roaming in summer might be exciting, but he thought it would be nice to have a place to come to in winter.

"School pretty soon," Ham said.

"You like it?"

"It's all right, but I don't like it."

"I never did either," she said. "I think most of it is just a waste of time."

Ham had *never* heard an adult say anything except that school was the best place in the world for kids, and how wonderful it was to get an education.

Ham asked somewhat warily: "But don't you think it is good to get educated?"

Lydia pushed a furrow in the ground with a piece of kindling. "There are lots of ways to get what you might call educated. I think a boy should get enough so he can hold down enough of a job to make a living. But I don't think any girl ever learned anything about loving and keeping house in a classroom."

[179

Ham would have liked to pursue the subject, but he thought he noted a hint of embarrassment, so he tipped the cup to let the last of the coffee run into his mouth. It was cold and bittersweet.

"Can I help with anything?" Ham asked.

Lydia looked around. "Well, I've got to go to the farm for a pail of water. If you want to hunt up some wood while I'm gone, I would appreciate it."

Ham went back to the fence row, and Lydia went up the long slope with a pail. He watched her go, and forgot about the wood until her long, slim legs had taken her around the corn crib and the golden hair had passed from sight. Then he scrounged for wood—oak and hickory—passing up the linden because it smoldered and smoked.

By the time she returned, he had a sizeable pile stacked near the tent on the north side where rain wasn't so likely to wet it.

"Have a cup," she said, dipping water from the pail with the cup he'd had coffee in. "It's cold. Icy. Delicious. Taste it when you drink it." Ham had never thought about tasting water before, but now he did.

Lydia went into the tent and came back out with an armful of blankets. She hung them in the sun along the fence. Then she dragged out two water-stained mattresses to air, and when Ham went to help her he saw that the tent was partitioned into two rooms, with a gray blanket hung from two cross arms extending from a center pole.

"That's a good pile of wood," Lydia said. "It'll make a lot of meals." Ham smiled that she should notice.

"What kind of flowers are around?" she asked.

"Back there, near the marsh, there's jewel weed," Ham said, pointing.

"They're tiny. They're beautiful. I think they're shaped like orchids."

"Want some?"

"Maybe about five. No leaves. Just the blossom."

Ham followed along the edge of the marsh to where jewel weed grew thick and high and green. The tiny flowers were like sparks of fire among the leaves. He picked five, each as tiny as a fingernail. When he got back she was coming from the tent with a tiny white vase so delicately carved Ham had to look closely to see that on it a boy and girl were embracing.

"I've had it since I was little. I don't know why I drag it around with me. I'll only lose it or break it."

She went to the fence for a stone, and put the stone a little way back from the fire. Then she put the tiny vase on it and poured a little water from the pail, and the water beaded on the sides of the white vase and darkened the rock. Then she took the five tiny orange flowers, put them in the vase, and sat back on the chopping block to admire them.

"What do you think?" she asked, turning away from the flowers toward the boy.

"Perfect."

"They are, aren't they?"

Ham nodded. Then when he looked up at the sun he saw it was pushing toward twelve o'clock, and they heard poles banging against the side of a boat. They both looked out over the marsh.

"Guess they're coming back," Lydia said.

It was his signal to leave so he started toward the fence corner. "Maybe I'll see you tomorrow," Ham said hopefully.

"Maybe," she said, and then again: "Maybe."

Ham crawled under the fence and through the tangle of vines. But instead of going directly up the hill, he waited to watch.

The scow maneuvered the path through the rushes with considerably more ease than it had on the trip out. In a couple days it would slide along the new trail almost as easily as on open water.

The men, their clothes still dark with the wetness of the river, dragged the scow to dry land. Then they began to unload the big, black, serrated clams into a pile alongside last years shells.

Ham marveled at the great number they had found, and wondered how they opened them so expertly and easily. He knew they used a knife. He also wondered how they searched for and found the pearls once the shell had parted.

He had tried it, but only rarely did he get a clam open without crushing it with a rock, and then he had to finger through a mess of clam shell and clam meat. He had never seen anything resembling a pearl.

While the men unloaded the boat, Lydia opened cans and poured their contents into a kettle. Building up the fire, she shoved the kettle over the flames.

There was little conversation. Once Lydia asked: "How's fishing?"

One man looked up and said: "Pretty good."

But then the other man said: "But they're probably all empty."

Now Ham could smell food cooking. It made his own stomach growl, so he headed up the slope to get dinner.

Twenty

THAT NIGHT Ham thought about Lydia in the bleached tent, on the water-stained mattress, and the two men sleeping just across from her behind the flimsy, gray blanket. He put the picture out of his mind and wondered, instead, what Lydia had been like as a little girl.

Did she have a mother and father, and were there brothers and sisters, and had she ever gone to church? Was she sad? And would she go on as a member of the pearl hunting team for the rest of her life, or would she someday come to a house and put furniture into it and maybe have children of her own?

Next morning he rushed through his chores and was in the grapevine corner early. He waited until the two men poled out into the river and then he went down the gentle slope to the camp site.

Lydia poured coffee for both of them and began brushing her hair. "I swear sometime I'll get it bobbed. Nobody wears long hair these days, but if I cut my hair, what have I got left?"

Ham would have liked to tell her, but of course, he didn't have the words to let her know that it wouldn't make any difference if her hair was long or short, so instead he asked: "Any pearls yesterday?"

"Darn few, and no good ones."

"Well, it's good to get some," Ham said.

"Pearls around here and in lots of places are disappearing," Lydia said. "It's getting so it hardly pays. But I don't know.

You keep at it anyway. It's kind of like a fever. Everytime you open a clam you have the feeling that this might be the one."

Ham thought about it. Finally he said: "But there should be pearls. In all the time I've lived here I've never seen anyone else hunt for them."

Lydia explained: "It's the rivers. They're filling with muck. They're polluted. A clam can't live in muck. There's no current. A clam has to have current to make round pearls. It has to be rocked gently in the current."

"What makes the pearls?" Ham asked.

Lydia stopped brushing and put her hands in her lap. "Different things. But mostly a piece of sand gets into the clam's craw, and it hurts, like when you get something stuck in your throat. You can cough it up, but the clam sometimes has a hard time letting the water wash away the sand. So instead it puts slime around the sand, and the slime hardens, so there are no sharp edges to hurt the clam. That's the start, and the more slime it puts around the sand, and the longer it is in the clam, the better the pearl. Providing," she emphasized, "the clam is rocking around enough so the pearl becomes perfectly round."

Ham was fascinated. Pearls were as foreign to him as elephants. He didn't even know anyone who had a string of real pearls, unless the strand Mrs. Van Stylehausen wore to church was real.

"It sure must take a long time to make a pearl," Ham said.

"Yes, I suppose so. I don't know too much about it. Mostly I hear the men talking, and I don't think they know too much about it themselves. We didn't used to look for pearls. We had an outfit over on the Mississippi, and we just fished clams for the button factories. Never bothered to look for pearls. But the price of shell went down, what with people using other things to make buttons, and so we sort of drifted into this racket."

Lydia's hair shone like golden sunlight. She put the brush away and hauled out blankets, and he helped her with the mattresses.

"How come living here you never hunt pearls?" Lydia asked.

"First, I never knew there were any. Then when I did know,

I didn't know how to go about it. Nobody around here ever hunts pearls. I don't think people even know there are clams in the river."

"Don't people eat them?" Lydia asked.

"No."

"Well, we don't either any more. But we used to. The tiny, green, tender ones."

"But you must get some pearls or you wouldn't hunt them," Ham said.

"Oh sure, we get some pearls. Sometimes we even get lucky. Found one on the Turtle River that brought us three hundred dollars. But mostly they are worth maybe five or ten cents, or a dollar or two. They use them to make children's jewelry."

Ham's mouth was open. "You mean," he exclaimed, "one pearl was worth three hundred dollars?" The thought that three hundred dollars might be hiding beneath the waters of his river staggered him. "I'd sure like to hunt pearls." He said it as much to himself as he did to Lydia.

"Well, why don't you?"

"I can't open the shells. I can sometimes find clams, but I have to smash them to get them open."

Lydia laughed. "It's easy finding clams. And it's even easier getting them open, but it can be awful boring if your luck's bad."

Ham kept thinking about the three-hundred-dollar pearl, and about how he could literally buy his way back, not only into the church, but into the good graces of his parents.

"In this river," Lydia was saying, "the best place for clams is on hard clay and at the bends, where the river turns. All you have to do is walk along, feel them with your feet, and then dive down and bring them up. Only the big black ones have pearls. The little green ones don't."

Ham asked: "How do you get them open?"

Lydia got up from the chopping block and walked to the fresh pile of clam shells and clam meat. A cloud of flies ascended. She stooped over and came back with a shell. Then she got a long fish knife and sat back on the block of wood.

"Now you watch," she said.

Ham came close enough so he could feel the warmth of her body and smell the perfume of her hair. She closed the clam shell, held it tight with one hand, and inserted the knife blade.

"You have to cut down in here." She indicated a place near where the clam was hinged together. "If you don't hit the muscle right away, keep cutting. Then the clam practically opens itself. It doesn't have any muscle left to stay closed."

Ham watched as she spread the black clam so its lustrous pink and pearly white interior was exposed.

"Then don't spill out the insides," she went on, "because if you do, you might lose the pearl. Feel along here." She held the clam so each thumb explored an area close to the hinge. "Most pearls, if there are any, will be in this area. But feel all through the meat because sometimes they aren't where they are supposed to be."

She handed Ham the shell. It shone like a gigantic jewel.

"When you feel something small and hard," Lydia went on, "it's likely you've got yourself a pearl."

Ham was being carried away like the generations of fortune hunters who had sired the likes of him.

"If you feel a pearl, pick it up carefully and put it into your mouth under your upper lip. It will be safe there while you work. Then when you get through, put your lips to a bottle and spit the pearl into the bottle. That way you won't lose it in the grass."

Ham ran his fingers over the unbelievably smooth interior of the shell. "You mean, that's all there is to it?"

"That's it," Lydia said, "but don't think that it isn't a lot of hard work, and for darn little money."

"But what if you hit a big one?"

"Don't plan on it."

Ham tossed the clam shell back on the pile, and the flies lifted in a black cloud. "It's like looking for buried treasure," he said.

Lydia laughed. "Maybe you're right," she said. "Maybe that's what makes me and those two boobs out there keep at it instead of settling down to decent jobs." A little sadness came into her voice. "Maybe we think that someday we'll find the big one so round and so perfect it will bring a thousand dollars."

Ham missed the sadness in her voice. He was already wrapped up in dreams of treasure, sunk right out there beyond the fringe of the marsh. Pearly treasure. Pink treasure. Waiting only for someone to discover it.

"Three hundred dollars," Ham was thinking, and didn't realize he had spoken his thoughts.

Lydia put the coffee pot back on the flat stone. "Don't go getting pearls in your eyes," she said, "or you'll wind up like us—always broke and always looking for the pot of gold at the end of the rainbow."

"But you found one!" Ham said.

"Yes, and we might go on for another ten years before we find another," Lydia sighed. "Meanwhile, we've got nothing. No dignity. Not even decency."

Any other time Ham would have been perturbed at the subtle change in Lydia. But like hundreds of thousands before him, the prospect of gathering in hidden treasures from an alien place suddenly relegated family, friends, God, creature comforts, and even this one woman, into a place where a man could close the door and be on his way.

"I can hardly believe it," Ham said, "that there are pearls out there." He had known it all along, of course, but never really quite believed it. Not until now.

Lydia, for the first time since Ham had known her, looked angry. "I shouldn't have told you," she said. "It will spoil everything. You'll get the fever. You'll turn into a drifter. You'll forget about the things we talked about, how a duck is a beautiful thing to watch. You'll forget where the flowers grow, and that there's something more to life than pearls. You'll get like they are. Then you won't see a thing except the slimy insides of the next clam."

Ham came back to earth, back to the campsite with its heap of stinking, fly-covered clam shells. He came back to this place with the odoriferous tarpaper outhouse just back of the tent and the beautiful jewel weeds along the marsh fringe. "I won't forget," he promised. "I won't forget any of those things."

Lydia composed herself and laughed. It was a low laugh, down in her throat—husky. "By the time it would make any difference in your life there won't be any pearls in this river. By that time it'll be a sewer."

But she couldn't shake Ham's enthusiasm. There *were* pearls here—not tomorrow—but right now, this day, and when you are twelve the future is only next week and manhood is a million years from yesterday.

Coffee bubbled out the spout and a steam plume leaped from the fire.

"More coffee?" Lydia asked.

"No, thank you." Ham didn't need coffee now, or at the moment, even Lydia.

He was handing Father Zamanski a ten-dollar bill from one pocket, and from the other pocket a whole handful of ten-dollar bills for a new Catholic school. He was watching his mother try on a new coat. Her's was older than he was. He had the kitchen table piled high with fragrant cigars and was telling his father to throw his old pipe into the outhouse.

"Come down out of the sky," Lydia said. Ham laughed self-consciously. "And stay out of the sky."

The boy poked at the callouses on his bare feet with a thumb nail. "I'll try to stay out of the sky," he said. "But it's fun going up there. It makes everything all right—for a little while anyway."

"But doesn't it hurt when you hit ground again?"

"Maybe, I suppose," Ham said. "I guess it does."

Lydia put a hand on his shoulder. Had it been any other woman it would have embarrassed Ham. But to have Lydia do it seemed perfectly natural. "Sure, it's fun," Lydia said, "and it doesn't cost a dime. And I guess it really doesn't hurt, because if you're like me sometimes that's the only way you can be happy. The only trouble is in not going too far. The trick is knowing you have to come down, so that when you do, you don't splash all over the place."

Ham thought he knew what she was talking about. "Maybe I'm only a kid," he said, "but I guess I've probably had my share of falls."

Lydia smiled. "Yes, I suppose you have. Yes, I'm sure you have. And it is good that a boy bounces. But remember there comes a time when you don't bounce any more, when you stay flat on your face. That is when you start hating it."

The morning ended abruptly with the sound of poles banging against the sides of the boat.

"They're coming," Lydia said.

Ham stood up to go. His eyes were still glistening.

"Beat it," Lydia laughed. "Beat it before you turn into a clam."

As he climbed the slope to the house, his dreams climbed with him, up and up to the pearly clouds. For the time being it was enough. He felt no urgency to eat.

After dinner he wandered north where he could get a better look at the river, to a place on a high, breezy hill where he could see it like a brown, living thing, writhing through the green earth.

Rock had trailed along and was yelping for help where he'd put a rabbit into a stone pile. Any other day Ham would have dug it out so the grizzly dog could have another run at it. But now all he wanted was to lie on the grass and watch the pearls roll in and turn into ten-dollar bills.

But even a dream can't hold at a summit. Certainly the pearl divers had never struck it rich. In fact his father had characterized them as "a miserable lot." But perhaps they did really make money, but squandered it. He knew they always had moonshine in camp. Then, too, they only worked three or four months, so maybe they made enough from their summer revenue to live for the rest of the year.

He had the dream building again, and if this time it didn't get all the way back up to the pearly clouds, it did get high enough to sustain him through that day. Maybe tomorrow he would find out.

Twenty-one

WHEN HAM WENT to bed there was a chill in the air, and he knew autumn was nudging summer. There was even a crispness to the stars, and everytime a breeze went through the oaks, his porch roof rattled with acorns. No crickets, no frogs—only fish splashing. And the herons, well oriented now, had no cause for calling out to get landing instructions.

Many teal and small birds had already left, and there were hawks soaring south, more strange hawks in high trees.

Mice were coming up from the fields to scout the buildings, and when the little owl found no moths, it whimpered until it caught one of the mice.

Young raccoons did some hunting on their own. Young skunks wandered off, and the occasional one never came to the home den again.

In the morning it was misty. The ribbon of river was white. The mist reached high as the low trees to leave wet tracks on the leaves. It softened sharp edges, as a dream can, and muffled sounds so ducks flew silently until they lifted to where their wing whips were audible on clear air.

Ham started early. He wore swimming trunks—blue, as was the style, with a white belt. Rock went with him. Mort begged to go, and even kept on begging from the shore until they lost him around a bend.

The boy went north against the current, because he knew the pearl divers were working to the south. He was headed for Big Bend. His anchor never brought up mud there because the bottom was solid. It was an arm-aching trip against the current, and by the time he got there, the sun had evaporated the mist and dried the grass.

Where a woodlot came down to the river he edged the boat close to shore and went over the side. The water was waist deep, so he roped the boat to his middle, and in the current, it tugged at him gently as he began probing the bottom with his feet for clams.

His toes felt a clam-shaped object immediately. He jarred it with his heel to loosen it and then went under to pick it up. It was a rock. He threw it back toward the middle of the river, and when it splashed, Rock raced back and forth in the boat looking for some leverage for a lunge.

Ham hoped he wouldn't jump. He'd have to beach the boat to get him back into it. He didn't want to waste the time. The dog whimpered, then sat on the stern seat, and when he saw nothing on the current, decided to stay aboard.

Ham shuffled along, his feet probing the hard clay bottom. He felt another object with his toes and knew instantly that it was a clam. He jarred it loose and went below and brought it up.

It was a giant as river clams go, black and grooved, hard and tight lipped. Ham tossed the clam into the boat, and Rock examined it with his nose. He poked at it with a paw, and when it didn't poke back, he ignored it.

Ham's toes felt a rock, but he had to be sure, so he ducked to retrieve it. Then he found two clams in quick succession. It was uncanny, he thought, how his toes could already discern a clam from a rock of the same size.

He moved slowly, the boat tugging at him from the end of its rope, and the small pile of clams grew to a sizeable mound. He knew it would be wiser to wait until he had half-filled the boat, but he couldn't wait. So he dragged toward shore, bending forward to keep the boat from swinging all the way around and downstream.

Where the sun lighted a scattering of brown-eyed Susans, he piled his clams. Then sitting cross-legged, he prepared to go to work.

Rock ran off to smell out what manner of creatures had passed that way in the night, and to see if there were any who had tarried and needed to be chased to their dens.

Ham slipped the knife between the tightly closed jaws of a clam and cut, but nothing happened. He edged the knife deeper and felt the clam close tighter. Then he rocked the knife, and the clam's jaws parted a little way to show what looked amazingly like a small, pink smile on a big, black face. He put his fingers in the crack, and the clam opened easily.

Then he probed with his thumbs on each half near the hinge, the way Lydia had showed him. He ran careful fingers under the flat slices of flesh, and juice ran down his wrists and dripped to his legs. He went over the clam a half-dozen times, reluctant to let it go. Then quickly he tossed it aside and grabbed for another.

Once again he found the muscle and opened the clam. Carefully as a duck steps among her own eggs while covering her nest, he fingered through the clam's insides. Again there was nothing. Now he hurried, spending less time on each clam, but when he had opened them all there was nothing.

Rock was back from his tour of inspection. He nosed the pile of clam shells and clam flesh, looked inquiringly at Ham, and then stood off to one side waiting.

Ham gritted his teeth. Maybe the next batch. He motioned Rock into the boat and waded into the water. He found clams immediately. He worked until he had a heap twice the size of his first harvest. The sun and his stomach told him it was nearly noon, but he couldn't go home now, not with such a pile of clams to be mined for their treasure.

He worked almost expertly, satisfying himself in a dozen fingerings that each clam had no pearls. He was sure when he sat down to the huge heap of clams that among so many there would be at least one with a pearl. But when the juices of the last bivalve were beginning to evaporate in the sun, he had failed again.

He walked into the water to wash off the slime and then lay on the bank. His back ached, and there was a throbbing at the nape of his neck. His finger tips were raw. His buttocks were numb from sitting on harsh grasses in wet swimming trunks.

Lydia had warned him. She had said it was a rough way to make money. But the men were finding pearls. If they weren't they wouldn't come back year after year.

Ham humped himself erect and went back into the water. He moved back and forth, deeper and deeper until the water was to his armpits. He kept at it until he was shivering and had to wade out into the sun for warmth.

Rock, bored with the whole thing, was glad to race away into the woods again. Ham heard him troubling something with sharp yelps and was almost tempted to go see what it was. Anything now. Anything rather than sitting cross-legged fingering through slimy clams while vicious deer flies dive-bombed and left red welts.

There were three clams left when Ham felt something. He rolled it carefully with his thumb, and then felt it with the tip of a more sensitive forefinger. It might be a pearl. He pushed the body of the clam to one side and carefully closed his finger and thumb over the tiny object. Then he brought it forth from the slime.

It was tiny and shaped like a horse's head. Then when the clam juice drained away it picked up a sunbeam and there, pink and promising, more beautiful than a cloud tinged with the rays of a setting sun, was his first pearl. He turned it to see the light change its colors. Then he popped it into his mouth, and carefully with his tongue, he hid the treasure beneath his upper lip.

He probed the last two clams more carefully, but they yielded nothing. Ham went to the boat and from a paper bag took out a glass saltshaker for which he had fashioned a cork stopper. He spit the pearl into the salt shaker. It slid slowly on the saliva to the bottom. He corked the shaker and then held it to the sun. His hand trembled. The tiny pearl quivered with light. He held it at different angles to see the light play color variations on it. His precious pearl, up from his mysterious river, pink and then not pink, but a whole spectrum hurrying.

He took the pearl to bed with him that night.

Next day he was back at another bend in the river. A cool wind was prodding a good run of waves, and sometimes, when he ventured out too far, they lifted him and their crests foamed over his head.

He found clams, but it was an arduous task. While opening them he shivered as clouds, which were boiling over the horizon, took turns at blocking off the heat of the sun.

When he finally gave up to go back he hadn't found a single pearl. That night neither food nor blankets nor even the pearl in the saltshaker could warm him. But the physical torture of the day was too much competition in the end for the turmoil in his mind, and so he slept.

If the next day hadn't dawned warm and sunny, Ham's adventure might have come to an end. He was ready to abort, but under such auspicious circumstances, and with nothing else to do, he went up the river again.

He had a bad run of luck finding clams and beached the boat the first time with only a dozen. The first two were empty, as had been the hundreds already fingered through. He spread the jaws of the third, and even before exploring it with his thumb, he saw a tiny cluster floating on the slime. He thumbed it, and his spirits soared.

There was not one pearl in the clam, but eight, including one nearly the size of a pea. None was round, but all had a good luster, and in the saltshaker they were such nuggets as have sent men scrambling around the world and clawing even at the hearts of mountains.

Ham was hooked. He was in and out of the water. He never felt the pain in his bleeding finger tips. The ache in his back belonged. Hunger was nothing. So goose pimples stood until his skin looked sick, and his eyes turned red from river water. When at last he stood, it was to walk bent over, but he had added three more pearls to his treasure of nine, and one was black, a mysterious black with a satiny shine.

Then each day jammed one right into the other. Every night he fell asleep even before his head hit the pillow. He grew thinner and thinner until he was like a whip of rawhide. He skipped chores, meals, forgot his toilet . . . And Lydia? Who was Lydia?

He was on the trail leading to the lode. He was getting closer and closer to stacks of prime beaver skins, to dark sink-holes of diamonds—on up the mountains of silver to where raw gold lay on top the earth. He was the first fortune hunter and all the fortune hunters, and now he couldn't turn back. And he might have gone on and on and on, if he had been a man, ripping his guts out on the ragged edges of jagged dreams. . . .

But he wasn't a man, only a twelve-year-old boy with a bristling father and a sad and worried mother—and a sin which must somehow be expiated.

Still he went to the river and increased his fortune by ten more pearls, and then ten more—until he had forty.

Meanwhile his eyes sank back into his head until they looked like smoldering coals. He began to cough, was feverish.

Yet he went to his boat every morning and cast it out into the current, even though he shivered in the sun, wasted like a heron held fast by a muskrat trap—thinner, thinner.

The end was inevitable. His father's patience, stretched farther than it had ever been, snapped.

Then when Ham tried to sneak away, they took his boat, dragged it out onto the bank, locked it to a tree. When he couldn't eat, they forced him to swallow soup, and when the soup wouldn't stay down they made him swallow castor oil.

Whether it was the castor oil or fear of his father that made him resign himself to the fact that there would be no more pearl hunting is difficult to say.

But he finally gave in, accepted the fact that his days as a fortune hunter had ended. Yet what pearls he had were always in his pocket, except at night when he slept with them under his pillow.

It wasn't until the Friday before Labor Day that he finally convinced himself, was reconciled to the fact that the pearls would do him no good unless he sold them.

He had, of course, known it all along, but it is one thing to know the truth and another to accept it. So finally on that Friday he took the dusty road to town, and going directly to the jeweler's, set the saltshaker on the glass counter and asked: "How much?"

Mr. Keener leaned forward, and adjusting his glasses, asked: "How much for what?"

Ham pointed. "For the pearls."

Mr. Keener picked up the saltshaker and shook it. The pearls caught the ceiling light and were iridescent. They glowed with soft pinks, snowy whites, sky blues—and the one, black and satiny.

"Where'd you get them?"

"From clams. In the river," Ham said.

"But I don't buy pearls. I don't buy anything. I'm not a jeweler. I wouldn't know a real pearl from a piece of paste. All I do is get in a few things like rings, watches, compacts, bracelets—things like that—and then I try to sell them."

Ham looked around. "There's a string of pearls."

Mr. Keener turned the price tag so Ham could see. The price was six dollars and ninety-nine cents.

"But who? I've got to sell them!"

Mr. Keener looked at the ceiling. He pursed his lips. "Hmmmm. Well, if you're going into Milwaukee sometime I could give you the address of some firms who make up jewelry. They might be interested."

"But I've got to have the money now," Ham blurted.

Mr. Keener spread his hands. "But I haven't the faintest idea what they are worth. I wouldn't know."

Ham didn't wait. He burst through the door and ran down the street. The rest of the day was an aimless, half-remembered day, like so many had been since they'd made him stop hunting for pearls. He roamed the sidewalks, back and forth, from one end of Greenville to the other. And when Old Oscar asked him what was wrong, he never heard. Then, as was necessary, he turned toward home and trudged along the dusty road, up and down the long hills.

He stopped at the Creek Crossing and looked down toward the bend where he'd drunk the moonshine. He'd almost forgotten the terrible sickness, though he could vividly remember how he had at first been lifted, so it seemed, as if a singing wind were whistling through his mind. Next to finding his first pearl, the first feeling of alcohol riding in warm waves through his blood vessels was like no other feeling he'd ever had.

Not even the feeling he got when he was close to Lydia could compare. Lydia! All the while he'd been pearling, he hadn't once felt a need for her. But now suddenly the need was strong. He wanted to see her, to talk to her, to get close enough to smell the perfume of her hair, feel the warmth of her body.

The pearl. The moonshine. And Lydia. Standing on the road he could still see the bright bottle riding high and empty on the current, shining in the sun.

Then it was gone, around the bend and out of sight. Oblivion. He felt a sudden urge to cast the pearls to the current. To watch the saltshaker float away, to let it come to some muddy end in a marsh or smash against a rock and spill his pearls so they'd be lost forever among the stones.

He turned to go, and his feet dragged. Then from the brow of the last hill, he could see, like a white stone far away, the bleached tent of the pearl divers. And he thought: Maybe they will buy my pearls. If they can make a profit, maybe they'd be glad to get the extra money.

Why not? If the pearls were worth twenty dollars, wouldn't they be willing to give him ten? If they were worth ten dollars, wouldn't it be to their profit to give him five? It would be a quick, easy, simple way for them to make money.

He hurried down the hill, cut across fields straight to his grapevine corner. He lay for a moment among the cedars, peering out through the vines. Then he crawled beneath the fence and started toward the tent.

The boat was in. Already there was a lantern burning in the tent, and he could hear voices—subdued. He trotted in all innocence across the clearing which separated his arbor from their camp. He came up hurriedly, almost breathlessly.

One flap of the tent was laid back a little. Ham took the pearls from his pocket with his right hand and pulled the tent flap the rest of the way back with his left. Then he stopped.

Lydia was naked on the mattress. Both men were naked too.

He must have made a sound, because Lydia lifted her head. Both men turned. He panicked and fled. He stumbled, falling into the still-glowing coals of the supper fire. He scrambled to his feet, spraying sparks. He ran so hard he never saw the fence and bounced back off it.

He lay gasping, and then when he could breathe, crawled under the wire. When he was in the long grass he stretched out and was still. And all he could see was Lydia . . . the nipple of one breast pink as a pearl, the inside of her thigh white as the inside of a clam shell, and the two men naked . . .

Twenty-two

SATURDAY DAWNED OVERCAST. First leaves were falling. Wind had an edge. Ham was in town, wearing his new shoes. His pearls were gone. He had dropped them when he fell into the campfire.

He was going to church, to confession. He had been ordered to, but that wouldn't have been necessary because he had decided to do it even before the ultimatum had been issued. In one hour he would breathe his sin through the latticework of the confessional, into Father Zamanski's hairy ear.

As on Saturdays, and especially this Saturday before Labor Day, everybody was in town. There would be two days without stores—Sunday and Monday—and on Tuesday school started.

The town was crowded. Shoppers from villages having fewer stores were buying in Greenville. Farmers from five and more miles around had converged to buy school supplies for their children, to buy clothes, staples, and often the meat they had originally taken on the hoof to the market.

Youngsters who knew Ham called out. Several tried to engage him in conversation. He contrived to elude them. He had no energy left for idle conversation. His never-wavering faith in miracles had finally abandoned him. It was finished. Now there was nothing except to endure.

He walked past Old Oscar who was on a bench in front of Hilgendorf's Hardware, and Ham knew by the bulge beneath his coat that he was well fortified against this gray day. He would have hurried past and ignored Oscar, except the man leaned forward and reaching out took his arm.

"Winter's coming," Oscar said. It was a peculiar thing to say, and Ham could think of no answer, so he nodded and agreed by saying: "Yeah, winter's coming."

Old Oscar shook his arm, as though demanding more attention. "It's going to be cold." Ham turned to look at the man. His eyes, usually so bright and brassy, were dull and lifeless.

Just looking into those eyes, the boy could understand what the man meant. It was going to be cold and bleak, and another summer was a whole lifetime away, a lifetime of church and school, and more church and more school.

"I hate winter," Oscar concluded, dropping his arm so Ham could continue on down the street.

Ham felt that he would hate this winter, too. He had never hated winter before. In the past, winter had been an exciting, exhilarating time. He had gathered together the town hound dogs and, though he had no gun, had taken them rabbit hunting. He had trapped the condensory creek for muskrats, and once he had caught a mink. There were snowball fights—and the short days were frosted with the breath of much excitement.

He turned off Main Street onto Oak, starting toward the park, and then turned on Elm instead. He approached Rosie Callahan's boarding house, an old, rambling white house with peeling paint and wicker chairs along the porch. Miss Mallow was coming down the steps. She was holding onto the arm of a man. Ham thought to run, but saw it was too late, so he only quickened his pace. He kept his eyes averted, hard on the sidewalk, but Miss Mallow was out on the main walk before he had a chance to get past. She stood right in his way and he had to stop.

"Well, Hammond! Hello!"

She turned to the man. "Hammond is one of my pupils. Well, he was last year. Who's your teacher this year?" she asked.

"Mrs. Greer."

"Oh, you'll like her. Natalie's a good teacher. Nice person, too."

Ham nodded. He knew Mrs. Greer. Everybody called her Greer the Grouch.

"Oh, Hammond, forgive me. I forgot to introduce you to my husband." Ham's head popped up. He looked at the man. "Meet Mr. Forester," Miss Mallow said with a flourish. Suddenly Ham realized that he was staring. He lowered his eyes.

"Marty, Mr. Forester I mean, is in insurance. With Hampton's Mutual. He's opening his own office here."

Ham chanced another look. The man was reed-thin. He reminded Ham of a black-capped night heron, especially the way his black hat sat on the top of his narrow head.

Miss Mallow (Mrs. Forester now) patted Ham on the shoulder. "It was nice seeing you, Hammond." The man never said a word as Miss Mallow swept him down the street, laughing and calling out to people to meet Mr. Forester. "We were married this summer . . . honeymooned in the east . . . in insurance . . . plays marvelous five hundred . . . have to get together sometime . . ."

Ham waited until her voice receded. Then he turned around and went back to Main Street. When he went past the restaurant Mr. Nero waved through the window. Ham lifted a hand and would have continued on, except the restaurant proprietor came to the door and called to him: "Come back, boy. Come back. I want to talk to you." Ham stopped walking, but he did not turn around. "Please. Don't be mad at me."

There was something in the man's voice a reaching out that hit a responsive chord. The boy turned. Mr. Nero walked toward him, put out a hand, and Ham took it.

"We be friends, boy? Forget what happened? It was nothing You shouldn't think about it." Mr. Nero shook his hand. "You thirsty? Want some soday? Come. Come, I give you some."

Ham shook his head. "Thank you," he said, "but I'm not thirsty."

"Sometimes, maybe. You just drop in."

"I will." A customer started up the steps and then went through the restaurant door. Mr. Nero turned and followed him in.

Mr. Van Stylehausen's Pierce-Arrow pulled up in front of the post office. In spite of himself, Ham stopped and caught his breath. Immaculate in a Palm Beach suit, the man looked straight over the head of the boy as though he didn't exist.

A small black and white fox terrier, which had sought refuge beneath the large metal mail box which stood on the sidewalk, came running out to bark savagely around the big man's ankles. Mr. Van Stylehausen never gave the dog a glance, though the red was creeping from beneath his collar into his face when he barged through the post office door.

At the corner Julius Freund, the weekend constable with his bright badge pinned to a blue blazer, was arguing with a farmer who was trying to park a wagon and a team of horses between two cars. The wagon was loaded with meal sacks from the mill.

"You can't do it," Julius was saying. "There's no place to tie horses. And who's going to clean up after you leave?"

The farmer, a burly man with a shock of rust-colored hair, got down from the wagon seat, and quieting the horses with a "so-so-so-so," ignored the constable. Taking the bridle of one of the animals, he led the team to the curb. When they had quieted, he went around to the back of the wagon, took out a concrete block, and bringing it to the curb, anchored his team to it with a lead line.

Julius Freund was fuming, but the farmer never gave him a second glance. Instead, he spit a long brown stream of juicy tobacco toward the gutter, and then with his freckled hands waving from enormous wrists, he walked up the street. In spite of his mood, Ham had to laugh.

Julius saw the laugh and lifted a hand as though to clout the boy. Ham ducked, ran a few steps, and then sensing someone was watching, resumed walking.

It was the Widow Theisen. He saw her out of the corner

of his eye. She was carrying a parasol. Why Ham couldn't guess, since it wasn't raining and there wasn't any sun. It was an old fashioned parasol, faded but still colorful, and she held it in white-gloved hands.

As soon as he lifted his eyes, the widow averted her's and moved on down the street. Ham slowed down in order to fall farther behind, but it wouldn't have been necessary because she turned in where Doc Shallock's white house stood back off the street.

She was halfway up the entrance walk when the doctor, carrying his black bag, came bustling out the door. The woman stopped and waited. When he saw her, Doc Shallock asked, "Did you have an appointment today, Mrs. Theisen?"

For a moment the widow was silent. Then she said, "Well, not exactly, but I was downtown, so I thought . . ."

The doctor cut her off. "I'm sorry. I just can't today. A cow kicked Tim Kurtz. In the head. I've got to get out there." He hurried on past her and climbed into the car. The widow stood looking, waving her parasol slowly, and Ham got the feeling that she looked like a last lonely leaf on a tree.

Now through a break in the trees he could see the cross atop the church. When he was little he had thought the cross was made of gold. He had been surprised to learn that it was really only tin and that it had gold-colored paint on it. Beneath the scudding clouds, it looked dull, as though it needed another, a fresh coat of paint.

He turned his eyes from the church cross and looked far up the street to where the bank clock was a white eye in the time-blackened bricks of the bank building. It was twenty minutes to four. He rehearsed, in his mind, what he would say.

"Forgive me, Father, for I have sinned. My last confession was three months and ten days ago, and since then I have committed the following sins: I have had impure thoughts about thirty times . . ."

But, how did you keep track of how many times you had impure thoughts. He didn't even quite know what constituted impure thoughts. Impure thoughts came and went. Perhaps, instead of saying "thirty times," he should say, "about every third day."

But maybe he should get right on with the big sin. Get it over first. Not wait until the end. Say it straight out: "Father, I stole from the church. Ten dollars. I took it from the collection basket, and I have not yet been able to make restitution."

As many times as he had envisioned himself kneeling in the gloom of the confessional, whispering the sin through the latticed wood, as many times as he had rehearsed it, as many times as it had followed him along the river during the day and haunted his nights, as many times—it still made him tremble inside when he thought about it.

If he had the ten dollars and could say, ". . . and I have the money, and at tomorrow's Mass I will make retribution by putting it into the collection basket . . ." If he could say that, the priest would be powerless to do anything except give him absolution, prescribe his penance, and tell him to ". . . go in peace, and sin no more."

But he didn't have the ten dollars, and he had no way of getting it.

Someone bumped him. It was High Pockets Garrity, the boy who always seemed to know everything about girls.

"Dreaming about some babe, Ham?" High Pockets asked. Ham shook his head. "Well, you sure were dreaming about something. Look where you're going. You're pushing people off the sidewalk."

High Pockets laughed, walked past, and then, as though remembering something, turned and came back to catch up with Ham. He took him by the sleeve and turned him around.

"Listen, boy, do I have something for you." Ham looked up at High Pockets who, though only in the eighth grade along with Ham, was almost as tall as his father. "Mabel Cushman and Marjorie Holman," High Pockets continued, "are going to meet me at four o'clock under the bleachers at the park. I think they've got something on their minds. Want to go along?"

That would be all he'd need, Ham thought. He had heard about Mabel and Marjorie. He twisted free from the bigger boy's grasp. "I got to meet my Dad."

"Too bad. This could be something. Want me to tell you about it later?"

Ham swung away, and without a word, crossed the street, ignoring the honking horn of an irate motorist. He looked down toward the equipment yard. Mort was on the seat of a Fordson tractor, pretending to be driving it. His father was nowhere in sight.

On the other curb, safe from High Pockets, he turned to look back across the street. The entire side of Hanrahan's Dry Goods store had been repainted. Where once there was an advertisement for Plow Boy tobacco, there was now an enormous picture of Martin Grosslire. He was pointing a pudgy finger, and beneath the finger were the words: "You! Don't forget to vote for Martin Grosslire for governor. Your man of integrity!"

In the picture, the senator's salt-and-pepper hair was brown and wavy. His white eye brows had been darkened. The triple chin was gone.

Ham turned away to look back up the street at the bank clock. Ten minutes to four. He should really be starting for church. He didn't want to have to wait in line. Waiting was the worst of it. Better to be there early, get right in, have it over with.

Well, there was some consolation. By this time tomorrow it would all be over. They planned to move tomorrow. There wasn't much to move. His father had already taken several loads of blankets, sheets, and clothes to the town house. There wasn't much more. Tomorrow night they would sleep in Greenville.

He'd miss the river. He always did. There'd be few things to listen to. The crickets, perhaps, and the church bell on the hour, every hour. A car passing. Somebody's dog barking. Voices perhaps, up from the street.

But there would be no fish splashing. No wings on the wind. Not likely an owl finally getting an answer. For sure

[205

no herons going south and coming in the dark to strange places, calling out in the night about what trees were high and safe enough to roost in.

There would be no acorns on the roof, no mice hurrying. The fox would not bark, nor would there be any young raccoons to squawl because a ring-tailed mother had disciplined one with her teeth.

He would not hear the river bumping the boats about, curling noisily over the willow roots, and there would be no roosters crowing long before dawn, all the way back across the gravel pit and up the slope to the red barn of the Gremminger farm.

He would miss the cool feel of the river lifting on the mist up the shore, all the way to where the porch screened out the last of the mosquitoes still whining hungrily for blood. He would miss the sun through the leaves, putting a patchwork of light and shadow on his cot. He would miss the smell of the marsh, as redolent with the odor of death as of life. Miss the cast of rain, running ahead of the clouds like a shadow of its own across the water. Miss the cool mud between his toes, the stones warmed by the sun waiting for his bare feet. Miss the high grass, bent to lie like a blanket, and the grasshoppers shooting out ahead like seeds snapping from the jewel weed pod. The crickets, so shiny in black, looking for places under rocks. The crayfish, armored with questing claws. Minnows skittering ahead of a charging pike. Carp rolling. Terns complaining in formation. Bright blue arrow of the kingfisher straight to the water. Sandpipers, scribbling and standing, scribbling and standing on the sand.

He would miss Rob MacQuarrie forever and always. But he would miss the river this year like he had never missed it any other autumn. He would miss it like a man misses something he will never love again with that first fierce intensity, when there was dew on the new and tender grass.

He would miss it, God, how he would miss it, because it was gone now, gone forever, and he knew that somehow, no matter how many more springtimes he lived to come to the river, it would never ever really be the same.

Ham slowed his pace. In front of Jumpy Jones's place was an old stake truck, and he thought he recognized it. It was piled high with camping gear and covered with an old, bleached canvas tent. Yes, it was. It was the pearl diver's truck.

He turned his eyes toward the building from which the resounding mixture of music and voices came. It sounded like a party. For a moment he remembered, and his mind pictured, how the inside of the Speakeasy looked the day he had caught the fish for Jumpy. The dim corners back from the bar where candles dripped wax to the bottles which held them. The girls, exciting in their tiny white aprons and their long black silk stockings. The smell of beer, rich like the marsh. The glint of glass in the candlelight, like moonbeams splintering on a ruffled river. The smell of people. The smell of girls.

He turned to retrace his steps when the door to Jumpy's place burst open and Lydia, her hair in disarray, came out onto the porch.

"I gotta get some air," she said, throwing back her head and brushing the hair from her face. "I just gotta get some air."

Ham started away, quickened his pace. She saw him.

"Ham! Ham!" she called. He wanted to keep going, and he wanted to turn around, to look at her. "Come here, Ham." The boy stood still, but he didn't turn. He could hear her coming down the steps. "Don't run away, Ham." He heard her shoes on the sidewalk. He could smell moonshine. He turned. Her eyes glittered.

"Ham, we hit it! The big one. Ham, we found the pearl!"

He tried to understand what she was saying.

"Don't you understand? The big one! Round and pink and big as a pup's nose!"

Still Ham didn't comprehend.

"A thousand dollars. Maybe two thousand. Who knows, Ham, maybe it will bring three."

Ham understood.

"Oh, Ham." She put a hand on his head and he tried to draw back. "It isn't as bad as you think."

But how could it be worse?

"Oh, Ham. Someday, maybe. You've got to understand about such things. There are maybe as many kinds of love as there are leaves on that tree. Maybe someday you'll know."

The boy started away. "I have to get going."

"Wait, Ham!" She grabbed his arm hard. "You wait here. Right here. Just one minute. Promise me?"

Ham started to object.

"Promise me, Ham!"

The boy nodded, and Lydia darted back up the steps and into Jumpy's place. He could see her through the open door. She went directly to the oldest of the pearl divers. The man shook his head angrily. Lydia went over and picked up a chair and lifted it as though to bring it down on the pearl diver's head.

The man took something from his pocket. Lydia put the chair down. She turned and came running through the door.

"Here." She thrust a ten-dollar bill into his hand. "We found your pearls where you dropped them."

Ham's eyes were fixed on the ten dollars, and then he turned and started away. When he was halfway up the block a rift in the clouds let the sun through. He looked back. Lydia was watching from the porch. The sun was golden again on her hair. Then she went inside.

He turned and could see the church cross now. He took a deep, deep breath, and it came out in a long, long sigh. Maybe it was over. Maybe. But something told him it wasn't, that this was only the beginning.

About the Author

There is not a more knowledgeable and articulate spokesman for the wonders of the outdoors than Mel Ellis. The author of the popular *Run, Rainey, Run; Wild Goose, Brother Goose;* and *The Wild Runners,* Mr. Ellis has been an associate editor for *Field & Stream* and the outdoor editor for *The Milwaukee Journal.* The author of many juvenile books and the nationally syndicated column "The Good Earth," Mr. Ellis makes his home in Wisconsin.